The Cuffing Game

ALSO BY LYLA LEE

I'll Be the One

Flip the Script

LYLA LEE

The Cuffing Game

HARPER
An Imprint of HarperCollins*Publishers*

HarperCollins Children's Books,
a division of HarperCollins Publishers,
195 Broadway, New York, NY 10007

HarperCollins Publishers, Macken House,
39/40 Mayor Street Upper, Dublin 1, D01 C9W8, Ireland

The Cuffing Game

harpercollins.com
ISBN 978-0-06-333041-2
Typography by Molly Fehr
25 26 27 28 29 LBC 6 5 4 3 2
First Edition

The Cuffing Game

PROLOGUE

Mia

It is a truth universally acknowledged, that when there is a hot person, there is also someone with a crush on them. This crush may be a secret or a well-known fact. It may be voluntary, or completely against their will.

Mia Yoon was no stranger to crushes. Hers lasted anywhere from a few seconds of daydreaming to years of secretly pining, regardless of whether she wanted to or not. Usually, they weren't mutual, so she ignored them. And that's exactly what she did when she developed an annoying crush on Noah Jang.

Or at least, she tried to. Because ignoring *Noah* proved to be impossible.

Mia couldn't remember when she'd started following Noah on social media, but before she'd seen him in class, before she'd even *set foot* in LA, she had watched his fame skyrocket over the last few years. Suddenly he was everywhere, all over her feed. Rich mahogany eyes and dazzling smile.

From her insignificantly small hometown of Bluebonnet, Texas, Mia had watched him do everything from lip-syncing in his bed to starring and directing in highly produced commercials.

She wasn't a fan of social media, but even she was begrudgingly impressed by the fact that, for several years, Noah posted almost daily, with an incredible range that went from tragic to comedic, from simplistic to awe-inspiring. This, she told herself, was why she hadn't gotten around to blocking him yet. And not just because he was incredibly hot.

But now, she wished she had. Maybe then he wouldn't have such a strong effect on her in person, dancing right in front of her, *shirtless*.

Those shoulders . . . was Mia's first attempt at a coherent thought. *And holy . . . abs*.

Never in her many years of envisioning her life in college had she pictured herself at a party, red Solo cup of SunnyD in hand, during the first week of classes. But her new roommate, Celine Huang, had insisted. And Mia had wanted to make a good impression on her, so she'd tagged along.

Unfortunately, Celine had ditched her for the first hot guy who walked past them, leaving Mia alone to fend for herself against the lure of Noah's abs. And eyes. Well, both. Mia liked both girls and guys, but guys like Noah reminded her that she was very much not a lesbian.

There were two other boys flanking him, executing the

same dance moves. But they could have been invisible as far as Mia was concerned. While the other boys looked like they were just going through the motions, Noah fully embodied them. An extra flick of his wrist. The almost too perfect curve of his smirk. As much as Mia hated to admit it, Noah had "star quality."

And she wasn't the only one caught in his siren song.

"Noah! Noah! Noah!" chanted the people around them.

Partygoers bobbed their heads and bounced along to the up-tempo K-pop song blasting from the portable speaker that someone had set up—for a reason unbeknownst to Mia—right by the drinks. Several people recorded the performance with their phone cameras.

Mia's heart beat faster and louder as Noah pulsed along to the music, running a hand through his hair before sliding it along his perfect chin in one fluid motion. His movements were graceful, yet powerful. Easy, yet heavily controlled. She shook her head, like that would settle her thoughts. He was a good dancer. So what?

But then, Noah leapt high and executed a flawless backflip.

Mia's jaw dropped. The crowd went wild.

One of the other boys spread his arms out wide, regaling everyone with a dazzling smile. Waving at a guy who was live streaming in the audience, he said, "Hey, everyone! Thank you so much for coming to our party. We're Alpha Tau!"

All three boys fist-bumped each other, drawing laughter from the crowd.

With a sheepish grin, the first boy continued, "I'm Thad, and these are my fraternity brothers Brent and Noah."

At his name, Noah tilted his head up in greeting. Cheers and screams erupted from the crowd, and the two other boys rolled their eyes in a good-natured way.

"Yes, yes, we know how much you love my Big, Noah," Thad teased. "If you're a guy and you want to be cool like him, or any of us really, rush our fraternity this week. We do a lot of awesome stuff, and this is just one of the many parties we'll host this year. We promise we're chill."

"Most of the time," Noah said with a dashing grin.

A few girls in the front row shrieked. One actually swooned, her beer sloshing as she almost fell to the ground.

Thad cupped his hands over his mouth and yelled, "Alpha Tau!"

Noah and his friends bowed, each adding a flourish, as a wave of applause swept through the crowd. Several boys in the audience hooted and threw their fists into the air.

Mia covered her ears and backed away from the crowd.

If frat parties were supposed to be the epitome of college social life, Mia wasn't sure if she wanted to leave her room ever again except to go to class. Books, movies, and TV shows provided her with enough entertainment, thank you very much. And neither of those involved yelling or underage drinking or one particular frat boy who was hotter than anyone had any right to be.

Thad and Brent joined the rest of the party while Noah remained behind. The live streamer ended the video and handed the phone over to Noah.

Mia wasn't drifting closer to eavesdrop. Okay, she totally was.

"You're so cool, man," the other boy was saying to Noah. "That backflip? Wow."

"Thanks, Kyle," Noah replied. "Appreciate you."

"No problem," the other boy replied. "Hey, what are you doing for the rest of the party? There are so many hot girls here. We did good!"

Noah ran a hand through his hair as he scanned the area. He did a double take when he saw Mia, standing by herself in the middle of the yard.

Oh, no.

She froze, like a deer in headlights waiting for imminent death.

His eyes widened.

Her cheeks flushed.

"They're all right," Noah said, turning back to Kyle. "Not really my type, though. I'm going to head back upstairs and call it a night. Best of luck with rush week!"

Not really my type.

Noah had looked at her *twice* before saying those words.

Indignation rose up inside Mia, a cold tightness that gripped her chest.

This is why some crushes are better off a secret, she thought.

Inside her brain, a fuse lit, rapidly growing into a fire of an idea. She had to go back to her room to write it down, ASAP. But she couldn't resist doing one more thing before she left.

Mia cupped her hands to her mouth and yelled, "Put a shirt on!"

A chorus of *ooh*s erupted from the crowd.

Noah turned back around to face her, raising his eyebrows. He'd said nothing but had somehow still got the last word.

Cheeks burning, she spun and ran as fast as she could back to her dorm.

And then, in the safe comforts of her own room, she dealt with her crush on Noah Jang by doing what she did best: she planned out a TV show.

PART ONE

Pre-Production

CHAPTER ONE
Noah

Mia Yoon hated Noah. Or at least, he was pretty sure of it.

He and Mia sat across from each other in the lecture hall, and Noah was grateful for the distance between them. Any closer and he'd surely explode into a thousand pieces from the force of Mia's glare.

"Short-form video is like cancer," she was saying, looking at him like *he'd* somehow given her cancer. "It's causing the death of cinema as we know it, since, these days, fewer people are interested in real stories and are obsessed with clickbait-y, dopamine-chasing content instead."

Noah furrowed his brow. Well, he *had* just been thinking of explosions. So maybe Mia had a point? But there was no way he was letting her win this easily. Not when she was on her high horse again.

He raised his hand, and before Dr. Thompson, their perpetually frazzled professor, could even finish nodding, Noah cut in, "On the contrary, one can argue that short-form video is one of the only things keeping movies alive in the first place."

Mia pressed her lips into a firm, unhappy line. She opened her mouth, then closed it again, and Noah smiled at how she was clearly stumped. "How so?" she asked, begrudgingly.

"Well, it's one of the main ways people find out about movies these days. Millions flocked to theaters for *Barbenheimer* because it became a trend on social media. And to this very day, people still discover classics like *The Godfather* or *Alien* because they stumble across random clips and fan edits on their feeds. Short-form is simply a—"

"You did *not* just say *Alien* is a classic."

"Well, it is."

"It's not."

All around them, the lecture hall erupted with protests. A house divided, hundreds of voices agreeing with either Noah or Mia. Others had something else to contribute to the discussion entirely, and someone even mentioned she watched *Alien* with her grandma "at least twenty times."

This, after all, was film school. None of them would have been there if they didn't have strong opinions about movies. Most of the voices he could make out seemed to agree with him, though, so Noah sat back in his seat, his arms folded triumphantly across his chest.

Mia scowled.

Noah grinned. He couldn't help it. He normally wasn't the competitive type, but when it came to Mia, he relished every victory. Despite being only a first year, she was just so sure of herself, a stickler for her high and mighty beliefs about *cinema*.

"All right, that's quite enough, class," Dr. Thompson said, waving his hands in an attempt to pacify the room. "Ms. Yoon and Mr. Jang, thank you for starting us off on such a . . . lively note. As always."

The class burst into laughter. Noah watched as a blush blossomed on Mia's face. He had to admit it: she was cute. It was too bad she was also an asshole.

As Dr. Thompson continued his lecture on . . . something, Noah entered the password on his laptop and went through his unread emails.

As a fourth year, Noah was only in this lower-division class because it was an arbitrary and totally unhelpful graduation requirement. If it had been up to him, he would have skipped the class entirely. He'd already learned most of the material the old-fashioned way, by going out there and shooting things with both a camera and his phone himself. Like a proper filmmaker should.

Unfortunately, the administration had disagreed, so he was stuck taking a class on creating content for social media. With mostly first years, second years, *and* a professor who followed him on said social media.

Dr. Thompson liked almost every video Noah posted. Noah didn't normally track who liked what video, but seeing the professor's avatar—an adorable golden retriever that looked like she was smiling—pop up in his notifications was always a highlight of his day.

It was the little things.

Noah would never admit it to her, but some part of him

was glad Mia was in this class. Dr. Thompson was probably a great guy—he at the very least had excellent taste in dogs—but he was a dull lecturer. Noah probably wouldn't even stay awake in class if it weren't for her.

He scrolled through his inbox some more before coming to a stop at a rather interesting subject line.

WANTED: CAST AND CREW FOR THE SPC'S NEWEST PROPOSED SHOW, *CAMPUS CRUSH*

Marlon University's Student Production Center—or the SPC as everyone called it—frequently sent out email blasts to recruit people for student-created movies and shows. Since he was already busy making his own things, Noah usually didn't even bother reading these emails.

But this one caught his attention. He didn't have a crush of his own. He was far too busy for that sort of thing. But he did love drama. Well, watching it anyway.

He opened the message.

Do you have an unrequited crush? Or do you want to work on a show about one? Then consider applying for *Campus Crush*! The show will follow four college students with unrequited crushes as they go about their lives and confess to the people they like. A cross between a reality TV show and a documentary, it raises the questions: What happens when we act on our crushes? And are

they worth our time? BIPOC and LGBTQ+ students are encouraged to apply.

Noah scrolled down to see what sort of evil mastermind had come up with this idea. When he saw who, he stifled a laugh.

Short-form-is-cancer-and-pop-culture-is-bad Mia Yoon was helming *a reality TV show.* Well, "a cross between a reality TV show and a documentary." Whatever helped her sleep at night.

Noah pressed his palm against his mouth. But the more he thought about it, the funnier it became. A small, strangled noise escaped from his lips.

"Mr. Jang, was there something funny about what I just said?"

Noah slammed his laptop closed. Dr. Thompson stood right in front of him, a perplexed look on his face.

Well, damn. Noah regretted sitting in the front row. He did so out of habit only because Mia did too on her side of the room. It made it easier to hear her when they were arguing. But maybe he needed to start sitting in the back.

He cleared his throat. "No, sir. Sorry, I was, um, thinking about something else. I'll pay more attention for the rest of class."

Everyone was staring at him now. From across the lecture hall, Mia smiled. She'd somehow gotten him into trouble without even trying.

Touché, Noah thought.

He was afraid the professor would ask to see his computer screen, but fortunately, Dr. Thompson moved on with a disappointed shake of his head. Noah wondered if he was ever going to see the professor's dog in his notifications again.

When the coast was clear, Noah reopened his laptop and starred the email from the SPC.

Even *if* he wanted to—which he did not—Noah didn't have time to be on Mia's show. But he'd still keep tabs on it. Just to see how things went.

CHAPTER TWO

Mia

ATTN: *Campus Crush* Cancellation Notice.

Due to insufficient talent interest in the program, this show will be canceled by the Student Production Center. You are welcome to submit revisions to the proposal by October 15th or retry in the spring semester.

When Mia read the SPC's email, she rolled out of bed and called her oldest sister, Jeannette.

"Yeah?" Jeannette said. "Mia, I'm driving to school right now so I can't talk long. What's up?"

Guilt and gratitude twisted together in Mia's gut, like it always did whenever she thought about Jeannette commuting to school every day from home. Two years ago, Jeannette had gotten into all her dream schools on the East Coast but had opted to go to the local state school fifteen minutes away from their house instead.

"Someone needs to stay behind and help Mom and Dad take care of y'all," she'd said when Mia had asked why. "It's also way more affordable!"

Besides Jeannette, Mia had three other sisters: Marie, Cara, and Lola. As the oldest, Jeannette really could have left them all to fend for themselves. But no. She had stayed so Mia, the second oldest, could move thousands of miles away instead. Her sister had sacrificed so much for her. And yet here Mia was, already a failure just two months into the semester.

She'd called Jeannette out of habit, because they always told one another about everything. But now she regretted it.

"Hello?" Jeannette said. "Mia, are you still there? If you are, talk now or call me back later. I'm seven minutes away from school."

Looking out at her sparsely decorated side of the dorm room, Mia sighed. She condensed the mini-rant in her head to one sentence, so she could be as small of a burden on her sister as possible. "My show is going to get canceled if I don't figure out a way to save it by next week."

"The dating show? How come? It was such a cool idea!"

"It's more of a documentary, but yeah. Not enough people signed up to be on it."

"That sucks. Why do you think that happened?"

"If I had to guess . . ." Mia pursed her lips. "I don't know enough people. No one wants to be on a show led by a freshman who is brand-new to campus."

"Aw, well, you just got there. Maybe you can try again later!"

Mia bit her lip. One of the biggest differences between her and her sister was how they saw the world. For Jeannette, the glass was always half-full. While for Mia, it wasn't a simple matter of the glass being half-full or half-empty. It was a question of *why* it was half-empty in the first place and what she could do to fill that glass back up.

Campus Crush may have *started* as something she'd invented to distract herself from her crush on Noah, but over the last couple of months, it'd become more than that. Thanks to the show—well, technically, the SPC—Mia had met Kallie, Damien, and Alex, her only friends so far at Marlon. And the four of them had sacrificed sleep—and a little bit of their sanity—to plan out the show and submit the proposal.

Their producer, Damien, was a senior, while Kallie, their cinematographer, was a junior. Both, like most upper-level film students at Marlon, already juggled an intensive schedule of working on studio lots and going to class. They'd barely managed to fit the show into their schedules as it was, and they would have even less time as they approached graduation. They didn't have a "later."

Mia was going to disappoint everyone.

"How about we take a few calming breaths together," Jeannette continued when Mia didn't respond. "Would that help?"

Take a few calming breaths was Jeannette's number-one mantra, the one that she told all her younger sisters. Those words had—admittedly—gotten Mia through the years she'd worked her butt off to get a full ride to Marlon, a fancy private school that their parents would never have let her go to otherwise. But this time, Mia's throat felt too tight. She wasn't sure if a few calming breaths would help with her current predicament.

"Mia?"

"Sorry, I have to go," Mia managed to say out loud.

There was silence on the other end. Mia didn't have to see her to know Jeannette was chewing her lip, a habit that both sisters shared when they had a lot on their minds.

"Sure," Jeannette said finally, her voice falsely bright. "I'm at school now so I'll talk to you later. Hope you figure things out!"

"Thanks, J. I'll keep you updated."

After they'd hung up, Mia opened the group chat she had with her friends and started typing.

Hey, y'all. Sorry but . . . She hit the backspace button. Already, her message sounded pathetic.

Some bad news. But not all hope is lost!

She groaned. She sounded like someone from a Shakespearean play.

Finally, she screenshotted the cancellation notice and shared it without any message.

Their responses were instantaneous.

KALLIE MARTIN (she/her): WTF??????

DAMIEN CARTER (he/him): Is this a joke?

ALEX DOMINGUEZ (they/them): What are we going to do now?

DAMIEN CARTER (he/him): Pray, I guess.

Mia watched as her friends' confusion and despair filled her phone screen, her own fingers frozen with dread. She stared at the blinking cursor but couldn't figure out what to say. What *were* they going to do now?

KALLIE MARTIN (she/her): We should just go indie. We don't need the SPC! We can make our own show!

DAMIEN CARTER (he/him): With what money?

ALEX DOMINGUEZ (they/them): Maybe we can try resubmitting next semester?

Mia went to her desk drawer and got out her four-year planner. It was obnoxiously heavy, practically a novel in its 140 pages of 48 monthly spreads and other helpful pages.

In the summer, after she'd registered for her fall-semester classes, she'd gone on the school website and found the previous spring's course catalog to make a list of the classes she'd have to take next. They were mostly GE classes like biology and math that were overly intensive but unfortunately required for her to graduate. She'd been planning on loading her spring semester up with such classes so she could focus on stuff for her actual major the rest of college.

MIA YOON (she/her): I can't do next semester, sorry. And I know Damien and Kallie can't do next year. I'll try to think of a solution. Will keep you updated.

Could we independently produce the show like Kallie suggested? Mia thought. *Set up a GoFundMe? Crowdfund on social media?*

The door to their dorm opened, and Mia jerked her head up to see Celine, her roommate, coming back into the room with a big box. It was 7 a.m. on a Monday, but she was already in full makeup. The only time of day Mia consistently saw Celine in their room was in the morning, since that was when she made her makeup haul posts or recorded her videos.

"Oh good, you're awake!" Celine said. "Good morning! I just got a new shipment of makeup, so I have to record a video. Hope that's okay!"

Mia collapsed back onto the bed and tried to match Celine's friendly and polite tone. "Yeah, you're totally fine. Thanks for the heads-up!"

Mia and Celine weren't exactly friends, but they were friendly enough that Celine knew about Mia's show, and Mia knew Celine was a beauty influencer who specialized in Asian makeup products. Other than that, they had virtually no overlap, since Celine hardly ever watched movies and Mia never went to parties. Well, besides the Alpha Tau one they went to during the first week of school.

Although Mia hardly ever wore makeup, she listened in as Celine recorded her latest video. Not only did her roommate give the best tips, but her voice was incredibly soothing, too.

Since she still had a couple hours until her first class, Mia rolled over until her face smooshed against her pillow. She must have dozed off, because when she next opened her eyes, Celine was back in her own bed, hugging her pillow close to her chest as she stared down at her phone.

"Ugh, he left me on seen again!" she whispered.

And that's when Mia got an idea. It most likely wouldn't work, but at this point, Mia was desperate to try anything.

"Hey, Celine?" Mia asked. "Do you have a crush on anyone? Ideally someone who goes to our school?"

It was a leading question, since Mia had heard Celine grumble to herself about this mysterious "he" several times in the past month, ever since she'd broken up with the guy she'd met at the Alpha Tau party.

Celine slowly blinked up at her. "Um, yeah?"

She sounded wary, and Mia didn't blame her. Just to be polite, Mia usually pretended she couldn't hear Celine whenever she talked to herself in their room. The actual conversations they had together rarely went beyond small talk. If Mia weren't so desperate, she wouldn't be talking to Celine about this in the first place.

"Great," Mia continued. "How would you like to be on my dating show? We're looking for more people to be on it, since it's in danger of being canceled."

"Wait, what?"

Celine dropped her phone into her lap and burst out laughing.

When Mia stared at her, completely serious, her giggles faltered.

"Oh, you're not kidding. Look, I'd love to, but I doubt my crush would ever appear on the show with me. He has over a million followers, so I'm sure a lot of girls are interested in him. Plus, he almost never replies to my messages."

An uneasy feeling spread throughout Mia, settling like a rock in her stomach.

Even though she already knew the answer, she forced out the words: "Who's your crush?"

"Noah Jang? He's a senior from South Korea."

Of course, it's Noah.

Mia scowled. "Ew."

Celine let out a pseudo-indignant gasp. "Wait, *what*? What's wrong with Noah?"

"Nothing. I just . . . know him, that's all."

Celine gasped for real this time. "And you're only telling me this now?"

"He's in one of my production classes. It's a lower-division course, but apparently, he procrastinated on taking it, so he's in it now as a senior. Noah's a classic example of what *not* to do in college."

But instead of looking horrified at Noah's failings, Celine only asked, "Is he as hot in real life as he is in his videos? Have you ever talked to him?"

Mia sat up. "Plenty of times. He's super annoying. He always debates things with me, like he can't stay quiet and let my opinion be heard. And he constantly tries to one-up me in class."

"Wait, this is perfect!" Celine enthused. "Well, not the one-upping part. But the situation in general. Mia, don't you see? I *have* to go on your show. And we have to convince Noah to be on it as well."

Mia nearly fell out of her bed. "What? *Why?*"

"Think about it," Celine replied. "Noah's a senior, and one of the most famous people on campus. I have a decent following as well. If we both appear on the show, with him as my crush, it's bound to get a lot of attention. Maybe it'll be enough for the campus TV station to un-cancel your show! And *I'll* finally get a chance to meet him and talk to him in person. A win-win!"

Making a show about other people's crushes was supposed to distract her from her own, *not* bring her into even closer proximity to him. And having to watch Celine potentially date Noah? It didn't sound like a win for Mia, at all.

She had no idea what her face was doing, but apparently her expression was concerning enough for Celine to say, "Um, you okay, Mia? Maybe you better lie down. Sorry, was my idea too unhinged?"

"No, you're fine. Sorry, let me think for a second."

Mia took a few deep breaths that would have made Jeannette proud.

Her thoughts whirled. But the more she wrapped her head around Celine's idea, the more she knew her roommate was right. If Noah and Celine couldn't bring more attention to her show, then no one could.

This was her and her friends' one and only chance to make this TV show. She had to take one for the team and try her best not to let her weird, complicated feelings about Noah get in the way.

Mia gritted her teeth, steeling herself against what she had to do next.

"Okay," she said. "I'll ask him."

CHAPTER THREE

Noah

"I need you to be on my show."

There was no *hi* or *how are you doing?* No, Mia went straight for his throat, as usual, with her razor-sharp tone.

Was this a dream? Noah actually wasn't sure. For some reason, Mia hadn't said a single word during today's lecture. And like magic, Noah had dozed off. He'd tried his best to pay attention, but Dr. Thompson had been going over framing, something he'd taught himself years ago. And Noah was still exhausted from staying up all night editing a project for a different class.

He rubbed the sleepiness from his eyes. When he reopened them, Mia was still there, looking as resolute as ever. Around them, the other students started filing out of the lecture hall.

So this was real then.

It was bizarre to see Mia standing right in front of him, on *his* side of the room, no more than a couple inches away from where he was sitting in his seat.

Noah resisted the urge to extend his leg and tap one of her pink tennis shoes. A childish impulse. But she was just *so* serious.

"*Campus Crush*?" he finally asked.

Mia nodded. "Yup. Someone nominated you to be on it."

Noah raised his eyebrows. "But I don't have a crush on anyone."

"The show follows four people *and* their crushes. You're someone's crush, and she nominated you to be on the show with her. And no, I can't tell you who it is yet."

Noah was already far too busy to add something else to his plate this semester. And even if he weren't, he wasn't sure if he'd ever want to be on a "cross between reality TV and a documentary" show like Mia's, where he'd likely be scrutinized for everything he said.

The best part about his short-form content was its high editability. Before he uploaded anything, he could watch it repeatedly and fine-tune everything he said and did to the nearest second. Sometimes, even more precisely than that. He presented himself to the world exactly how he wanted to appear.

That would be impossible with longer media, especially when he wasn't the one shooting or editing. His palms grew sweaty just thinking about it.

But since he didn't want Mia to know how nervous he felt, he said, "I'm too busy this semester. Plus, what if the person who nominated me is a sasaeng fan?"

It was only after he said it that he realized Mia might not know what that term means. From her last name, he knew she was ethnically Korean, like him, but during first-week-of-school icebreakers, she'd said she was born in *Texas*, out of all places.

He had no idea if Mia could even speak Korean, so he added, "Sasaengs are obsessive fans who stalk K-pop stars and other celebrities and terrorize their lives in South Korea."

Mia's brows drew together into a flat line. "I know what they are. And you are *not* famous enough to have sasaeng fans."

Noah hadn't meant to offend Mia, but clearly, he'd struck a nerve. He looked away apologetically and shrugged. "You don't know that. We *have* gotten creepy mail to the fraternity house before, so the possibility is always there."

"Okay, fine. The person who nominated you isn't a sasaeng fan. She's perfectly normal."

"So you know who it is."

"I never said I didn't."

Noah started packing up his things. "You know, Mia, you have a funny way of asking people for a favor."

Mia gritted her teeth for a second before opening her mouth. Noah half expected her to yell at him when, in a strangled voice, she said, "Sorry. I'm just so used to arguing with you."

A wheezing sound came from Mia's mouth, causing

Noah's eyebrows to shoot up with concern. A few seconds later, he realized that *this* was her attempt to relax. Some kind of meditative breathing technique, maybe?

Noah thought about telling her that whatever she was doing, she was doing it wrong. But he held his tongue. She'd just *apologized* to him for the first time. He could be civil. For now.

The breaths seemed to have worked, because Mia spoke much more slowly and calmly as she said, "Listen. This could be good for both of us. Are you happy being single?"

Noah flinched. Nice or not, she'd somehow gotten *even more* direct. He was usually good at talking to people, but Mia's frankness made him stumble on his words.

"W-what? How do you know I'm not dating anyone?"

She shrugged. "Just a lucky guess. I figured you'd be the type to be super public about your relationship if you were."

Noah frowned at Mia's assumption. But in truth, he had no idea how he'd act in a relationship. Before college, he'd been too busy studying English and doing everything else he could to get into Marlon. Then, over the last three years, he'd bounced like a ball between classes, the fraternity, and work. A part of him had always assumed he'd eventually meet someone. And yet, here he was now. A fourth year who had never really dated anyone.

Now that he thought about it, he was probably the only brother in his fraternity who hadn't had at least one girlfriend. His chest suddenly felt empty.

"Well? Are you happy?" Mia asked again. "Being single?"

In the now almost-empty lecture hall where time seemed to have stopped, Noah quietly said, "No, I guess not."

"Okay." Mia opened the Notes app on her phone. She took another deep breath and, as if reading off a teleprompter, continued, "Then what reason do you have to not be on the show? You've literally been voted the most eligible student bachelor at our school. If people hear that you're on the show, they'll flock to it to learn more about you. *Campus Crush* isn't like your usual content. It'll have quiet moments and heart-to-heart conversations that will give you space to be vulnerable and open, something you can't do with your normal 'unattainable cool dude' online persona. Everyone will eat it up, and you'll most likely end up with someone. Either because you meet them on the show or because a viewer will want to date you after seeing you open up, on-screen. It'll be a win-win, either way."

"Wait, did you take notes on me? And my content?"

Although he had many fans, no one had analyzed either him or his work as thoroughly as Mia had just now. Or at least, they'd never been brave enough to do it in front of his face. It was bold. Surprising, even. And it was the exact thing that made Noah wonder if he should take Mia more seriously, after all.

She opened her mouth to reply when someone coughed.

They both jumped and looked up to see a very tired-looking Dr. Thompson.

"Can you two please take this somewhere else?" the professor asked. "It's 10:15 p.m., and I'm not allowed to leave students alone in this building at night."

Noah blinked. Fifteen minutes had gone by, just like that.

"Noah, please," Mia said, surprising him even more. "My friends and I worked hard on this show. I don't want all of that to go to waste. At least give me a chance to continue this conversation somewhere else."

Mia was *begging* him now? The world was going to end before the clock struck midnight. He was sure of it.

Even so, Noah found himself saying, "All right. Let's meet up sometime else then. To keep talking."

There was no harm in meeting with her once, was there?

After shooting Dr. Thompson an apologetic look, he pulled up the Calendar app on his phone. "Just one moment. Sorry, Professor."

Noah's schedule was already full of big, ugly blocks that made up different facets of his life, from the monstrous chunks of time that film school classes required, late into the evening, to the hours he carved out for either the gym, his content, or the catch-up calls with his mom and brother back in Seoul.

"My calendar's a mess . . ." Noah trailed off as Mia opened up *her* calendar. It was somehow even more terrifying than his.

"How are you even alive?" he asked, in both horror and awe.

Mia shrugged. "My calendar."

A grin threatened to make its way across his face. To any other person, the differently colored and sometimes even overlapping boxes of his own calendar would also seem nightmarish, when in reality, they were the keys to his survival, too.

Noah had entered into an alternate universe. He never thought he'd be able to relate to Mia.

Dr. Thompson coughed again.

"I can do Friday night at eight," he told Mia. "You live on campus, right? By Carlisle Library, since you're a first year? How about Ground Smoothie? I think it's one of the few places on that side of campus that's still open then."

"Ground Smoothie? Where's that?"

Noah smiled triumphantly. Finally, something Mia the Know It All didn't know about. "Oh, you've never heard of it? I have to say, I'm surprised."

Mia scowled. "Just tell me where it is."

"It's by C Dorm. They have good milkshakes and smoothies, but they also grind and brew their own coffee, hence the cursed name. If you don't know where it is, I can send you a location pin—"

"I'm fine," Mia cut in. "Thanks."

Ground Smoothie was so infamously hard to find that Noah was ninety-nine percent certain that Mia would *not* be "fine." "Are you sure?"

"Yup."

Noah let it drop. He was fully grinning now. Her stubbornness to do everything herself reminded him of his Little, Thad, when *he* was a first year. The best he could do, he'd learned, was provide his contact information so they could reach out to him if they needed help.

When he gave her his number, Mia made a face, like she found the very gesture highly offensive.

"Right," she said. "See you."

CHAPTER FOUR

Mia

It took Mia the rest of the week to get over the full force of Noah's real smile. Or the fact that he'd just casually given her his number. Everything about him was so infuriating. His personality, his good looks . . . *everything.*

No one should be that hot, she thought as she followed Google's directions to Ground Smoothie.

She shuddered. Debating him from all the way across the lecture hall was one thing, but being *that* close to Noah had been nerve-racking. Her legs had shaken the entire time. And she had barely been able to think straight.

Was this how people felt whenever they did VIP meet and greets with K-pop stars? But Noah wasn't even an actual celebrity. And he was more like an antihero protagonist of a K-drama than a member of BTS.

Thank God she'd taken notes to prepare for their conversation. Her mind would have gone blank otherwise.

The directions on her phone led her to C Dorm, but she couldn't find any signs for Ground Smoothie. She made three laps around the dorm before giving up.

Of course, Noah would tell her to meet him at some weird, fake location.

She thought about calling him, but she doubted he'd given her his real number. If he was that worried about sasaeng fans, why would he give her his contact information so easily? This was probably all just one big prank.

She sighed and started to walk away.

"Hey, over here!"

Mia followed the sound of Noah's voice. He stood in front of the very dorm she'd just walked past several times.

Tonight, Noah was wearing khaki shorts and a navy-blue tank, and Mia realized this was the first time she was seeing him wear casual clothes in person. Sure, he'd been shirtless at the Alpha Tau party, and he wore all sorts of outfits in his videos, but he normally wore only long-sleeved dress shirts and other relatively formal clothes to class.

Mia tried not to stare at his shoulders, zeroing in on his face instead.

"Ground Smoothie is *in* C Dorm?" she asked. "Why didn't you just say that?"

"Well, it's not. It just looks like it. Ground Smoothie was the original dining hall for all first years, before they built a bigger one between B and C. And hey, I offered to help."

Mia frowned as they made their way to the other side of C Dorm. This time, she could clearly see how what she'd assumed was part of C Dorm was an awkwardly shaped, separate structure with its own entrance and set of windows.

The buildings were so similarly painted that there was no way she could have ever distinguished between the two on her own.

She hated to admit it, but Noah was right. She could have used his help.

Noah walked to the door with the leisurely gait of someone who'd been down this same path countless times. A flash of envy shot through Mia. She wished she had even an ounce of his self-assuredness, something she painfully lacked as a freshman who still got lost around campus without—and sometimes even with—Google Maps.

I just got here a couple months ago, Mia reminded herself as she followed Noah. *It'd be weird if I knew everything already.*

Noah pulled open the heavy door, his arm muscles straining from the weight. This time, Mia couldn't stop herself from staring. Wow, Noah *definitely* worked out.

"Um," he said. "Ladies first."

It took Mia a couple seconds to realize that Noah was staring back at *her.*

Her brain short-circuited. She dropped her gaze, but not before Noah shot her a confused look.

Despite the name, Ground Smoothie turned out to be more of an artsy cafe than a dingy smoothie shack. Her eyes were still adjusting to the dim light, so she couldn't see much except for the brightly lit center stage, where a girl with lavender-colored hair sang an acoustic guitar cover of a Taylor Swift song.

"Go find us somewhere to sit," Noah said. "I'll order our drinks."

Mia frowned. "What? No, I can buy my own milkshake." *This isn't a date!* she added in her head.

But Noah shook his head. "It's more efficient this way. Just tell me what you want. Chocolate? Strawberry?"

"Coffee," she answered without hesitation. "I want a coffee-flavored milkshake. If they have any."

Back home in Bluebonnet, when Mia ordered coffee past a certain time of day, she'd without a doubt get a few *bless your heart*s and questions about her well-being from her mother, her sisters, and other concerned individuals.

Noah, however, just gave her a conspiratorial wink. Like he understood.

Mia's heart fluttered. She tried to ignore it but then heat rose up in her cheeks. She rushed away before Noah could notice, turning back around only when she was several feet away.

Thankfully, he wasn't even looking at her. He was too busy ordering.

She sighed in relief and looked for somewhere to sit.

Aside from the stools that lined the coffee bar, the only other seating was beanbags that littered the floor around the stage. After several minutes of tiptoeing around the already occupied ones, Mia finally found two large yellow beanbags on opposite sides of the room.

She tried lifting one up. It didn't budge.

"Hey, do you need help with that?" asked a nearby guy.

"Nope!" Mia said, in what she hoped was a cheery voice. "I got it!"

She put more force into it. The bag still didn't move. With a growl of frustration, Mia put all her strength into lifting but then lost her balance. Before she could even process what was happening, she tumbled onto the beanbag, flopping down belly-first onto the plush fabric.

A few people gasped, while others laughed. The music stopped, and Mia looked up in horror to see that even the girl onstage was staring at her, her mouth a wide O of silent, secondhand embarrassment.

But the worst part of it all was that Noah now stood behind her, their drinks in hand. His expression was unreadable.

She flinched back, expecting him to say something mean.

Noah wordlessly shifted the drink carrier to one hand and held the other out to her. When she grabbed onto him, he helped her up.

Mia couldn't help but notice how he moved so effortlessly, like she weighed nothing. Before she could be *too* amazed, though, Noah let go the second she was back on her feet, so suddenly that she almost lost her balance. With a look of great discomfort, Noah flexed his hand, as if merely touching her had repulsed him.

"Here." He handed her the drink carrier before gripping the beanbag on opposite sides.

Noah was in an awkward position, bent at his knees, so it really shouldn't have been attractive. But Mia couldn't stop staring at him as he lifted the big beanbag up from the floor.

People around them whooped and hollered.

"Noah! Noah! Noah!" chanted a nearby boy.

A dashing grin flashed across Noah's face, immediately covering up the awkward expression he had before. It was so fake that Mia immediately wanted to leave. And she would have, too, if it weren't for her friends.

When Mia had broached the idea of having Noah on the show, she'd expected mixed reactions. It wasn't a shocker that Alex, who unabashedly watched all of Noah's videos, said yes. But Kallie didn't even like guys, and Damien quite literally once said, "Noah's content gives me a headache." And yet everyone had spammed the group chat with YES YES YES when she told them she was meeting up with him to discuss the show. They all agreed he was their best bet to save *Campus Crush*.

"Where should I put this beanbag?" Noah asked, bringing her back to the present.

Mia waved him over to where the other unoccupied beanbag was, and he set the first bag down in front of it.

Thankfully, by the time Mia and Noah had settled into their seats, the performer had resumed singing. Everyone was back to doing whatever they were doing before.

She handed Noah's drink—an iced Americano, no straw—to him.

And then they just sat there. Face-to-face.

Mia took a sip of her coffee milkshake and shifted uncomfortably, accidentally digging herself deeper into the beanbag. She'd felt nervous talking to him after class, but that didn't compare to how on edge she felt now, outside the familiarity of the lecture hall.

When Noah had described Ground Smoothie, she was expecting more of a boba shop vibe. Some place they could still have a relatively formal conversation. Instead, they were at this quasi-lounge area with live music and dim lighting. They were sitting on *beanbags*, their knees almost touching because of his stupidly long legs.

This was the closest she'd ever been to Noah. And unfortunately, even in the dim lighting, it was the perfect distance to clearly make out his long, dark lashes and chiseled jawline. It was the perfect angle to see how the stage lights bounced off his eyes, making them even more mesmerizing than they normally were when he stared at her in class.

This was the face that enchanted over a million people into following him on social media.

A chill went down Mia's spine. She shivered.

Noah sat up, before relaxing back into his beanbag.

"Sorry," he said, his eyes dipping down to her crossed arms. "I'd offer you my jacket if I were wearing one."

Mia narrowed her eyes. "And why would you offer me your jacket?"

Noah frowned. "A habit of mine, I guess."

"It's a habit of yours to give just any girl your jacket?"

He shrugged. "When they're cold, yes. It's called being a gentleman."

"More like being a flirt."

Noah looked down at his smartwatch. "Let's cut to the chase. I thought about it more, and I won't be able to join the show unless you make some changes."

Mia blinked. Well, he hadn't said *no*. "Like what?"

"First off, I can't film during the semester. It's too short notice and my schedule's already full. I could probably do winter break, though."

Mia bristled. "And why should we change everything to fit *your* schedule?"

He took a sip of his coffee. "It's not just me that's busy, though. It's the middle of the semester. A lot of people have their commitments already laid out. Some probably even have their winter breaks planned."

Mia bit her lip. She had to admit that Noah had a point. After all, *she* was one of the latter. Christmas was a big deal in her family, and she'd bought her plane ticket back home for the last day of finals—a full week before Christmas Eve—before she'd even left for Move-In Day. Her heart squeezed just thinking about the possibility that she might not get to go home for winter break this year.

"Also," Noah continued, "you might have a better chance of getting greenlit by the SPC during break."

"And why is that?"

"Fall is the hardest time of year to get a show made through the school, since everyone comes back from summer vacation with tons of new ideas," he explained with another sip of his drink. "And a lot of students rent the same equipment for class projects, so there's always a shortage of cameras. Spring is hard too, but it's still easier than fall. Winter, though . . ."

"No one's using school property," Mia finished with a sigh. Another point for Noah and his logic.

Hoping Damien, another senior, would disagree with Noah, Mia sent him a text. But before she could even put her phone down, it buzzed in her hand. Damien was always a quick responder, but this was fast, even for him.

That's very true. I agree with Noah.

Mia wanted to growl in frustration. She would have too, if she and Noah were back in class and not out in public. She'd already caused a scene in Ground Smoothie. The last thing she wanted to do was become the center of attention again.

"Okay, fine," she said. "*If* we can find enough people to commit to the show during winter break, we can do it then. What else?"

Mia's heart was beating fast. This meetup was supposed to be *her* pitching the show to Noah. But he'd somehow completely derailed everything in one fell swoop.

Noah blinked at her. His eyes met hers briefly before darting away. This was the first time she'd ever seen Noah look so nervous around her.

Anxiety had already been building up inside Mia's chest, but now it rushed in. It felt like the world was spinning.

"What is it?" Mia's voice came out sharper than she intended it to be.

Noah slowly took a sip of his coffee. "You need to rebrand the entire show, maybe even tear it apart and rework it from the ground up."

"*What?*"

Mia stood up, and then immediately sat back down again when the people around them glanced her way. So much for not being the center of attention.

"Think about it," Noah said. "There has to be a reason—maybe multiple—why not enough students signed up to be on your show, why you even need *me* to help out in the first place. I saw the email blast for it, and while the idea seemed interesting, it was also confusing. A cross between a reality TV show and a documentary? What even is that?"

"Like *Terrace House*," Mia explained, using the comparison that she and her friends had thought of during one of their meetings. "You watch four people go about their lives and hopefully confess to their crushes. But since it's unscripted, the outcome is unknown, so it's more like a documentary where you observe what happens."

"Ah. See, that'd be nice for an art film for older people," Noah replied, so matter-of-factly that Mia wasn't even offended. "Or maybe even an audience in another country. Take it from someone whose fanbase is mostly American college students. They love *drama*. All my flashy videos with fast music and lots of movement do well. The quieter slice-of-life ones? Not so much. You need to grab a viewer's attention. Maybe even make it into a straight-up dating show with challenges and contrived scenarios like *Love Island* instead."

Mia's head spun. "You want to make my show *Love Island* for college students?"

Mia didn't even watch *Love Island*, or any reality TV shows at that. The only exposure she'd had was through Jeannette and Cara, who showed her clips of the UK *Love Island* and gave play-by-plays of all the drama, badly executed British accents and all.

"Not exactly." Noah sat back in his beanbag chair. "For one, it'll be winter. Which *can* get cold in LA. Maybe we could rent out one of those luxury cabins in Big Bear. Oh! And since it'll be cuffing season, we could call it *The Cuffing Game*!"

Even in all his many different types of videos, Mia had never seen Noah like this. His breathing was uneven. His eyes wide in a way that reminded Mia of her friends' during their late-night production meetings at Carlisle, Marlon's twenty-four-hour library. The passion in his voice. His slightly flushed face.

Noah, she realized, was excited about *her* show. Or his version of it, at least. And unfortunately, seeing him like this was having an effect on *her*. It was intoxicating, and her skin buzzed. Mia was in deep trouble.

She coughed. "This is a lot. You're asking us to make so many changes. I'm going to have to check in with everyone and see what they think."

"Sure, of course."

Technically, she could text the group chat right then and there. But Mia's hands were shaking too hard to write up a proper message. She balled them into fists and looked up to see that the lavender-haired girl had finished performing. A skinny blond boy was now screaming into the mic, singing—or trying to sing—a punk rock song that Mia didn't recognize.

Mia felt like screaming too.

"Also, the cabin in Big Bear," she managed to say. "How do you expect us to be able to afford that? The SPC will only help us with equipment and permits."

He shrugged. "We can crowdfund on social media. I can take care of that part, don't worry."

He was just so confident, making everything sound easy. Out of sheer pettiness, Mia hoped her friends would say no, or at least give him a lot of trouble. That'd show him.

"Thanks for your time." She stretched out her hand in her best attempt to remain professional. "We'll be in touch."

Noah glanced down at her hand but made no move to shake it.

Of course he wouldn't, Mia thought bitterly, reminded of his extreme reaction to the last time they touched.

She let her hand drop.

Noah gave her a tight grin. "Looking forward to it."

Mia tossed out her milkshake and made her quick escape.

CHAPTER FIVE

Noah

When the words "Grumpy Mia" flashed on his watch, Noah almost fell off his electric longboard.

He rarely assigned nicknames to his contacts, but Mia had earned it. After their meetup at Ground Smoothie, she'd just texted him, This is Mia. And in class the following week, she'd gone back to bickering with him as usual. It was like he'd never gone out of his way to help her with her show.

Exhaustion already weighed him down like a bag of bricks. He'd just wrapped up a several-hours-long night shoot on campus for one of his senior production classes. He could just let Mia's call ring. Or even hit decline.

But it could be an emergency. Mia hadn't even called him when she was lost, so she must have had a really good reason to be calling him now.

To avoid crashing into any pedestrians, Noah got off his board and started walking the rest of the way to the fraternity house. He popped in his earbuds and took the call.

"My team loved the idea," Mia said. "And so did the SPC." Instead of sounding happy about this development, however, her voice was tight as she continued, "They think it has the potential to attract a lot of people. We can film and air episodes during winter break, since we can just upload videos onto the SPC YouTube channel ourselves. The only disadvantage is that no one will be in the office to help if there's an issue, but I'm sure we can handle things on our own. I mean, it's just a dating show. How complicated can it get?"

"That's great." Noah tried to keep his tone light, but he must have failed because Mia asked, "Um, are you okay?"

He grimaced. He must have sounded *really* bad for *Grumpy Mia* to be worried about him. Maybe it was a good thing he'd decided to walk the rest of the way home.

"Yeah. Just got done with an exhausting shoot. Anyway, when and where will we be filming, exactly?"

He paused at an intersection to open his Notes app.

"They suggested we do five days in Big Bear as the main location of filming and maybe do a big finale on the beach, *Bachelor*-style, if we have enough left from our budget."

Adrenaline shot through Noah as he jotted down what Mia said. Oddly enough, talking to her about the show was giving him more energy, not depleting it. Then again, Mia always had this effect on him in Dr. Thompson's class, so maybe he shouldn't have been surprised. Even though they hardly ever agreed, he enjoyed talking to someone who was as obsessed with film as he was.

That was when he remembered a very important detail.

"Wait," he said. "You hate pop culture. Are you *really* okay with the bastardization of your brainchild?"

Back at Ground Smoothie, Mia's eyes had flashed when Noah suggested the changes, like she was about to throw her drink at him and stomp out. Even now, she didn't sound particularly happy about her own show getting approved.

Instead of answering his question, Mia scoffed. "I do *not* hate pop culture."

"You said *Alien* isn't a classic. The same movie that the *Guardian* called a masterpiece. Even Roger Ebert gave it four stars."

Mia let out a long sigh. "I liked the *Barbie* movie. And that's as pop culture as you can get."

"Eh, with very heavy-handed philosophical themes—"

"I'm hanging up. I can't believe you just dissed *Barbie*."

"I didn't!" Noah said quickly. "I liked it. Watched it four times. While the doll itself is pop culture, the *movie* has an intellectual, high-culture side to it. It's not the epitome of pop culture."

"You watched *Barbie* four times?"

"Yes. My English is decent, but it's still my second language. I watch most Hollywood movies twice to understand all the jokes and themes fully. For *Barbie*, I watched it two other times with Korean subtitles, once with my mom and once with my brother. Hey, you never answered my question."

Mia was silent. If it weren't for the barely audible sound of her breathing, he would have thought she'd hung up.

By then, Noah had reached his room in the Alpha Tau house. He sprawled out on Fossil Couch, so named because it'd been passed down from fraternity brother to fraternity brother for an unknowable number of years.

Mia let out a breathy sigh.

"I'm not happy with it," she finally said. "But I *think* I'll be okay with it. As long as it doesn't get too toxic. My friends love the changes you suggested, and so does the SPC. My main priority is that it gets made and everyone is proud of it in the end."

"All right then." Noah got back on his feet and started pacing. He'd been in many projects, both his own and others', in the last three years, but this was his first time getting involved in a reality TV show. *And* the first time he'd have to star in any kind of long-form production himself.

His throat tightened just thinking about all the heart-to-heart conversations he would need to have on camera. Three years of making all sorts of short videos, and nothing had fazed him like this. But maybe this sort of new experience would be good for him. And he was always pushing his own boundaries when it came to filmmaking.

Mia's voice cut through his musings: "Are you still there?"

Choosing to focus on the far-less-intimidating production side of things for now, Noah asked, "When do we need to raise the money by? And start casting for the rest of the contestants?"

He was about to write down Mia's response when someone hammered on his bedroom door. Noah opened it to see Thad, who was all out of breath. His Little's usually slicked-back brown hair was a puffed-out, tangled mess, like he'd been running around the house.

Noah raised his eyebrows.

"Hey," said Thad. "Sorry. But did you tell Kyle that he can have a party in the backyard?"

"Just a sec," Noah told Mia. He put himself on mute before responding to Thad. "What? No. I haven't seen him all day. I just came back from campus a short while ago."

"That son of a . . ." Thad let out an exasperated groan. "I *thought* it was weird that he said you out of all people wanted to throw a party."

Noah smirked. Out of all their fraternity brothers, Noah was known as the "antisocial" one. Thad and Brent, who were now both officers, didn't pester him to come out to events he didn't want to attend, and, in exchange, Noah helped them with recruitment every year. It was a nice trade-off.

"Is Kyle giving you a lot of trouble?" Noah asked. "I didn't know he was that kind of guy, to be honest."

Thad exhaled. "I hate to say it, but yeah. He keeps lying and trying to get away with stuff. Man, being a Big is hard stuff. Was I this bad, too?"

Noah shot his Little a fond smile. "Nah, you made things easy. I was in the middle of something, but let me know if I can help out in any way."

"Appreciate it, bro." Thad nodded and left.

Noah unmuted himself and said to Mia, "I'm back. Sorry, fraternity business."

"Er, okay," she replied. "Anyway, the SPC wants us to have a concrete plan on how we're going to crowdfund by next week. They also said we won't be able to officially cast anyone else until we raise enough money to make everything happen."

"I'll start promoting the show on my social media then. The sooner we get started the better."

Noah got out his phone from his pants pocket, his head already swirling with ideas.

"Yup," said Mia. "Do you want to brainstorm together?"

"No. Just send me the sign-up link for the show."

There was a pause. Mia's voice pitched higher, like she regretted asking Noah for help. "Uh, okay. Good luck, I guess?"

"Thanks."

Noah opened up his apps and got started.

CHAPTER SIX

Mia

Mia stared, transfixed, at the video playing on Alex's phone.

Since Noah had told her he'd "get started," she'd just assumed he'd have some kind of update for her by their next production meeting at Carlisle. What she didn't think would happen was . . . whatever was happening on the phone screen right now.

Noah danced to a cute, poppy girl-group song, swaying his hips and making heart signs with his fingers. Instead of smirking or playing it cool like he usually did in his videos, Noah smiled, so brightly that Mia sat back down in her conference room chair. And immediately got back up again. Because her friends *could not* find out about her crush on Noah.

When they started working together, when *The Cuffing Game* was still *Campus Crush*, she didn't tell any of her friends about her feelings because they simply seemed irrelevant. But now, this was all just embarrassing. What kind of showrunner would they think she was if they knew she had a crush on one of their contestants?

Mia willed herself to calm down. She glanced around the room, but luckily her friends hadn't noticed her overreaction. In fact, they were too busy reacting to Noah themselves.

"This is the first time Noah has ever smiled like that in his content before," Alex said in an awestruck voice. "Even in the funny videos, he always keeps a straight face. Wow, I'm in love."

"He's not *that* great." Damien rolled his eyes.

"Agreed," Kallie replied. "And judging by the comments, this video is rather polarizing. But I think that's intentional. Given the over-a-million view count."

"Posting a video that's so shocking and out of character that people debate about it in the comments," Mia said, trying her best to keep her voice flat and sound only mildly interested. "That's a smart way to make sure your content gets pushed onto a lot of people's feeds."

As the music continued in the background, Noah stopped dancing to say, "Hi, everyone. Have you ever wanted to be on a dating show? Or see your friends on one?

"Or maybe you want a chance to date me, Noah Jang. Well, if you're a Marlon University student, your chance has finally come. Nominate your friend—and their secret crush—to be on *The Cuffing Game*, *the* hottest dating show created by Marlon University students, for Marlon

University students. More details coming real soon, but I promise you, it's going to be *good*. Before we start officially casting anyone else, though, we need your help to make this show happen. You know where to go for more info."

Alex turned off their phone screen before the video could replay.

"He's made several more of these," they said. "With various hooks and formats. But that's the most popular one so far."

For a moment, no one else said anything. Kallie sank further into her chair. Alex stared off into space like they were a TV show character breaking the fourth wall. Damien glanced at Alex and shook his head, running a hand over his cropped Afro.

"Was this his idea or yours?" he asked Mia.

Mia raised her hands up in a sign of innocence. "Entirely his. I just told him that the SPC gave us the okay to start crowdfunding."

Kallie pushed her laptop across the conference table so they could all see the screen. "I have to hand it to him. He knows what he's doing."

On her computer was an email from the SPC that was cc'd to all four of them.

It read:

Congrats, TCG team! We are happy to inform you that you've received a record number of applicants. You

have also officially met the recommended production budget for the show, so consider yourselves officially greenlit! Please see below for the link to the shared drive that contains the suggested production timeline and all the entries so far. We're so excited for this project. Thank you!

Until now, Mia had assumed all the emails from the SPC were copy-and-paste form letters, impersonal and devoid of any feeling whatsoever. Or at least, that's all she'd been getting from them until now. The difference between failure and success was jarring, and it'd just taken a few videos by a popular influencer. By *Noah*, no less.

You did what you needed to do to save the show, she reminded herself. But she couldn't shake off the feeling that she'd made a deal with the devil.

On her own laptop, Mia opened the shared drive from the SPC in one window and the text conversation she had with Jeannette in another. After glancing at the suggested timeline, she sighed and sent her sister a text.

MIA: Hey, J. Can you do me a favor? I'll owe you big-time when I get home for break.

Jeannette's response was instantaneous.

JEANNETTE: Sure! What is it?

MIA: Can you tell Mom and everyone else that I won't be coming home until Christmas Eve? They'll take it better coming from you.

Due to their parents' infamous love for Christmas, Mia's family started their festivities on December 1, opening Advent calendars and putting up decorations all around the house. Although Christmas Eve would be a perfectly reasonable time to go back home for the holidays to some households, it was considered late for hers.

MIA: And *don't* tell Mom or Dad that this is for my TV show.

JEANNETTE: Wait, did you get it approved? Congratulations!

MIA: Thanks. And yeah, it's looking like we'll wrap on the 23rd, which means I won't be able to fly home until the morning of the 24th.

JEANNETTE: Well, I guess that can't be helped. I'll tell them you failed math and have to stay behind to do remedial classes.

MIA: Kind of scary how fast you came up with that lie but sounds good. Thanks.

It was bad enough that their mom already thought Mia had "abandoned" everyone by moving thousands of miles away to study *film*, something that would "only make her a starving artist in the end." Mia didn't need to add any more wood to that fire. In some families, Mia, who had gotten a full-ride scholarship to one of the best film schools in the country, might have been a favorite. But to the Yoons, she was the black sheep while Jeannette was the golden child who had stayed close to home and majored in accounting, something perfectly practical.

"Okay, so we have two hundred entries and counting," Alex said, pushing their boxy green glasses up their nose. "How many people are we thinking in total here? Five? Ten?"

Everyone turned to Mia. She immediately switched to the other window on her computer.

"Sorry," she said. "I was telling my family I have to stay in LA a bit longer for break."

"You're fine," Damien replied to Mia before looking at the others. "Most of the cabins I found seem to cap at around fifteen people, and there's four of us. So around ten contestants, but make it an odd number so we can eliminate one person on the first night."

"That's something else we need to figure out," Kallie said. "The structure of the show and how we're going to keep eliminating them after that."

Mia's head whirled. She hadn't even thought of eliminating

people, but if this was a dating show—with all the drama—then they'd need to contrive ways to bump people off. Even the idea made her slightly queasy.

"We're doing six days, right?" Damien asked. "Why not just make it simple and do an elimination every other night? We can have challenges and random events here and there that'll also change things up, but the gist will be that whoever can't pair up—or *cuff*, if you will—with someone else gets eliminated until we're down to the last remaining couple. We can change some things later on, too."

An elimination every other night? Mia took a deep breath to settle her stomach. Making *Campus Crush* into a zesty reality TV dating show called *The Cuffing Game* had already been a huge shift. But it seemed like with every new idea, it was becoming more and more a totally unrecognizable show to the one she'd first envisioned.

"You'll learn quickly that the industry revolves around collaboration," one of her professors had said in the first week of classes. "Sure, we have auteur directors like Christopher Nolan, but even they still work with crews of other talented people. And for TV, we have writing rooms, where a *team* of writers work on scripts for shows. Not just one person."

Mia knew all of that in theory, but it was harder in practice, especially since she'd spent the last ten years coming up with ideas for shows alone in her room.

"Mia?" Kallie asked. "Are you feeling okay?"

Mia blinked and looked around. All three of her friends were staring at her now, various looks of concern on their faces.

"Yeah!" Mia exclaimed, putting some extra energy into her voice. "Sorry, some part of me is still reeling from all the changes we're making to the show."

Kallie frowned in understanding. "Yeah, we *are* making a lot of changes. Are you okay with them?"

"It may be *our* show, but it's still *your* original idea, Mia," Damien said, matter-of-factly. "You're allowed to say if you don't like something. Trust me when I say that Hollywood can be a dog-eat-dog world. If you don't speak up, people can walk all over you."

Mia shook her head. "It's not that I don't like it per se. It's just a lot. You know I don't like surprises. Or change."

Damien nodded. "Even so, *please* don't hesitate to speak up if I, Kallie, or Alex say anything you don't like, okay? We're not in Hollywood yet. And we're all in this together. If you're not comfortable with any of the changes we're making, we don't have to do them."

A burst of warmth and gratitude loosened the knot in Mia's chest.

"Right," she said, looking around the room. "I'll probably want to make a few adjustments here and there, but let's discuss and plan out the details some other time, since we should pick the contestants ASAP. There *is* one thing from our original idea I'd like to for sure bring in, though. If everyone else is okay with it."

"Yeah of course," Kallie replied. "What is it?"

"You know how, with *Campus Crush*, we planned to have interviews of the people with crushes? It'd be cool if we kept that part. Sort of a confessional interview at the beginning of each episode."

Damien nodded approvingly. So did Kallie and Alex.

"That sounds cool," Alex said. "How about you and I handle that part, since Kallie and Damien will already have a lot on their hands?"

"Yeah, that's perfect." Mia smiled. "And, going back to the entries, how about we divide them so we each review fifty? Unless that's too much."

Damien stretched out his fingers and moved his head from side to side, getting into full producer mode.

"It *is* a lot," he said. "But we should sort through them all by tonight since we have so many other things to take care of. We only have a month left until the first day of shooting."

"Sounds good," Mia said, trying to settle her nerves. At least they had a plan. "Let's get started then."

Through the glass walls separating the different conference rooms, Mia could see other student groups working on their own individual projects, burning the midnight oil as many often did in Carlisle.

This is going to be the first of many sleepless nights, Mia thought.

But instead of feeling weary, Mia felt almost giddy as she started flipping through the entries. After months of planning something that they weren't even sure could be a real show, here she and her friends were, one step closer to making their dreams into a reality. Her fingers tingled with excitement.

They hadn't reached Hollywood yet, but they were getting there.

LIST OF CONTESTANTS FOR *THE CUFFING GAME*

The following version of this document is meant for the ***crew*** *of* The Cuffing Game *ONLY! Please make sure to erase* ***crush information*** *and* ***internal notes*** *before sending it to the contestants. Thank you! —Mia*

CELINE HUANG
Sophomore

Major: Business

Zodiac Sign: Aries

Hometown: San Diego, CA

Crush: Noah

Internal Notes: She's my roommate, but if I show bias toward her in any way, PLEASE tell me.

NOAH JANG
Senior

Major: Film

Zodiac Sign: Leo

Hometown: Seoul, South Korea

Celine's crush

MATÍAS CISNEROS
Sophomore

Major: Communications

Zodiac Sign: Cancer

Hometown: New York, NY

Crush: Jack

BETHANY DARNELL
Freshman

Major: Biology

Zodiac Sign: Sagittarius

Hometown: Austin, TX 🤠

Crush: Jack

Internal Notes: Most people nominated Jack, so we were bound to have repeats, honestly.

JACK MILLER
Junior

Major: Psychology

Zodiac Sign: Taurus

Hometown: Atlanta, GA

Matías's and Bethany's crush

Internal Notes: We're super lucky we got him on this show, with how he's so famous and all. Thank God football season is over.

SHIRIN AHMAD
Sophomore

Major: Engineering

Zodiac Sign: Libra

Hometown: San Francisco, CA

Crush: Tiana

Internal Notes: She's best friends with Tiana

and has had a crush on her for ten *years but is too scared to ruin the friendship.* 😭

TIANA WILLIAMS
Sophomore

Major: Computer Science

Zodiac Sign: Aquarius

Hometown: San Francisco, CA

Shirin's crush

CALEB JACOBSEN
Junior

Major: Political Science

Zodiac Sign: Gemini

Hometown: Raleigh, NC

Crush: Carlos

CARLOS MANALO
Senior

Major: Architecture

Zodiac Sign: Pisces

Hometown: Los Angeles, CA

Caleb's crush

PART TWO

Now Airing

DAY ONE

THE CUFFING GAME

Behind-the-Scenes Contestant Interview

CELINE HUANG

MIA: *[from behind the camera]* Hey, welcome, have a seat. Please look at the camera and state your name, year, major, and your crush.

CELINE: Hi! Thanks for having me. Ooh, so cool. Is this like one of those one-on-one interviews that they have for reality TV shows? I feel like I'm on *The Kardashians*.

MIA: Yeah, so, you're the first person to be interviewed. I'm going to give you a quick rundown before we begin. My voice will be edited out later so it's just you talking to the camera. We'll also edit out any awkward parts so don't worry if you stumble on your words. But for now, please state your name, year, major, crush, and any other information you want to share.

CELINE: *[coughs and gives her biggest smile]* Hi, my name is Celine Huang. I'm a sophomore. I was born and raised in San Diego, but my family is originally from Shanghai. I'm going back there to visit my relatives after this, actually! We go every year. Anyway, you may know me from my YouTube channel, *Makeup with Celine*. I'm a business major and my crush is obviously Noah Jang.

MIA: Sorry, why obviously?

CELINE: Noah is so *dreamy* and he's the closest thing to a K-pop star we have at Marlon. Although, come to think of it, I've never heard him sing . . . but whatever. He's an amazing dancer. I've been watching his videos since I first came to campus. The fact that I'll meet him in person soon is . . . wow, I hope my mind doesn't go completely blank.

MIA: Well, good luck. And what is the thing you're most looking forward to on the show? Besides meeting Noah?

CELINE: Honestly, just the chance to unplug and find true love. *[makes a heart with her hands]*

MIA: And by true love, do you mean Noah?

CELINE: Of course! I won't have eyes for anyone else.

MIA: No matter what?

CELINE: No matter what.

CHAPTER SEVEN

Noah

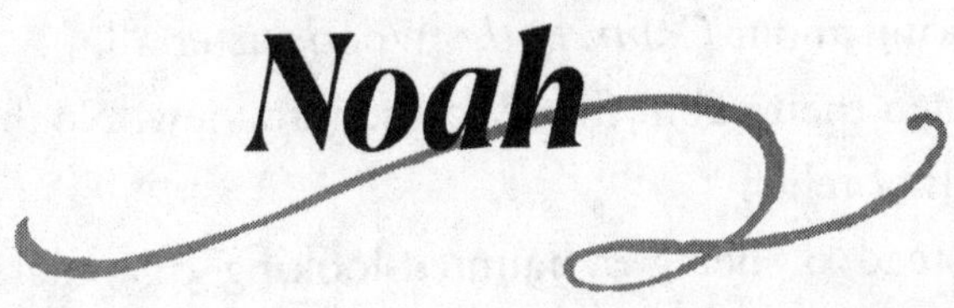

If someone had asked Noah how he'd planned on spending his last winter break from school, he would have said something like "swimming in the Florida Keys" or "skiing in Aspen with Thad." He definitely wouldn't have said, "staying in a cabin in the woods with a bunch of strangers."

Cabin in the Woods, Noah thought. *Now that was a great movie.*

Noah smirked as he thought of how Mia would react if he said her show reminded him of the horror-comedy movie. She'd probably pass out in frustration.

But as he drove his Jeep farther up into the mountains, that spark of amusement slowly died out. Throughout his time at Marlon, Noah had heard his fraternity brothers talk about going up to ski in the Big Bear Lake area. But they'd all failed to mention just how *remote* everything was despite being less than three hours away from LA.

Goose bumps ran down his back. The road was windy, and whichever side wasn't lined with snow-covered trees had scenic yet humbling views of the surrounding mountains. He gripped the steering wheel until his knuckles went white and glanced at the colorful line of rubber ducks on his dashboard for fortitude. Maybe he shouldn't have been thinking about *Cabin in the Woods* after all. . . .

When their cabin finally came into view, Noah breathed a sigh of relief.

Instead of being a haunted-looking dilapidated shack, their lodging was more of a two-story mansion made of polished wood that looked like it could be on *Selling Sunset*. He'd heard through the SPC grapevine that the *Cuffing Game* team had managed to raise a record-breaking amount for the show. It was nice to see that money being put to good use.

Noah parked in the line of vehicles in front of the lodge and opened his car door. In just a split second, the freezing mountain wind cut through him, chilling him to his bones. He immediately shut his door again.

Although he was born in Seoul, his last three years in LA had softened him up, chipping away the tough, winter-resistant shell he'd had back home. He was wearing a heavy black coat and a thick blue scarf, but somehow, it wasn't enough.

Drawing his clothes tightly around himself, he watched as the people in front of him slowly got out of their cars. They all had their backs to him and were bundled up in winter wear, so Noah couldn't make out much. But he counted six contestants, excluding himself. Which meant they were missing two.

He spotted Mia going from car to car, greeting everyone. When she got to his Jeep, though, she stopped in her tracks. Noah lifted a hand to give her a small wave, but she only widened her eyes in response, giving him a tight grin before turning back around toward the lodge.

Okay, he thought. *I see how it is.*

He guessed her reaction was to be expected. Only a couple days after their surprise phone conversation, he and Mia had gone back to their usual, comfortable routine of arguing with each other in class. Then finals had hit, and Noah hadn't seen her since they'd turned in their exams. Most of their interactions together this past semester had consisted of arguing. What were he and Mia supposed to do when he arrived at Big Bear, miraculously make peace and engage in friendly conversation? Noah did have his optimistic moments, but he wasn't delusional.

He shook his head, reminding himself of why he was here in the first place. He wasn't here to talk to *Mia*. The girl who nominated him could be right in front of him, walking to the house this very second.

Noah relaxed his shoulders, gathered up his things, and headed into the lodge.

The interior of the house was surprisingly cozy. Brown leather couches and a set of incredibly comfortable-looking turquoise lounge chairs faced a brick fireplace that already had a warm, welcoming fire in full swing. Large windows looked out onto the wooden patio outside and the snowy trees that surrounded the house in all directions.

Everything was perfect, until Noah turned the corner and saw a big grizzly.

He jumped, an embarrassingly high-pitched yelp escaping from his mouth, before he realized the bear was a statue.

Heart still pounding, Noah had placed a hand on his chest when he heard a barely restrained giggle. He turned around.

Three girls stared at him with great amusement by the foot of the winding staircase.

Before they'd left for Big Bear, Mia had sent them all an email with the address of the cabin, the names and basic information of all the chosen cast members, and the contact information of the crew, in case of emergencies. So technically, Noah knew the names of these girls. He just didn't know who was who.

The one who'd giggled, an East Asian girl bundled up in a white Fendi down jacket and pink skirt, still had her hand over her mouth. She looked familiar, although Noah couldn't remember how he knew her. The other two girls, clearly friends from the way they stood together, also smiled at him in recognition. The first was Black and had on red wintry athleisure gear while the other was Middle Eastern and wore an elegant green coat that accentuated her hazel eyes.

"Don't worry," said the third girl. "Grizzlies were eradicated from the area a hundred years ago. You'll still find black bears around, though. I looked it up."

"Or worry, because poaching sucks," her friend added. "It's a matter of perspective."

"Truly," Noah agreed.

Running a hand through his hair, he gave them what he liked to call his "social media smile." It was more of a mischievous, Flynn Rider smirk, but "social media smile" had a better ring to it. He'd learned through trial and error that most people liked this smile more than his real one.

The first two girls' faces lit up, while the third narrowed her eyes.

"Hi, Noah!" said the first girl. "I'm Celine. It's so nice to finally meet you in person!"

Her words and tone implied they'd interacted with each other online before, but Noah wasn't sure when or how.

Maybe we DMed each other? he wondered. *Exchanged a few words in the comments section?*

Admittedly, he interacted with a lot of people online. You had to, to boost reach for the algorithms. The girls he'd learned to flirt with, while with the guys, he tended to spam the fire emoji or send short, encouraging phrases like "Let's go!!!" Many of these interactions blurred together at the end of the day, even more so when people used random, anonymous usernames like they often did on social media.

"Hey," he said breezily. "Nice to finally meet you in person, too."

"I love your content!" said the second girl. "I'm Tiana. Nice to meet you!"

"And I'm Shirin," the third one said. "She always sends me your videos. They're okay."

"Haha, thanks. Nice to meet you ladies, too."

Noah waved goodbye at them as they went up the stairs to their rooms. When they were out of sight, he replayed the brief interactions he had with each of them in his head. Shirin didn't seem to like him very much, so she was probably not the girl who had a crush on him. But maybe Celine or Tiana.

Before he headed upstairs himself, Noah looked up and found two small cameras attached to the ceiling. One was pointed directly at him and the staircase, while the other looked toward the adjacent kitchen area.

Along with the address to the cabin, Mia had included in her informational emails a consent form that gave the crew permission to film the contestants all week. They were going to be recorded doing everything from going on dates to doing completely mundane things like getting up from bed or eating breakfast. Mia had also mentioned that there would be cameras throughout the house.

We probably won't use most of the footage from these other cameras, her email had said. **In fact, our editor is going to wipe them whenever they finish editing an episode since they**

have limited storage. Since our crew only has two main cameras, and we can't always catch everything that happens in a single moment, we'll have the smaller ones around the house in case we miss something.

Noah waved at the camera overhead before going up the stairs.

There were seven bedrooms, all labeled according to the first seven letters of the alphabet. Noah had been assigned to Bedroom D with Matías Cisneros, a second year. The door to the room was closed, but when Noah turned the knob, it swung open easily.

"Wait!" a voice yelled when he entered the room. Noah froze. "Oh, wow. It's really you! You're Noah Jang, right?"

A long-limbed, brown-skinned boy with curly black hair and glasses was reading a thick fantasy book in one of the beds. His suitcase lay haphazardly unpacked in the middle of the room, with clothes and toiletries taking up nearly the entire floor.

Noah raised his eyebrows at the mess. He hadn't shared a bedroom with anyone since he was a first year living in an on-campus dorm. This was going to be interesting.

He stepped around the boy's stuff to shake hands with his new roommate. "Hey, nice to meet you. Matías, right?"

"Yup, nice to meet you too! It's wild how we're here, isn't it?"

At first, Noah had thought Matías was yelling, albeit in a cheerful, not angry way. But now he realized the boy was just naturally loud, perpetually speaking like his statements all ended with exclamation marks. Noah's lips twitched. It took some getting used to, but it was quite fun.

"Yeah," Noah replied. "Who knows what'll happen this week . . ."

Noah gingerly maneuvered his bag to his side of the room and was about to lie down on his bed when he got a feeling that he was being watched. He looked around.

"The camera's on the dresser across the room," Matías said, before reopening his book.

"Ah," Noah said. Sure enough, on the dresser, with the red recording light on, was a small camera.

Matías kept his eyes on his book as he replied, "Luckily, we can just cover it up with something if we need privacy. I think they did that intentionally. I'm more worried about the overhead ones, but thankfully those are only in the hallways."

Noah made a mental note to do a full sweep of the house later. But for now, the adrenaline that had built up inside him during the drive was dissipating, and all he wanted to do was sleep.

"Contestants, please gather around the firepit in the backyard," Mia's voice rang loud and clear all around the room. "And don't forget to bring your phones and any other telecommunication devices you brought with you today."

"What in the Big Brother nonsense was that?" Matías grumbled.

It took Noah a second to realize that this *wasn't* one of his nightmares and that Mia's voice had really come from the ceiling. He opened his eyes to see his roommate unhappily peering up at an intercom speaker overhead.

Great, he thought. *Just what I need. PA messages from Mia.*

"Maybe we can spray some water onto it with the showerhead," Noah said wryly as he got up from bed.

"Ha, I wish," replied Matías. "I don't know if you heard but it sounds like they want us to gather in the yard. Apparently there's a firepit? I guess everyone's finally here."

"Nice. Do you think they'll actually take away our devices?" Noah asked as he picked up his phone from the bedside table.

Matías shrugged as he also grabbed his phone. "It said so on the email, right? I've seen a lot of reality TV shows that don't let contestants use their phones, so it's not that unusual. It'll be like a social media detox, I guess."

Noah winced. Before he'd moved to LA and started content creation, he wouldn't have even thought twice about the term "social media detox." But now, after years of being entirely dependent on his phone and smartwatch to not only make a living but also communicate with his family in South Korea, Noah's hands grew clammy.

The two boys put on their coats and went downstairs.

Frigid winter air instantly hit them the moment they

stepped outside. They shivered violently, and Noah gritted his teeth, hoping they wouldn't have to stay outside for long.

Seven other contestants sat around the thankfully already-lit firepit behind the lodge. Besides the three girls from before, the only person Noah recognized was Jack Miller, the star athlete who had led their school to victory this past college football season. The other three, a tall blonde wearing a pink tracksuit, a Southeast Asian boy with a shaggy shock of hair, and a lanky, long-haired redhead, were total strangers to him.

In total, there were four girls and five guys.

Uh-oh, Noah thought. Things were already starting off on a dramatic foot.

Before he and Matías could join the firepit circle, Mia stepped in front of them with a small, portable safe box.

"Phones and other telecommunication devices, please," she said.

Matías went first, gladly tossing his phone into the box before sitting next to Shirin. Noah slowly handed in his phone and smartwatch.

"It's like we're going to jail," he quipped.

Mia rolled her eyes. "It's only going to be for six days. Even less than that, if you get eliminated before then."

"Oh, believe me when I say you won't be getting rid of me that easily."

"You don't even know what the show is going to be like."

Although Noah had come up with the idea to transform *Campus Crush* into *The Cuffing Game*, he and Mia had agreed that he should be kept in the dark about any and all plans after that, just to keep things fair for everyone else.

Noah raised his eyebrows. "Whatever it is, I'm ready for it."

Mia fixed him with an all-too-familiar glare.

Heat rose up inside Noah as he stared back at her. A part of him was still aware that the other contestants were waiting for him to join them by the fire. But it was as though he and Mia were back at Marlon, electricity crackling between them like they were mortal enemies in an anime.

Suddenly, Mia rubbed the corner of her eye, creating a small, dark smudge.

And just like that, Noah snapped out of it.

"Wait," he said. "Are you wearing *makeup*? And *contacts*?"

In the four months he'd known Mia, Noah couldn't recall seeing her wearing anything else but her usual glasses, T-shirt—with a hoodie, if it was cold outside—and jeans. And because she never wore makeup, he'd assumed that that was just her thing.

But now, as a real blush bloomed across her cheeks, Noah noticed how they also had a faint shimmer of artificial pink. Her heart-shaped lips were cherry red, and although it was very slight, her eyes were lined with eyeliner that made them look bigger than usual.

And her hair. Her hair was down, in dark waves that pooled across her shoulders.

Noah put a hand over his mouth. This was a Mia he'd never seen before, and he had no idea what to do.

"Yeah?" Mia frowned. "So what if I am?"

Noah only then realized that, in his shock, he'd stared at Mia for *too* long, way beyond the socially appropriate amount. She looked pissed.

He shrugged and glanced away in an effort to break the tension between them. "Looks nice. But also, you smeared your eyeliner. You should probably fix that before we start filming."

Mia narrowed her eyes at him and reached into her pocket for her phone.

Someone grabbed Noah's shoulder.

Noah bristled, his heart rate skyrocketing from the sudden physical contact. It was a good thing they weren't filming yet, because for a split second, he grimaced in what was probably a very unflattering way.

"You must be Noah," said a low, matter-of-fact voice behind him. "We simply *do not* have time right now for . . . whatever it is you're doing. Please go to Alex—they're with Matías right now—to get miked and then join everyone else at the firepit."

Noah turned away from Mia, who was now fixing her makeup with her phone camera, to look at the speaker, a vaguely familiar Black boy holding one of the cameras.

"Damien Carter," he said. "We took Intro to Cinema together as freshmen, although with a class size of three hundred fifty students, I don't expect you to remember me. I myself only know you through social media, since we never talked to each other in class. Now, shoo. We're already behind schedule. Alex, mike him."

Alex, who reminded Noah of a tomato with their short, dyed-bright-red hair and green, squarish glasses, got Noah miked up and ready to go. As they were working, the final crew member, a white girl with a blond pixie cut, came by with the other camera.

"Hey," she said. "I'm Kallie. Nice to meet you."

"Noah. And likewise."

When Noah finally settled into his seat at the firepit, everyone stared at him.

Noah squashed down his discomfort, forcing himself to put on a neutral, vaguely friendly face.

"Hi, everyone," he said. "I'm Noah. It's nice to meet you all."

His words were met with a mix of cheerful greetings and disgruntled noises from the other contestants. They all seemed to know who he was, but not everyone looked happy to see him.

Mia bit her lip. "All right then. Sorry for the delay. Now that everyone is ready, let's get started so we won't finish filming too late at night."

The crew introduced themselves to the contestants, and then Mia went in front of the cameras.

Kallie said, "Camera is rolling."

"Sound, speeding," added Alex as they held up the boom mic.

Noah braced himself, fighting the thundering of his heart.

"Action!" Mia said. "Hi, everyone. I'm Mia Yoon, your showrunner and host. Welcome to the very first night of *The Cuffing Game!*"

CHAPTER EIGHT

Mia

A thrill ran down Mia's spine as she looked at all the contestants one by one. She and her crew had memorized names, faces, and crushes before they'd left for Big Bear, but none of that compared to seeing everyone in the flesh. Everything was just so real now. This whole day, despite Noah's presence, was a dream come true.

The back of her neck prickled from the gaze of both cameras, but she tried her best to ignore them, focusing on the people in front of her instead.

"Thank you all for coming," she said. "*The Cuffing Game* is a dating show run entirely by Marlon students, for Marlon students. You have been chosen to be a contestant because you are either a crusher—someone who has a crush—or you are someone's crush. If you're a crusher, you can win the game by cuffing with your original crush *and* lasting all six days of the game. If you're a crush, you win if you last that long and cuff with someone who likes you back. Hopefully this is the crusher who anonymously nominated you to be on the show, but it doesn't have to be."

Caleb, a long-haired redhead, raised his hand.

"Yes, Caleb?" Mia asked.

"What if you're a crusher but end up liking someone else in the show?"

Everyone laughed, and Jack exclaimed, "This man, right here!"

Mia winced. "Well, I'd hope your crush is strong enough to last more than a week if you nominated them to go on this show with you."

Some people said, "Ooh," and Mia continued, "Y'all *are* giving up some of your winter break for this, after all. *But* if you do end up developing feelings for someone else, you are more than welcome to try dating that other person later! Just not on the show, out of respect for your original crush. The only exception is if, for some reason, your crush gets eliminated before you. *Then*, you can cuff with someone else and still be eligible to win the game, as long as the new cuffing is mutual."

Bethany tossed her ponytail to one side and raised her hand. "If you're a crusher, it's probably best to confess and cuff with your crush as soon as possible, right? So no one steals your crush from you?"

"Not necessarily," Mia replied. "I mean, you can. How you want to approach things is entirely up to you. But every crush has the right to refuse. And if a crush says no, then that'll be an automatic elimination from the game for the crusher."

Nervous murmurs erupted from around the firepit. Most of the crushers, like Shirin and Matías, looked terrified, while the crushes, like Noah, seemed intrigued but otherwise nonchalant.

"Oof," said Bethany. "Understood. So, basically, we need things to be mutual."

"Yup, the last thing we want is for someone to end up in a cuffle that they don't want to be in."

"Cuffle?" Shirin repeated. She frowned, as if the very word offended her. "What does that mean?"

"A cuffed couple," Mia explained, trying her best not to blush. When she and her friends had made up their own words for the show, it'd seemed cute and clever. But now, under the scrutiny of all nine contestants and the two cameras, Mia wasn't so sure. Maybe they'd overdone it a little.

But then, from behind her camera, Kallie grinned and gave her a thumbs-up.

Mia relaxed her shoulders and smiled. Right. In the end, this was *their* show. They could do whatever they wanted with it.

She waited to see if anyone else had any questions. When nine pairs of eyes silently stared back at her, she went on, "For the next four days, including today, there will be a random event, like online viewer voting or a competition. These events will determine your fate in the game, because how you do in them will determine the order you choose your cuffing partner. Whoever fails to cuff with someone else at the end of each day will be eliminated until we have the final three cuffles, of which the winning pair will be determined via audience vote during our live streamed finale on the twenty-third and receive five thousand dollars."

Caleb let out a low whistle. "Five thousand dollars in less than a week? Nice!"

Noah, Jack, and Bethany kept somewhat neutral expressions, while Matías and Shirin still looked frightened. Carlos and Tiana frowned, as if they were still trying to piece out why they were even here in the first place, while Caleb smiled like it was the best day of his life. And Celine? Celine looked so hopeful that Mia's own heart beat a little faster.

Mia was about to go on when Noah raised his hand.

She braced herself. "Yes, Noah?"

"So, what is the random event for today?"

Mia gritted her teeth, hoping Noah wouldn't go back and forth with her like he did in class. This was definitely not the time or place.

"I was getting to that," she said, trying her best to keep her voice even. "Tonight's event is speed dating. You'll have the chance to talk to whoever you wish for short periods of time. If you're a crusher, hopefully you'll get a chance to talk to your crush! Whoever you end up talking to today, please remember that you *and* another person have to agree to cuff together by the end of the night. Otherwise, you'll be eliminated."

The contestants warily eyed each other, like they were all afraid the others would send them packing. The tension in the air was so thick, Mia could have cut it with a knife.

And then, of course, Noah raised his hand again.

Mia tried her best not to sigh in exasperation. "Yes, Noah?"

"For these dates, do we have to stay outside, or can we go back into the lodge?" he asked. "The firepit is nice and all, but I prefer indoors."

Some of the other contestants made sounds of agreement, and everyone, both cast and crew, turned to look at Mia. Not for the first time, she resented Noah's entire existence.

The original plan was to record everyone talking to each other around the firepit, since that would make it a lot easier to film the group. But of course, Noah *had* to randomly suggest an alternative.

She exchanged glances with her crew. Damien looked indifferent, but both Kallie and Alex gave her a pleading look. Since Kallie was the principal cinematographer and Alex was the editor who was going to have to piece all the different clips of footage together, Mia didn't blame them. If everyone split apart, it'd be hell to record and edit this episode.

Mia tried to think of a compromise that could keep everyone warm without making postproduction hell.

"You're welcome to go back inside," she finally said. "But please keep to the living room or the dining room, since that's where most of the overhead cameras are. Please be sure to stay near a camera so we can see and hear your conversations."

"Cool," Noah replied. "I call dibs on the turquoise lounge chairs! I saw a couple cameras near there."

Mia hadn't known the "turquoise lounge chairs" even existed. And apparently, she wasn't the only one, because several other people shot Noah confused looks.

Noah would *pick the most random piece of furniture . . .* Mia thought.

She almost rolled her eyes before remembering she was still being recorded. It took everything to keep her face blank. "If no one has any other questions, let's get started! Feel free to wander into the rooms I mentioned!"

They stopped recording, and Mia relaxed her shoulders as everyone got up. She was officially done hosting for today, since all the work she had to do now was behind the scenes. Quickly, she tied her hair into a messy bun. It was a relief to be able to look sloppy again.

Before any of the contestants could leave, Damien held up a finger. "Wait, one more thing. The cameras around the house are lower quality, so Kallie and I will come around with the main cameras so everyone can have equal screen-time with the higher-quality video and audio. Please let us know if you haven't been recorded by a main camera by the end of the night."

"Good point, Damien," Mia said. "Okay, everyone, go!

Feel free to go inside and mingle! But also, whether you're a crush or a crusher, be sure to remember your objectives for the night!"

Noah was the first to leave, presumably heading for the "turquoise lounge chairs." Most of the other contestants walked aimlessly about, trying to decide where to go. Only Celine seemed to know exactly who she wanted to talk to, making a beeline for Noah.

Mia had to hand it to her. Her roommate wasted no time when it came to getting what she wanted.

"Mia and Kallie, go follow Celine," Damien said. "I'll stay here and film whoever leaves next with Alex."

"Maybe I won't use the boom mic for this portion and instead mainly rely on the audio from the lav mics," Alex said, already looking stressed. "Since I can't be in multiple rooms at one time. I wish I could clone myself!"

Mia winced. "Sorry, Alex."

Alex shrugged. "It's fine. Noah had a point. It's a lot colder out here than we thought it would be. It happens."

Mia grabbed a tripod and caught up with Kallie, who'd resumed recording as she trailed after Celine. When she saw Mia, Celine waved at her before wincing.

"Wait, sorry," she whispered. "I'm supposed to pretend the camera isn't there, right? I'm so used to my vlogs, where I wave and talk directly to everyone."

"It's fine," Kallie said. "We can always edit it out later."

Sorry, Alex, Mia thought. *Again*.

The three of them found Noah exactly where he said he'd be, stretched out on one of the turquoise chaise longues in the living room. Cushioned against the plush fabric of the chair, Noah lay with his eyes closed, as if he were taking a nap. Mia had to hand it to him. The lounge chairs did look super comfy. She was almost jealous.

Celine's eyes darted from Mia to Noah, like she wasn't sure what to do.

"Should I wake him up?" she asked quietly.

Noah bolted up in surprise, like he hadn't been expecting anyone to come over to talk to him.

What is this clown doing? Mia bit back a laugh.

"Hey," Celine said with a strained smile. "Mind if I join you?"

Noah coughed. "No, not at all. Come have a seat."

As Celine settled into the other chair, Mia helped Kallie set up the camera on the tripod.

A weird sense of déjà vu filled Mia's head when she saw the two contestants on the viewfinder. Not too long ago, she and Noah had sat just like this on the beanbags of Ground Smoothie. Granted, it'd been a business meeting. Not a date. But still, a lump formed inside Mia's throat.

She pushed it down and took another step back. "Are you two ready?"

Noah and Celine nodded at her.

"Action! Go ahead and start the conversation."

"So, you're from Korea, right?" Celine asked Noah when

they resumed filming. "That's so cool. What's it been like to go to school here?"

"It's been mostly good," Noah replied. "The language barrier was hard at first, but I adapted quickly. In Korea, I learned basic English in school and self-studied with American movies and TV shows. And when I came here, I got into a fraternity. Living in the house *definitely* helped a lot. It was like an immersion program."

Celine laughed, and Mia winced at how unnaturally high-pitched the sound was. That was *not* her roommate's normal laugh. She must have been really nervous. "Wow, that's impressive that you're going to school using your second language! *And* you're in a frat!"

Noah gave Celine what Mia now recognized as his fake influencer smile. It was handsome, charming even. But it wasn't like the ones that naturally sprung up on his face when he was talking. His real smiles were a lot less polished but—Mia begrudgingly admitted—*cuter*.

"What about yourself?" he asked. "Are you from Asia or were you born here in the US?"

"I was born in San Diego," Celine replied. "So I'm barely fluent enough in Mandarin and Shanghainese to understand my relatives when I visit them once a year."

Noah shrugged. "That's good that you know both, though. Even if it's a little bit. And San Diego can still feel like an eternity away with LA traffic."

"Right?"

Celine laughed again, and as they continued talking, Mia couldn't help but notice how good they looked together. With her flawless douyin makeup and long, gorgeous hair, Celine looked amazing. And Noah . . . well, he was Noah. Perfect, as always. At least physically. Mia felt like she was watching a rom-com.

Even though she absolutely did not want to ever date Noah, in this one moment, Mia wondered what *she* would look like on the screen in Celine's place.

But as soon as she did, she had to stifle a laugh, earning a panicked glance from Kallie.

"Sorry," Mia mouthed, moving farther back from the camera.

She didn't think she was ugly, but she was no influencer. The only reason she was able to put on makeup tonight was thanks to Celine's videos. And even then, if Noah's reaction was any indication, it'd still turned out terribly. Her hair had been nice at least, but she'd hastily tied it back earlier, so it was probably a messy bird's nest again.

As she watched Celine and Noah ease closer together on the lounge chairs, Mia concluded she would look ridiculous in Celine's place. She and Noah were just so different from each other that the viewers back home would surely laugh at them.

Celine tucked her hair behind her ears, recapturing Mia's attention. "So . . ."

Noah cocked his head to the side. "So?"

"Okay, sorry if this makes things awkward, but I have to address the elephant in the room!"

Mia bit her lip, wondering what her roommate was going to say.

Noah gave Celine an apprehensive look. "What is it?"

"You're like . . . famous," Celine continued. "Why are you even here? What made you agree to be on this show?"

Mia could have imagined it, but Noah's eyes seemed to shift focus, looking up from Celine to where *she* was standing behind the camera. Mia frowned and crossed her arms.

Noah's reaction was immediate. His head tilted up, definitely looking at her this time. He frowned before focusing on Celine again. So she *hadn't* been imagining things.

"Ah," Noah said, smiling again as if nothing had happened between him and Mia. "Just because I'm 'famous' doesn't mean I have a whole line of people waiting to date me. All the content I produce takes a lot of work. So I haven't had much time for relationships."

A small line formed between Celine's perfect brows. "Then why start now?"

Mia stared down at the floor, pretending not to care about Noah's response. But she had to admit that she was also curious. Although she *had* worked hard on her initial pitch, she'd been surprised when he'd agreed to be on the show. Even more so since he'd never said exactly why, just that he didn't want to be single.

"Well," began Noah, "what can I say? I'm a hopeless romantic at heart. My older brother, Jae-hyun, always says that after college, dating becomes a bunch of apps and algorithms. I don't want that. I want to meet someone face-to-face. I want *real love*. This is my last winter break ever. I want to fully take advantage of that time and meet someone as organically as I can, before it's too late."

"Aw!" Celine gushed.

Kallie also made some kind of adoring noise, which was saying a lot. Noah gave the camera a dashing smile before leaning back again in his seat. There he was. Noah Jang, charming as ever.

A million protests built up inside Mia. She covered her mouth, and it took all of her self-control to not burst out laughing at Noah.

Really? The guy who literally said that every girl at a party wasn't his type thinks he can meet someone organically on a dating show?

She rolled her eyes. That, at least, she could do behind the camera without disrupting the scene. Or so she thought. Noah shifted his gaze again, his eyebrows arching up slightly, as if to say *Really?*

Mia turned around. There. Now Noah couldn't see her reactions.

"I'm a huge fan of your videos, by the way," she heard Celine say. "You're just so handsome and genuine! I don't know how you do it."

Genuine? Mia scrunched up her face. Good thing she'd had the foresight to turn away.

Noah's social media presence was many things. Cool. Flashy and charismatic. Funny, even, on the rare occasions he did comedy skits. But *genuine*? Even after years of watching his content and several hours of *specifically* studying him to pitch the show, Mia couldn't pin down what kind of guy he really was. How was any of that genuine?

"Thanks," Noah replied smoothly. "And how about you?"

"I'm a makeup vlogger," Celine said. "I don't have as big of a following as you, but I'm getting there."

"Wow, that's awesome. I'll have to give you a follow sometime."

"You already do. We DMed each other a few times."

Mia widened her eyes, whirling back around just in time to see Noah freeze. Celine sat back in her seat, like she knew she'd dropped a bomb.

"Ah," Noah said. "Sorry, I get a lot of DMs. They all blur together."

Underneath her makeup, Celine turned splotchy. "I see," she said evenly. "Well, it's okay. There's a way you can make it up to me."

Noah raised an eyebrow. "Oh?"

"You can cuff with me, because, surprise! You're my crush."

Mia covered her mouth and tried her best not to scream.

CHAPTER NINE

Noah

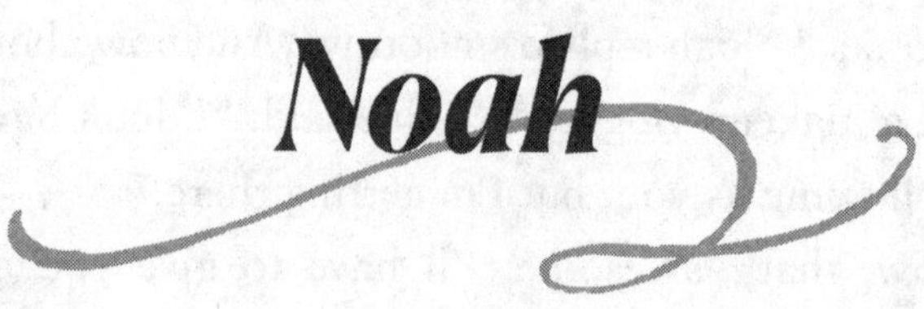

Noah blinked back at Celine. Here they were, not even ten minutes into their conversation. And somehow, not only did he already know who his crusher was, but she expected him to cuff with her *now*.

He hadn't even gotten a chance to talk to the other girls yet. Wasn't this supposed to be speed dating?

In an ideal world, Noah would have been able to tell Celine, "Hey, I think you're cool. But I need to get to know other people first before I commit." But this wasn't an ideal world. This was *The Cuffing Game*, where, by telling the girl in front of him "not yet," he would automatically cause her to be eliminated.

Who came up with these stupid rules? Noah thought. But of course, he knew exactly who.

He shot Mia a glare before turning his attention back to Celine.

The girl's eyes were wide with terror, like she'd belatedly realized what she'd just done.

Noah wanted to sigh or shake his head, something to

help alleviate the pressure that was building up inside of him. But he couldn't. He'd watched enough *Love Is Blind* and other reality TV shows to know that the camera was often unforgiving. Any sort of negative body language could reflect badly on either himself or Celine.

He had no idea how popular *The Cuffing Game* was going to be. But he had to be careful, just in case. Anything could be misconstrued or made into a viral video by people online.

He briefly closed his eyes and then gave Celine what he knew was a charming smile.

"Sure," he told her. "I'll cuff with you. I'd be an idiot to say no."

It wasn't a total lie. Sure, he still wished he could get to know the other girls. But Celine had not only nominated him to be on this show but also quite literally risked it all for him. The least he could do was give her a shot.

Celine threw her arms around Noah.

He stiffened and put up his hands, too caught off guard to control his reaction.

"Oops, sorry," Celine replied, backing away. "I got too excited there."

He forced out a laugh, turning away so neither she nor the camera could see the discomfort in his eyes. "No worries. You just surprised me."

And it's been several years since anyone's hugged me like that, he added in his thoughts. Of course, he couldn't say that part aloud, since people would probably think there was something wrong with him. But it was true. Growing up, the only people who really hugged him were his mom and his brother. And it'd been three years since he had seen either of them in person.

Most people in school gave Noah a wide berth, like his social media fame created some kind of invisible force field around him. Besides the occasional, brief bro hugs with his fraternity brothers, no one touched Noah, period. And he was perfectly fine with that. In fact, it now startled him whenever someone *did* touch him.

"Um, Noah? Are you okay?" asked Mia.

Noah sharply looked up to see that all three girls were now staring at him. The camera was off, safely pointed down toward the ground. Had they wrapped for the day? He hadn't heard anything, but maybe he'd been too lost in his thoughts.

"Sorry," he said. "I'm still tired from the drive. I had an early start to my day, since I had a lot of posts to schedule before I left."

"Aww, I totally get it," Celine replied. "Because same!"

But behind her, Mia narrowed her eyes, as if she could tell he'd told a half-truth.

He let out a quick breath, only now realizing how light-headed he was.

"I'm done for today, right?" he asked Mia. "I'm gonna get some water. I think I might be getting altitude sickness."

Mia's face shifted to an unknowable expression, and it took Noah a few seconds to realize she was *worried* about him. Grumpy Mia, actually concerned about his well-being.

Hell was about to freeze over.

"If you and Celine are both sure about your decision to cuff with each other, then yes, you're done for now," she said. "But we need you to come back later tonight to film the cuffing reveals. Kallie and I are going to film another pair, but in the meantime, go drink water and eat something. You *really* don't look good. Celine, you should grab something, too. Help yourselves to anything that's in the fridge, since we bought those supplies for y'all."

"Wow, thanks!" Celine exclaimed. "Come on, Noah! Let's go eat dinner."

Noah had been planning to chill in his room, but he said, "Sure." He couldn't remember the last time he'd eaten anything.

They wandered into the kitchen, where Noah drank some water and zeroed in on a box of Uncrustables, his favorite American invention. He grabbed a sandwich while Celine grabbed a ready-made chicken Caesar salad.

He'd hoped to have a break from talking, and maybe even a chance to listen in on the other contestants, but that proved to be impossible. While they ate their food at the kitchen table, Celine talked to him about everything, from her favorite foods to all the makeup she put on today. It was like they were still on their date.

At first, Noah tried his best to engage in conversation, nodding and responding at appropriate times. But when he stopped to chew, he had a horrifying realization.

It didn't matter whether or not he responded. Celine kept

talking anyway, sometimes even with her mouth full. There was a small camera right above their heads. Fortunately for Celine, she happened to be sitting with her back turned toward it. The camera couldn't see the salad in her mouth. But Noah could.

He snuck glances up at the kitchen clock and was relieved when, thirty minutes after they'd sat down to eat, Mia's voice came from the speakers: "Contestants! Please regather around the firepit."

Noah let out a quiet sigh of relief. For the first time in his life, he was glad to hear Mia's voice.

"Ooh," Celine said. "I wonder who cuffed with who!"

They threw away their trash and headed back outside.

"Hi, all," Mia said when everyone was settled around the firepit. "I hope you enjoyed getting to know each other. It's time to announce the cuffles. When it's your turn, please stand up and link arms with your chosen match. Does anyone want to go first?"

Celine jumped to her feet and loudly declared, "Noah and I have decided to cuff with each other!"

It took all of Noah's self-control not to wince. If he told Celine the truth and said he was having second thoughts, he'd embarrass her in front of everyone *and* get her eliminated. It was far better to let her down gently tomorrow, when they could hopefully each cuff with someone else.

Noah stood up and linked arms with Celine, giving everyone his best fake smile. "Haha, yeah, we have."

Ever so slightly, Mia bit her lip. But before he could think much of it, she turned around and said, "Okay. We have our first cuffle of Day One. Anyone else want to go next?"

Matías and Shirin exchanged glances, then both stood up.

"We've decided to cuff with each other," Shirin announced.

They also linked their arms and stood next to Noah and Celine.

"We both made it through the first round," whispered Noah, raising his hand to give Matías a fist bump.

"Huh? Oh, y-yeah."

Matías half-heartedly bumped his hand. Noah frowned. Granted, he had known Matías for only an hour or two, but his roommate, who'd been loud and outgoing before, was now sweaty and quiet. He was even shaking a little. Noah made a mental note to check in on Matías when they were back in their room.

Tiana cuffed with Jack, and Caleb with Bethany, leaving Carlos sitting by himself on the bench. They all turned to look at him.

"Carlos," Mia said. "I'm sorry but as the last remaining uncuffed individual, you are now eliminated from *The Cuffing Game*. Would you like to say any parting words before you leave?"

"Um, sure." Carlos looked around at the other contestants. "Well, that was fun . . . I guess? I'm still not sure why I'm here, to be honest. *One* of you had a crush on me, but no one fessed up. Which I understand, since it's only Day One. If you're my crusher and still want to chat at the end of this, DM me when you have your phone back, okay? Have fun, do crime, et cetera!"

"Except, maybe *don't* actually do crime," Mia said, leaping in front of the cameras. "Carlos, thank you so much for your time and for the . . . very interesting goodbye. Everyone, thank you so much. I hope you enjoyed the first day of *The Cuffing Game*. You're now free to go back to your rooms."

The camera crew wrapped up for the night, and the contestants got up from the firepit.

"Good night, Noah!" Celine said, giving his arm a playful squeeze before she left.

Every muscle of Noah's body tensed up. But he made himself relax. He wished she'd stop touching him.

"'Night," he replied with the best fake smile he could manage.

Before he went back upstairs, Noah glanced over at Matías, who seemed to be in deep conversation with Shirin. Well, at least that cuffle seemed to be a good match. Rather than stand around and accidentally third wheel, Noah decided to scout for the overhead cameras before returning to bed.

It'd only been Day One of *The Cuffing Game* and already Noah wanted to sleep a thousand years.

THE IN-BETWEEN

CHAPTER TEN

Mia

"What happened?" Mia hissed when the crew met up for the night in Alex and Damien's room. "Wasn't Carlos someone's *crush*? Why did he get eliminated?"

They had until midnight to edit and submit all the footage for episode one. But first, she had to understand what was going on.

Alex shrugged.

Damien sighed and said, "A rather *interesting* phenomenon happened tonight. But before we discuss, we should set up the production room so we have a space to review all the footage from today. And Alex can start editing."

"Good idea," Mia replied. She snapped a quick picture of the bedroom's original setup so they could put things back where they belonged at the end of their stay.

The bedroom had originally been a quaint kids' room, with sky-blue painted walls, two hotel-quality twin beds, and cotton candy–pink rocking chairs. While Damien and Alex scooted the two twin beds to the far-left corner of the room, Mia and Kallie brought in two long desks and chairs they'd found in the other rooms. Afterward, they carefully placed the cameras onto the desks along with all the other equipment they'd borrowed from the SPC. And, as a final touch, they set up their external hard drives and laptops. By the time they were done, with all the connecting wires and whirring electronic devices, the bedroom resembled a semiprofessional editing room.

Just looking at their setup sent a thrill up Mia's spine. Her first-ever production room, hopefully the first of many more.

The only things they left untouched were the rocking chairs, "for our great amusement and possibly also our sanity," as Alex had said.

Damien sat in one of the chairs, contemplatively rocking back and forth as he said, "So anyway, from what I could gather, no one except Celine cuffed with their actual crush. Everyone else just paired up with their friends or people they were the friendliest with. The biggest offenders being best friends, Shirin and Matías. I think we scared them a bit too much with the 'rejected crushers immediately get eliminated' rule."

Mia winced. "Maybe I should have worded that differently. Or encouraged them to actually try cuffing with their crush more."

"It's okay," Kallie replied. "It was your first time hosting, so it's natural that you made a couple mistakes. You did great, overall! I can't believe you don't watch any reality TV."

"Thanks! I researched a few shows before I got here. And I grew up watching clips here and there, thanks to my sisters," Mia said. "But yeah, anyway, people are cuffing with their *friends*?"

Damien nodded at Alex, who opened one of the video files on their computer. It was a clip of Matías and Shirin sitting together at the kitchen table.

"We filmed these two right before Noah and Celine sat down for dinner," Damien explained. "They were the first cuffle we had, actually."

Alex hit play.

"We don't have to cuff with the person we have a crush on, now, right?" Shirin was saying in the video. *"It's only the first round, so we just need to pair up with literally anyone to make it to the next one."*

"Pretty much," Matías said. *"No way I'm trying to cuff with my crush this early! It'd be too embarrassing if he said no. How about we cuff with each other and try our best to make it through the early rounds first? We can't be eliminated if we stick together, right?"*

"Right."

Alex hit pause. "And they're not the only cuffle that did this," they said with a chagrined expression. "Tiana and Jack are also acquaintances. I think they had a class together or something, from the conversation I watched at least."

Mia groaned. "Do they not realize this is a *dating* show, not a friends show?"

"I mean, in a way, Matías and Shirin are right," Damien said with a shrug. "It's still early on, so they're playing strategy. It's kind of funny, actually. Makes great television."

"But what's going to happen to Caleb now that his crush is gone?" Mia wondered out loud.

"It didn't seem like he had any trouble finding a replacement," Damien pointed out. "Since he cuffed with Bethany instead. I was filming him today, and he didn't react at all when Carlos got eliminated. Which was both impressive and concerning at the same time."

"I know, right?" said Kallie. "You'd think he'd care more about his crush. . . . Poor Carlos."

Mia frowned. "Maybe Caleb's main goal is to survive."

It was entertaining TV, for sure. But it didn't feel authentic, like she had dreamed of the show being back when she first came up with the original idea. The new reality TV element was already creeping in, and it was unstoppable. Her stomach twisted into knots. "He did seem pretty excited about the cash prize," she added.

"People are so unpredictable," Damien remarked. "The beauty of unscripted television."

Alex sat down in front of their computer with a heavy sigh. "Hopefully we can compile all the clips into a comprehensible episode. Truly looking forward to later into the competition when things will be more streamlined. And we'll have fewer people to keep track of."

Without editing, footage was just that: footage. Random

clips of interactions that didn't have a story. It was only when the clips were strung together that they formed a narrative. Editing wasn't Mia's, Kallie's, or even Damien's forte. But that was why they had Alex.

"Let's get to work, team," said Damien, effortlessly stepping into his lead producer role. "Try to prioritize footage from the main cameras tonight, since we should have more than enough content from all the dates we shot today. Alex, how about you start editing Mia's intro? Meanwhile the rest of us can sift through the different dates and flag which clips you can use. First things, first, though: Mia, you and I should grab food for everyone from the kitchen."

Mia nodded. "Sounds good," she said, just as Alex replied, "Aye, aye, captain."

As everyone got to work, Mia's heart nearly burst with excitement.

They were doing it. It wasn't exactly what she had imagined, but she and her friends were really making their own TV show.

CHAPTER ELEVEN

Noah

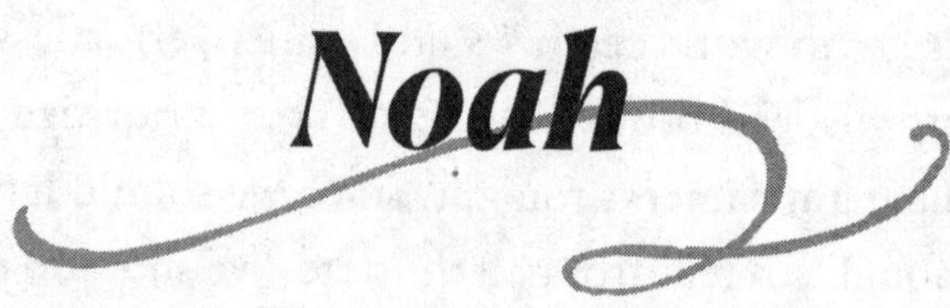

Noah had just finished showering when Matías's voice came from outside the bathroom door.

"Um, Noah? Are you in there?"

Noah wrapped a towel around his waist before stepping out. "Yeah, what's up?"

Matías's face turned bright red as he widened his eyes. "Oh, sorry, I wasn't sure if it was you because of the . . . music. I thought a girl accidentally wandered into our room or something."

Noah followed Matías's gaze back toward his old iPod, which was currently playing "Long Live" by Taylor Swift through his portable speakers.

"I can't shower without my playlist," Noah said. "I wasn't sure if they'd actually take our phones, so I brought this ancient hand-me-down iPod I got from my older brother, just in case. Matías, you look like you're about to suffocate. You can laugh at me, I don't care."

Matías burst out laughing, guffawing so loudly that Noah couldn't help but grin himself.

"What can I say? It's relaxing," Noah went on. "My brother's really into Taylor Swift and Selena Gomez, so he'd always have their music playing in our shared bedroom when we were kids. And now I find it comforting."

Matías laughed even harder, falling backward into his bed. Noah gave him a minute, taking that time to return to the bathroom and get fully dressed in his pajamas.

"Whew," Matías said when he'd finally calmed down. "Well, feel free to play whatever music you have in our room during our week here! And thanks for the laugh. After how tense tonight was, I needed it."

Noah smiled. "Sure thing. Speaking of which . . . are you okay? You didn't look too good back at the firepit."

Matías's face fell. Noah wondered if he should have even brought it up at all.

"Yeah, about that." His roommate buried his face in his hands for a moment before continuing, "I cuffed with my best friend because I doubt my crush likes me back. It seemed like a good idea when Shirin and I first thought about it. Funny, even! But once we were all gathered around the firepit again, it hit me that I couldn't confess to my real crush. And it sucked."

"Wow." Noah sat down on his bed.

"Sorry! That was probably too much, too soon. Especially since we only met a few hours ago."

"No, you're fine. I just . . . don't know what to say."

Noah leaned back, eyeing the camera on the dresser. He had a special love for Thad and his other fraternity brothers, but unless there was some sort of issue, their conversations back at the house were usually surface level, just talking about hot girls or the next tailgate. And that was exactly what Noah preferred.

Now, in this small bedroom with Matías, someone he barely knew, Noah felt out of his element, more so with the camera recording their every word. He grabbed one of Matías's shirts from the floor and threw it over the device. The microphone was probably still recording what they were saying, but he felt better knowing he at least wasn't being watched.

"Why couldn't you confess to the person you like?" Noah asked, finally managing to coalesce his thoughts into a tangible question.

"Well, it's complicated. I don't want to tell anyone who my crush is yet, since once I say it out loud, everyone at school will know. And so will the people who *don't* go to Marlon but still watch our student programming on YouTube. The person I like is a guy. I'm out, so that part is fine. But I don't think *he's* into guys. I could make a total fool of myself."

Ah. Noah wanted to say something kind, something that told Matías that he was an ally. But he didn't want to sound too cheesy or randomly talk about his gay brother when Jae-hyun wasn't even relevant to the conversation. The fear of saying the wrong thing jumbled up the words in his head.

The only thing he could get out was a stupid joke. "It's not me, is it?"

A pillow flew toward him, almost hitting his head.

"Noah, you're so full of it!" Matías said with a laugh. "Even if it were, I said I don't want to tell anyone yet, remember?"

"Yeah, I know. I was kidding."

Noah took a deep breath, growing serious. He and Matías barely knew each other, but he didn't want this moment to pass without him saying something actually beneficial.

He tried again. "Look . . . if you want me to shut up, tell me. But the entire reason you came on this show is because you want a chance with the person you like, right? You're literally sacrificing your winter break for this, like Mia mentioned back at the firepit. Don't you owe it to yourself to at least try talking to him, even with all the risks?"

For a long moment, Matías didn't answer.

Noah panicked. "You can ignore what I said and do whatever you want—"

"No, you're right," Matías cut in. "Might as well just go for it, right?"

"Yeah. Also, I know Marlon is generally an open-minded campus. But if anyone gives you a hard time for liking guys or anything like that, you let me know."

He held out a fist. Matías bumped it and replied, "Thanks, that means a lot, really. I have no idea what the show has in store for us, but let's try our best to have each other's backs while we're both here."

Noah smiled. "Deal."

DAY TWO

THE CUFFING GAME

Behind-the-Scenes Contestant Interview

CALEB JACOBSEN

MIA: Hi, Caleb! Thanks for joining us. Please state your name, year, major, and crush.

CALEB: *[while addressing the camera]* Hello, world! Haha, I've always wanted to do that.

MIA: Name, year, major, and crush?

CALEB: Caleb Jacobsen, junior, political science, and Carlos. Before his unfortunate elimination. RIP. Carlos, if you're watching this and if you're interested, you know what to do. Slide into those DMs, will ya? Because I can't do that yet.

MIA: So yeah . . . that happened. How are you feeling about not having the chance to confess to your crush?

CALEB: It's a bummer, especially since he got eliminated on the first night.

MIA: Did you talk to Carlos at all while he was here?

CALEB: Nope, didn't get a chance. I honestly thought I had more time. Lesson learned. Luckily Bethany and I got along well, so we're cuffed together now.

MIA: So I'm assuming you like girls, too?

CALEB: Hm? No, I'm gay. Like Pete Buttigieg.

MIA: Wait, what? Then why did you . . .

CALEB: *[leans forward]* The other contestants won't be able to see this until they get out of here, right?

MIA: Right . . .

CALEB: Bethany doesn't like me, either. Or at least not in that way. She likes Jack, but she's too scared to confess right away. And I want a chance to win the money. Might as well try since I'm already here, right? So I agreed to cuff with her when she asked. I don't know how long I can last in the game but . . . *[shrugs]* Should be fun!

MIA: That's amazing. Well, I'm wishing you the best of luck. Thanks for coming on!

CALEB: Thanks for having me. Carlos, if you're watching, DMs!

CHAPTER TWELVE

Mia

Throughout the next day, Mia refreshed the YouTube page of the first episode of *The Cuffing Game*. At first, there were only a dozen views. Then fifty. By noon, the view count had exponentially grown, so that it was getting hundreds of new views every few minutes. It was dangerously addicting. And gratifying, given how hard she and her friends had worked on the episode the previous night.

Last night, editing the first episode had been a lot more difficult than any of them could have ever imagined, and by the time they had uploaded the final product, they'd each taken turns sitting in the rocking chairs whenever they felt overwhelmed. Despite all this, Mia had felt giddy just knowing they finally had created a tangible *something*, the first episode of their show.

And now it was out in the world for everyone to see.

New comments appeared every second, and back in the room she was sharing with Kallie, Mia carefully read them one by one. Celine and Noah were the clear crowd favorites, cemented by the results of an online poll Alex had included at the bottom of the page. They'd given the viewers until 5 p.m., Pacific time, to get their votes in before they resumed filming today, but now Mia wondered if they should just call it. Comment after comment said that Noah and Celine looked perfect together, like two celebrities in a rom-com.

Mia flung her phone across the room.

Sure, she'd had the same exact thought when she watched their date. But thinking something to herself was one thing—having the entire world agree was another.

Since there was still some time left before she had to play host again, Mia returned to bed and checked the group chat she had with her family. Her mom and her sisters had sent a bunch of cute photos from yesterday. She smiled as she looked through the snapshots of Cara and Lola wearing matching Christmas pajamas, Marie flipping off the mall Santa, and Jeannette and their mom holding up their hands to their foreheads in dramatic fainting poses while surrounded by groceries from Costco and H Mart.

Someone knocked on the bedroom door.

"Mia, are you in there?" Damien called. "We start in twenty."

"Yup, I know!" She stood up and took a deep breath.

The time flew by as Mia got dressed and did makeup—skipping the eyeliner this time. Then she was back at the firepit, in front of the cameras and the eight remaining contestants.

Some people, like Tiana and Caleb, looked well rested. While others looked worse for wear. Noah in particular, although still his usual polished self, had noticeable dark circles under his eyes.

Did he not get any rest? Mia wondered.

"Hi, everyone," she said. "Hope you're all having a good day so far. The viewers are loving the show. Last time I checked, we were already at ten thousand views! The first episode of *The Cuffing Game* is already the most-watched video on the SPC YouTube channel."

Every contestant except Noah gasped in excitement. Instead of looking pleased, he narrowed his eyes.

"Are these all Marlon students?" Celine asked.

Mia shook her head. "I doubt it, since anyone can watch the videos on YouTube. Unless half of the entire undergraduate population at our school really did watch the first episode, which would be amazing but unlikely. It's amazing, especially for the first episode! People are invested already, which leads me to the random event for Day Two: online voting. On the page for the first episode, the viewers were asked to vote for their favorite cuffle so far."

Matías pulled at his hair. "Wait, people voted for us? Based on the conversations we had yesterday?"

Mia gave him an apologetic smile. "Yup, sorry we didn't

tell y'all in advance because we didn't want it to affect your behavior."

The contestants nervously glanced at each other, and then at Mia.

Her stomach twisted. She was still coming to terms with what she had to say next. But in the end, she knew she had to keep things strictly neutral and professional. No one could know her real feelings about the voting results.

"We asked viewers to rank their favorite cuffles, and this pair won over people's hearts with their amazing chemistry," she said, neatly summarizing what she'd read in the comments. "Congrats, Noah and Celine, you two won today's random event!"

She was going to leave it at that, but behind the cameras, Alex beckoned to the two contestants.

Begrudgingly, Mia added, "Please come stand next to me."

"Yay, Noah, way to go!" exclaimed Matías.

Everyone else cheered as Celine and Noah got up from their seats. Mia had known what was coming, but nothing could have prepared her for how absolutely awkward it was to stand in between her crush and her roommate. As the cameras panned from Noah to Mia to Celine, and back again, she wondered what she'd done to deserve this highly specific and laughably tragic experience of having to third wheel on her own show.

Keep smiling, Mia reminded herself. Her face muscles ached.

"Noah and Celine," she said. "As a reward for being the crowd favorite, you two are eligible for a bonus random event: an intimate second date by the firepit tonight."

"Yay!" Celine jumped up and down, clapping her hands.

Noah, however, looked surprisingly . . . constipated. Or at least, that was the best way Mia could describe the look on his face. It was jarring to see him lose control of his expression on camera. She wondered if she should warn him but decided against it. Since she was currently being filmed too, she had to remain neutral.

And it was deeply satisfying to see Noah look ugly for once.

Maintaining her bright and cheery smile, Mia turned to the other contestants.

"While Noah and Celine are doing their fireside date, the rest of you are welcome to mingle like you did last night," she said. "While Kallie and I film the date, Damien and Alex will come around to record your conversations."

Mia paused for dramatic effect.

"At the end of the night, you may choose to either cuff again with your current partner or cuff with someone else. And yes, this means that you can theoretically 'steal' someone else's partner, as long as the person you want to cuff with agrees to cuff with you, too. So be thinking about who you want to cuff with as you mingle!"

A chorus of *ooh*s and laughter came from the contestants.

"All right, let's get started!" Mia exclaimed. "Noah and

Celine, please sit back down in front of the fire. Everyone else, please return to the lodge."

When Noah and Celine had settled around the firepit, Kallie repositioned her camera so it was pointed right at them. Celine looked excited and happy, but Mia couldn't help but notice how Noah squirmed in his seat. Eyes wide, he looked like he was having an existential crisis.

It was already turning out to be a fun night.

CHAPTER THIRTEEN

Noah

Noah was trapped. What had started as a simple act of kindness had escalated out of control. There was no way he could uncuff from Celine now, not when they had been voted the most popular cuffle. Not when they were supposed to have an intimate one-on-one fireside chat tonight that thousands of people would later watch from their homes.

He supposed he could still dump her since, technically, there wasn't anything stopping him from doing whatever he wanted. But that could potentially create a lose-lose situation. He would embarrass Celine, *and* he could quite possibly make things hell for himself. There were too many dating shows out there with contestants getting villainized all over social media just because they'd been honest about how they felt. Noah didn't want to be that person.

Sweat prickled his forehead as he warily glanced at the camera. He couldn't remember the last time he was this nervous about being recorded.

"Hey, Noah," Celine said when they started filming. "How are you doing?"

Get ahold of yourself, Noah thought, shaking his head from side to side.

"I'm doing great," he lied. "How about you?"

Seemingly oblivious to Noah's inner turmoil, Celine beamed. "Amazing! I'm so glad we're getting this cute date."

Movement in his peripheral vision made him look up. Mia was staring at him from behind the camera, like she always was. She'd strangely been more smiley than usual today, but now, when their eyes met, she furrowed her brow and jerked her head at Celine, as if telling him to pay attention to the date.

Noah glanced back at Celine, just as she said, "So I know we talked about a lot during our first date. But one thing we didn't talk about is our hobbies. What do you like to do besides school and work?"

He nodded, grateful to all that was good that at least *this* question was one he could answer easily. "I like watching movies and TV shows, especially Hollywood ones, which is how I ended up going to film school here. And I like dancing, working out, and making content, so in my free time, I'm always going to the gym or driving around, scouting new shooting locations around SoCal."

Celine stared at him like he'd sprouted an additional head.

"Um," she said. "So basically, you have no other hobbies besides work?"

"Well, like I said, I like to work out and dance . . ." He trailed off, remembering how he'd definitely made videos of himself doing both. "Ah. Yeah, I guess I don't have much of a life beyond watching and making content."

Noah saw some movement again. He looked at Mia out of the corners of his eyes. She was covering her mouth, and her shoulders were shaking. Was she . . . crying? No, she was *laughing*. Mia was laughing at him. For what? For being honest?

Anger flashed inside him. The urge to get up and call it quits, to loudly declare to the camera that he couldn't do it anymore, rose up in his chest. But just as he was about to stand, Celine said, "I like watching movies, too, but older ones, like *Roman Holiday* and *Singin' in the Rain*. They're comfort watches for me on hard days."

Okay, *now* Celine had Noah's full attention.

"You love old classics?" he asked, looking back toward her. "I like those, too. I watch everything, really, from horror to rom-coms to anime. But I have a special love for old Hollywood movies, too, since I grew up watching them with my mom. What's a recent favorite movie of yours, though? Like, from the last ten years."

Celine scrunched up her face in a cute way. "Ooh, if I had to pick . . . Does it have to be a rom-com?"

"No, any movie."

"Okay, then, *A Star Is Born*. The one with Lady Gaga and Bradley Cooper. Not really a comfort movie, but still good. I cry every time I watch it. And the music is amazing!"

Noah smiled. "Oh, yeah, of course. I really thought that movie deserved more Oscars."

"You don't agree with the *Oscars*?" Celine asked in a teasing way. "Who do you think you are? Snob!"

Noah gave her a mischievous grin. "Hey, when you watch three to five movies every week for school, you form opinions, okay? I talk about cinema all the time with my fraternity brothers, even the ones who aren't in film school. I even talk about movies while playing beer pong."

"Critiquing *cinema*, the classic frat boy pastime."

"Obviously."

Celine giggled again, and Noah felt his shoulders loosen up. The date was going a lot better now, which was a huge relief. Maybe he'd been too harsh with her the previous night.

After all, Celine was gorgeous. Her pink sweater dress perfectly complemented the rosiness of her cheeks, and her knee-high white boots made her legs look flatteringly long. She had good taste in movies and was funny, too, sometimes. So what if she talked with her mouth full during meals and sometimes steamrolled him in conversations? No one was perfect.

The best part was, once things really got going between him and Celine, Noah didn't think once about the camera, nor the audiences that would watch them tomorrow. Or about Mia behind the camera, laughing at him. Instead, as they continued talking, Noah's eyes lingered on Celine's bright eyes and pink, glossy lips.

He had watched enough dating shows to know that, technically, kissing on a second date wasn't too fast. But watching people kiss on TV felt drastically different from being the person to actually do it himself.

Out of nervous reflex, Noah glanced up. And almost jumped out of his skin when he saw Mia *glaring* at him from behind the camera. He shook his head and looked away.

Trying his best to pretend the camera wasn't there, Noah gently brushed Celine's hair away from her face and cupped her chin with his other hand. Softly, he said, "I know it might be too soon. And feel free to say no if you're not comfortable with it yet. But can I kiss you?"

Celine nodded, a smile blossoming on her face as she peered up at him through her long eyelashes. When her eyes fluttered closed, Noah leaned in and let their lips brush together in a light, soft kiss.

Celine let out a small gasp, and as she kissed him back, Noah did his best to keep his thoughts focused on the here and now. And not the fact that tens of thousands of people were going to see this moment tomorrow. Or the fact that Mia was still there, watching from behind the cameras.

CHAPTER FOURTEEN

Mia

Kissing on the second date? On camera?

Mia was glad the viewers wouldn't see the disgusted look on her face. She was baffled by how fast the scene had escalated. One moment, Noah and Celine were talking about Noah not having any hobbies besides work—which Mia related so hard with, she couldn't *not* laugh—and the next, the cuffle was *kissing*!

Mia knew from her sisters' recaps of *Love Island* and other dating shows that kissing on the second date wasn't *too* bad. Apparently some people even made out in the first episode. But it just wasn't for her. She'd kissed only one other person in her entire life, and it was Lacie Donovan during their junior year homecoming dance, when it'd felt like the stars had aligned and they were destined to be together. And then Lacie had dumped her not even a month after, anyway. Because that was usually how Mia's luck in love went.

As grossed out as she was by Noah and Celine's kiss, Mia

had to admit that, in the context of the show, it'd *seemed* right. And, curled up together by the firepit, they looked super cute together, too. The viewers back at home were going to eat this moment up.

As the showrunner, Mia was satisfied. This, after all, was exactly what she'd wanted. Her very own show. An amazing crew to help her produce it. And talent like Noah and Celine, who were interesting enough to hook audiences so people would want to tune in to the show every day. They were perfect, even better than she thought they could be.

But then why did Mia feel so . . . off? A sick feeling nestled into the pit of her stomach. If she hadn't been too caught up with the viewers' reactions to the first episode to eat anything all day, she'd have thought it was because she had food poisoning.

I'm probably just hungry, Mia thought, even when a part of her knew that wasn't the real reason.

She shook her head at herself. This was only the second day of filming, and there was still a lot of work to do. Something could go wrong at any moment. She didn't have *time* to get distracted by her complicated feelings about Noah.

Before she could dwell on them for long, though, Alex came running back outside.

"Mia! Come quick! Damien told me to come get you."

Kallie swung the camera toward Mia and Alex.

"Sorry!" Mia shouted at Celine and Noah. They jerked apart. "Y'all are done for the day! You were great!"

Heart pounding, Mia ran back into the house with Alex and Kallie. As her eyes took a few milliseconds to adjust to the bright light of the dining room, Mia hoped *and prayed* that no one was hurt.

Bethany stood at the table with a chair fallen behind her, while Jack had his hands outstretched like he was trying—unsuccessfully—to calm her down. The other contestants stood in a circle around the two, while Damien was recording everything from a corner of the room.

Mia didn't know much about Bethany, other than that she was also from Texas, albeit a whole different part of the state than Mia herself. With her sharp green eyes and her long blond hair tied into a high ponytail, Bethany reminded Mia of one of the cheerleaders at her high school.

"Well, then I don't know why we're wasting our time," Bethany was saying, loudly enough for everyone to hear. "Good luck with whoever you end up with. I'm leaving!"

She stomped away, leaving Jack alone in her figurative dust.

"I'll go talk to her," Alex whispered before they ran after Bethany.

This could not be happening. "Cut?" Mia said in a shaky voice. She let out a quick breath and yelled, "Cut!"

After Damien and Kallie stopped recording, Mia asked Jack, "What *happened*?"

"Well, she confessed that I'm her crush," he replied, looking at her with wide eyes. "And I said I didn't feel the same way. She didn't take it very well."

"Ah," said Mia. Her heart still felt like it was about to leap out of her chest.

"And I got it all on camera," Damien said. "I'm actually glad she's eliminated now, because sheesh! There's a fine line between *good* drama and too much."

Mia took a few breaths, trying to calm down. Everything was going to be fine. And no one was hurt. This was just a brief bump in their shooting day. She had to keep reminding herself of that.

At that moment, Bethany and Alex returned to the living room. Noah and Celine also came back inside the house, looking very confused.

"Did everyone get a chance to talk to whoever they wanted today?" Mia asked all the contestants. Luckily, her voice, at least, was steady. "Raise your hand if you need more time to decide who you want to cuff with today."

Everyone stayed still.

"Okay then," Mia said to her crew. "Let's resume filming. Kallie and Damien, please direct your cameras toward me."

When they began rolling again, she called out, "Contestants, please come stand in the living room with your arms linked with your cuffed partner from the previous night. It's time to determine the cuffles for Day Two."

She waited for everyone to get into their cuffles before continuing, "Noah and Celine, since you two were the most popular cuffle, you get to decide first. Would you like to stay together for Day Three? Or would you like to cuff with someone else?"

"We'd like to stay," Celine said. "Or at least I would."

"Me too," said Noah.

If they were at school, Mia would have commented on the weird look on Noah's face. But since they weren't, she cleared her throat and moved on.

"Tiana and Jack," she said. "You guys were the second cuffle. Would you like to stay together or cuff with someone else?"

Tiana and Jack looked at each other. Jack shrugged.

"I'm honestly okay with whatever Tiana wants to do," he said.

"Let's stay," Tiana replied.

Jack nodded, and the two remained standing with their arms linked.

"Great," Mia replied. "The third cuffle in terms of audience votes was Bethany and Caleb. But Bethany, you confessed to Jack, your original crush, and he said no. I'm sorry to say that you are now eliminated from *The Cuffing Game*."

Bethany sighed. "Whatever."

She walked off before Mia could ask her if she had any parting words.

Mia turned to Caleb. "Um, so with Bethany gone, is there anyone else you'd like to cuff with?"

Caleb looked at the other contestants. The other contestants stared back at him.

"Matías?" he said at last.

Matías's eyes widened. He looked back and forth between Caleb and Shirin before saying, "Sorry, I'm not interested."

Caleb shrugged. "Fair enough. Let me guess, you're straight?"

Matías winced and shook his head. "No, you're just not my type. Sorry!"

Beside him, Shirin covered her mouth with her hands, like she was trying hard not to make any noise.

Caleb barked out a laugh. "Amazing. Just my luck."

"Sorry, Caleb," Mia said. "You've been eliminated. Is there anything you'd like to say before you leave?"

Caleb turned to the other contestants. Placing his palms against each other, he said, "Well, it's been fun, folks. Both my crush *and* my backup are gone now, so sucks for me. See ya on the other side."

"He's making it sound like he's dying," Mia heard Matías whisper to Noah. A small quirk appeared on the other boy's lips.

Mia tried her best not to smile.

"All right," she said when Caleb had left. "That means both Bethany and Caleb are now eliminated from *The Cuffing Game*."

Mia turned to face the final cuffle.

"Matías and Shirin, I'm sorry, but you two were the least popular cuffle, probably because you admitted on camera last night that you're really friends who just cuffed together to survive."

Everyone laughed.

"Yeah . . ." Matías said sheepishly. "No surprise there."

"The good news is," Mia said, "since you guys still have each other, you are safe from elimination for today."

The cuffle cheered, and Mia finally let herself smile.

"And that's it! Everyone, thank you so much for yet another . . . *eventful* day of *The Cuffing Game*! Y'all are now free for the rest of the night. Just a heads-up, we will have an *early* start tomorrow morning, so please get some rest!"

When they finally stopped filming, Mia exchanged glances with her crew. Alex's eyes were wide, while Damien and Kallie looked exhausted. Somehow, today had been even *more* chaotic than the previous day. And now they had to go upstairs and edit all the footage.

Mia could only wonder what *tomorrow* would bring.

THE IN-BETWEEN

CHAPTER FIFTEEN

Noah

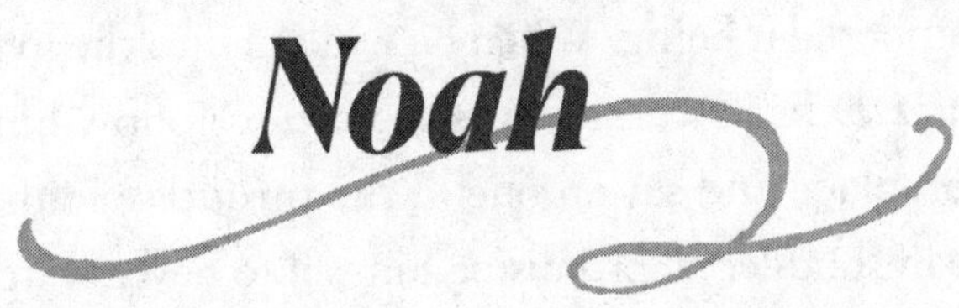

At half past two, Noah was still awake. He'd tried sleeping several times, doing everything from flipping to any angle he could turn his body without breaking his back to putting on the well-worn but miraculously still fuzzy blue socks that his mother had given him before he first left for college three years ago. He even counted sheep to two hundred before accidentally digging up repressed memories of a disturbing Icelandic lamb movie he'd watched a few years back.

Finally, Noah sat up. In the other bed, Matías was completely knocked out, snoring like a small airplane about to take flight. Noah envied people who could sleep so soundly. Meanwhile Noah had trouble not only falling asleep but also staying unconscious for eight hours.

He put on his coat and shoes and walked out into the hallway. Snores—some quiet and others less so—came from behind the doors of the bedrooms he passed on his way to the stairs. The dark wooden floors and red Persian rugs that had previously looked cozy during the day now looked downright creepy, and the wooden boards of the stairwell creaked under Noah's feet.

It was chillier downstairs. Or at least, colder than he remembered it being. When he walked into the living room, the grizzly bear statue's eyes seemed to follow him as he lit the fireplace and sat on one of the turquoise lounge chairs.

Noah shuddered, promising himself to never watch obscure horror movies again. Or at least not ones with animal-headed people like *Lamb*.

He'd just bundled up in a blanket by the fire when a rustling sound came from outside.

When he first heard of the Big Bear Lake area, Noah had been excited by the possibility of encountering a real-life bear. Now he wasn't so sure. Still, curiosity piqued, Noah went against his better judgment and slowly approached the sliding doors leading out to the backyard.

He was almost at the doors when he heard a crash. Heart thudding in his chest, Noah raced back to the kitchen to grab the biggest frying pan on the dish rack. He then gingerly slid the patio doors open, ready to swing at the first sign of fluffy black ears.

Hesitantly, he called out, "Hello?"

Something rustled in the tall bushes. Noah squeezed his eyes shut and swung into the air.

"Hey, watch it!" said a familiar voice. "What the hell are you doing?"

Noah opened his eyes. Mia was crouched on the ground, her arms flung up above her head. She held a flashlight in one hand, and her cheeks were red from the cold.

Noah dropped the pan and tentatively held out a hand.

Mia glared at his palm for a few seconds before taking it.

"Sorry about that," Noah said, pulling her up. "Thought you were a bear."

"Uh, no. I'm way too small to be a bear."

A grin slipped onto Noah's lips. "Maybe a cub."

Brushing the snow off her clothes with her gloved hands, Mia asked, "So, why are you still up?"

Noah shrugged. "Couldn't sleep. Obviously."

Mia narrowed her eyes. "Sure, obviously."

"How about you? You look like you've been out for a while."

She shrugged. "Just taking a walk."

Noah frowned in confusion. "This late? And why were you in the bushes?"

Mia made a face. "I tripped. And before that, I had some things I needed to do for the show, so I took care of that."

Noah stared at Mia for a long moment, peering down at this enigma of a girl who took walks past two in the morning with nothing but a flashlight and her pink puffer jacket to protect her from the wilderness. Back in class, he'd always thought Mia was a little strange, but Mia out in the wild was *fascinating*.

"You do know there are black bears out in the woods,

right?" Noah asked. "And coyotes, probably. You should bring bear spray next time."

"There won't be a next time," Mia said, rather mysteriously.

She shifted her weight, and Noah was suddenly, acutely aware of how close they were to each other. She was a head shorter than him, but she defiantly stood straight with her chin tilted up, like she was trying to make their height difference smaller.

His eyes lingered on her still-red cheeks before he made himself look away.

The dark, snow-covered forest around them was surreally serene, like they'd stepped into a separate plane of reality. Without quite knowing why he did what he did, Noah sat at the firepit and lit the fire.

Fully expecting her to ignore him and go back inside, he gestured at Mia, inviting her over. To his surprise, she did, and they sat next to each other in complete silence.

"So . . ." Noah said after a while. "What do you think of the show so far?"

Mia stiffened, immediately on guard. "What about it?" she asked sharply. "You know I can't tell you much."

"I know. But I'm not asking so I can get tips. I'm just trying to have a conversation. We don't even have to talk about me. I'm genuinely curious how the show has been for *you*."

Mia opened her mouth and then closed it again, like she was trying to figure out what she could and couldn't say.

"Well . . ." she said at last. "It's been surprising so far. Which, from what I've heard, isn't necessarily a bad thing when it comes to reality TV. But things are already a lot more dramatic than I thought they'd be. And . . . tough, personally. Still fun, but overwhelming. When we cast people, I thought I knew what would happen on the show. But when we put everyone together, things didn't go the way I thought they would, at all."

"Like what happened today with Bethany? And Caleb?"

Mia's eyes widened. "Yeah! That was so stressful. I was spiraling the entire time."

Silence fell between them again, until the only noise Noah could hear for miles was the crackling of the fire. It was a quiet that unnerved him, especially after three years of living in a noisy fraternity house.

Trying to break apart the stillness, Noah asked, "Is there good Korean food in Texas?"

Mia scrunched up her face at the random question.

"Or even Korean food at all?" Noah added.

"It's not as good as LA's, but it's pretty decent. The food wasn't why I moved here."

"Then why? Did you want to escape the cowboys?"

Mia rolled her eyes. "The only cowboys I ever hear of on a day-to-day basis are the football team. Yes, my family lives in the middle of nowhere, and yes, some people *do* have horses, but the only time I see actual cowboys is at the state fair."

"And you've lived your entire life there? Have you been to Korea?"

He'd asked the question out of sheer curiosity, but Mia bristled.

"Yeah, I have," she said, not meeting his eyes. "We went to Seoul once when I was little. But I don't really remember it. I'm from a big family and traveling internationally is too expensive with so many people. My sisters and I . . . we're pretty Americanized. We can understand Korean but can't speak much of it. And our family doesn't celebrate any Korean holidays. The only holiday my parents get really into is Christmas, to the point that we used to put on our own family Christmas plays when we were younger."

Noah's eyebrows shot up. "Family Christmas plays? How many siblings do you have?"

"Four."

"Jesus, five kids?" Belatedly realizing his reaction might have been rude, Noah added, "Is that normal in Texas?"

"Not at all, at least not in the part I'm from. My parents like to joke that they stubbornly kept trying for a son. To this day, none of us are sure how true or false that statement is."

"Stubborn, huh? Must run in the family."

He expected Mia to glare at him and was caught off guard when she let out a genuine laugh. Her face lit up in a way Noah wasn't prepared for. The light, surprisingly cute sound was so different from her usual sarcastic laughs that his brain short-circuited a little.

"I *know*," Mia continued, oblivious to the way Noah's heart now beat faster. "I'm self-aware. My parents and I both don't know when to give up."

She giggled again, and this time, Noah laughed with her. He was still smiling when he asked, "So how did you end up in LA, then? If not the cowboys . . . did you want to escape from your sisters?"

Mia frowned. "Not really. I mean, you're on the right track, because I *did* want to escape *someone*. But it wasn't my sisters. Or cowboys. My parents and I don't agree on a lot of things."

Now that sounded familiar. "Like what?" Noah asked.

"Well, my mom wanted me to stay in state for college, for one," Mia replied. "Study something easy and get married to a rich guy."

Noah winced. "She sounds very traditional."

"Yeah. My younger sisters are still in middle school and high school, but my mom is probably going to pressure them to find husbands when they're older, too. I wish she'd just *trust* us to figure out how we're going to support ourselves."

"How about your dad?" Noah asked. "Does he feel the same way?"

"My dad is more supportive, thankfully. But I can just *tell* by the anxiety in his eyes that he thinks I'm wasting my college scholarship by studying film."

"So that's why you try so hard in class." The words came out of Noah's mouth before he could stop them. "You're trying to prove your parents wrong," he quickly added, so Mia wouldn't think he was being mean. "I'm guessing you're the same way in all of your classes?"

Mia's eyes widened in surprise. "Yeah, I am. But that's only part of the reason. It's also because of my sisters. My older sister, Jeannette, stayed home for college. For me. For my parents. For everyone, really. And I love her so much. But I want to set an example for my younger sisters, so they know it's okay to dream bigger."

Noah leaned back, slowly nodding as he thought about all those months he'd spent making fun of Mia for being such a try hard. Guilt knotted his stomach as he thought of all the times he'd teased her. "I respect that," he said. "Really."

Mia blinked, as if she couldn't believe what he'd just said. She stared deep into the fire for a long moment before asking, "Hey, can I ask you something?"

"Sure," Noah said.

"Earlier, you said my mom sounds very traditional. And although I've heard stories, I don't know what actual Koreans in South Korea are really like. Are they as homophobic as people say they are?"

Noah drew in a sharp breath. "Well, not everyone is. I'm not, for one. But a lot of people still are, especially the older generations. Why?"

"Well, I'm bi, and my crush in high school was a girl. My parents didn't like it when I went to homecoming with her, but I was never sure if it was a Texan thing or a Korean thing, or both."

Noah clenched his hands into fists. Suddenly he was back home in his family's apartment in Seoul, hugging his brother as he cried after yet another one of their father's hateful rants.

"I'm sorry to hear that," he finally said. "I can't speak on the Texas part, but it's definitely a traditional Korean thing, too. My brother's gay, and my father made his life—all our lives, honestly—a living hell."

"That's rough," Mia replied. "Is that why *you're* here?"

"Part of it. My brother's two years older, and after he moved out, I became the next target. I'm straight, but Father Dearest found other things to pick on me about. Unfortunately for him, I fought back. And when I told him I wanted to go to college abroad, he funded my education *just* to get me out of his hair."

"Wow," Mia said. "Good for you, though. I'm glad you could get away."

"Yeah. He's the reason I go by Noah."

"Noah isn't your real name?"

"Noah *can* be a Korean name. But it's my English nickname. My real name is Dae-hyun."

A shiver went down his spine as he realized this was the first time he'd told anyone why he went by Noah. Every day, he posted content that millions of people watched. He danced in front of crowds shirtless. But somehow, in this one moment, he felt more naked and vulnerable than ever before.

Mia could easily take him down at this very moment,

attack him while he was at his most exposed. He held his breath against the thumping of his pulse in his ears.

But instead, she simply asked, "Why Noah, out of all names?" And then she scrunched up her face as if she was trying to solve a perplexing puzzle.

Noah's shoulders relaxed. He'd never thought he'd be grateful for Mia's usual scrutiny, but *this* at least was familiar. He'd seen this same expression many times before while they debated everything from cinematic techniques to artistic authenticity.

"I had a flare for the dramatic," he said, and then, at Mia's eyebrow raise, he clarified, "Okay, I still do. But just like the biblical Noah starts over again after the destruction of the Flood . . . I felt like I was restarting my life when I came here. It was liberating, to name myself. To not go by the name my father gave me and to live a whole ocean away from everyone I knew back home."

Everything had tumbled out of Noah like he'd been under some spell. He searched Mia's face, anxiously watching for a reaction.

Her slightly widened eyes reflected the warm light of the fire. For once, there was no judgment. Just interest. And, surprisingly, the faint hint of understanding.

I guess we have more in common than I thought, Noah realized.

Even so, he'd reached his limit. He had shared too much of himself and was desperate to divert the attention away from himself. “Is Mia your Korean name or English?” he asked.

“Korean. It’s actually Mi-ah, but they spelled it the English way to make things easier for me. I do also have an American name, but it’s my middle name, Elizabeth. It’s funny because *mi-ah* has a negative meaning.”

“‘Lost child,’ right? That’s why I wasn’t sure.”

“Yeah.” Mia let out a small laugh. “Despite the meaning, my parents liked how the name sounded, and after giving my sister an old-fashioned name, they felt creative and put their own positive spin to the word. I’m ‘lost,’ but only because I’m forging my own path. They regretted it later when I told them I was going to film school.”

A laugh burst out of Noah, free and uncontrollable.

“That’s clever,” he said, feeling his lips twitch up in a smile. “And you really are forging your own path. Or at least, that’s what it sounds like from what you’ve told me. It’s great.”

Mia stared at him with her mouth slightly open, taken aback. Silence stretched between them again, dampened by the snow and the late hour.

Suddenly Mia’s phone buzzed and lit up with a notification. Before it went dark again, Noah got a glimpse of the lock screen. *4 a.m.* Somehow, an hour and a half had already passed since he first got up from bed. And he’d barely noticed the time go by.

When he looked up from her phone, there was a peculiar

expression on Mia's face that he'd never seen before. Her cheeks were flushed, but he wasn't sure if that was because of their conversation or the heat of the fire. What he did know was that he couldn't stop staring at her rosy cheeks, or the way she nervously bit her lip when she noticed him staring.

Mia hurriedly got to her feet. "We should probably get to bed." Without so much as a second glance, she said, "Bye!" and ran back into the lodge.

Noah remained seated for a long moment before going inside himself.

This time, as he walked through the lodge, he didn't think about the creepy darkness. Instead, he thought about Mia and how *confusing* she was. She supposedly hated his guts. And yet she'd just completely opened up to him and had somehow gotten him to do the same.

Talking doesn't mean anything though, does it? he thought. *This was our* one *good conversation in several months. And we're both in film school, so of course we have more in common than we want to admit.*

Back when Noah was a first year who didn't have any friends in the entire United States of America, and even before he'd gotten close with his fraternity brothers, he'd volunteered to work on student production sets so he could meet more people. Even though the hours were long and he got paid only through craft services that were of questionable nutritional value, he made his first nonfraternity friends through those student films.

These friendships had been intense but short lived, since he'd spent twelve-hour days with these strangers and gotten to intimately know everyone before they all went their separate ways when the project wrapped, never to speak to each other again.

This is just another case of on-set comradery, Noah told himself. *That's all.*

DAY THREE

THE CUFFING GAME

Behind-the-Scenes Contestant Interview

MATÍAS CISNEROS

MIA: Hi, Matías, thanks for joining me. Please state your name, year, major, and crush.

MATÍAS: Hello, I'm Matías Cisneros. Sophomore, communications major, and my crush is . . . *[pauses and whispers while holding his hands to his mouth]*

MIA: Sorry, what was that?

MATÍAS: Jack. My crush is Jack Miller. Who's probably everyone's crush, which is why I'm saying it out loud, because he probably won't even see this.

MIA: I mean . . . he might! You never know.

MATÍAS: True. But anyway, I doubt he likes me back. You saw him rejecting Bethany.

MIA: Last night was *so* much. Is that why you didn't try to cuff with him these last couple of nights?

MATÍAS: Yup. I mean, come on. Bethany and Jack look so good together, like Taylor Swift and Travis Kelce! And that wasn't enough for him. He'll probably reject me, too, and everyone will see me get humiliated from whichever country they're at for winter break right now. People watching me get rejected from literally all the continents except Antarctica? Not exactly my idea of a good Christmas present!

MIA: I think some people might actually be in Antarctica right now for a research program. Since it's currently summer there. I remember reading about it in a brochure while I applied to Marlon.

MATÍAS: Great! People will also see me get rejected in Antarctica. How lovely!

MIA: Can I ask you a question that I think our viewers would also want to know the answer to?

MATÍAS: Sure, go ahead.

MIA: I get why you didn't cuff with Jack. But why did you cuff with your friend, Shirin Ahmad? Twice?

MATÍAS: *[nervously laughs]* Sorry, we were both too scared to even talk to our crushes. Are we disqualified?

MIA: No, not at all. Like I said, it's fine as long as it's mutual.

MATÍAS: Okay, good. It's just been all too much. My crush is the next all-American NFL superstar! *[laughs]* As for Shirin . . . well, she can talk about her situation herself, if she wants to. But the stakes are also high for her.

MIA: Okay, our time is up, but I'm wishing both you and Shirin the best. Just know that you don't have to do or say anything that makes you uncomfortable. And remember to have fun!

MATÍAS: Thanks, Mia. And I'll try!

CHAPTER SIXTEEN

Mia

After interviewing Matías early in the morning, Mia, still groggy eyed and exhausted from her late night with Noah, stumbled back into her room. Kallie wasn't in her bed, probably getting breakfast with the other crew members downstairs.

Mia knew she should eat something, too, but she wasn't hungry. If anything, she wanted to go back to sleep. But she couldn't. Not today, when they had an early-morning start to the shooting day. She chugged a few gulps from the water bottle she'd left by her bedside and plopped down in front of the intercom that linked to the speakers around the house.

"Attention, contestants," she said. "Please report to the front of the lodge. We will start the random event for today in twenty minutes."

She looked at herself in the mirror before heading downstairs. Her hair was messy, and there were big dark circles underneath her eyes, making her look like a raccoon. She splashed icy cold water onto her face and shuddered.

It had been even more freezing last night, and yet she'd barely felt the cold while she and Noah sat outside, talking for who knew how long. Granted, they'd had the firepit, but if it hadn't been for the snow dusting her hair and coat at the end of the night, she'd have forgotten she was outside at all.

Idiot, she thought to herself. *Why did you spend so long talking to Noah? He literally kissed Celine yesterday.*

There was a sharp rap on the door. Mia looked up to see Damien standing in the doorway.

"What happened to you?" he asked. "You look like a hot mess."

Mia groaned. "I know I do."

"Did you not sleep after we finished uploading the episode last night?"

"I did, but clearly not enough," Mia replied, suddenly glad that she and her friends had never figured out how to set up cameras around the firepit.

She would have told Damien and her friends about what happened last night, but she wasn't sure what had happened. And she didn't want to create unnecessary drama, especially if the weird tension she'd felt between herself and Noah was all in her head.

"Do you want me to ask Alex if they can be the host today?" Damien asked. "So you can relax behind the camera?"

A surge of gratitude filled Mia. Damien was always

looking out for her. They all were, since every member of the crew tried their best to take care of the others. But Kallie and Damien, as the two upperclassmen, *especially* took their roles seriously. They were the mom and dad of their little queer film production family.

Mia splashed another handful of water onto her face.

"No, I'm okay," she replied. "I got this. Thanks, though."

Damien frowned, looking unconvinced. "If you're sure."

Mia dried her face and took a big breath.

It was time for the third day of *The Cuffing Game.*

Mia stood behind a pile of shovels as she waited for the contestants to gather around her in the front yard. The snow had picked up after she'd gone to bed last night, providing the perfect amount between the house and their cars for today's random event. Mia couldn't have planned it better herself.

When Noah arrived, sne did a double take. He somehow looked even more exhausted than Mia felt, with even *darker* circles than the ones he had the previous day. Somehow, his fatigue gave him a brooding quality that made him hotter, reminding Mia of the tortured Byronic heroes of her favorite shows. As she watched, he pinched the bridge of his nose and briefly closed his eyes, like he had a headache.

Mia started to feel bad about keeping him up late, but then stopped herself.

He was already out and about before we started talking, she thought. *And I warned him and everyone else we had an early start today.*

Mia didn't realize she'd been noticeably staring at Noah until he met her gaze. "Just for the record," he said, "no, I will not help you bury a body in the snow."

"Huh?"

"The shovels. The ones suspiciously in front of you right now?"

Most of the contestants laughed, although some, like Matías, sounded nervous.

Mia's cheeks burned as she turned away.

"This isn't some sick and twisted game where you're going to kill off whoever is eliminated, right?" asked Matías. "Like in *Squid Game*?"

"No, of course not!" Mia replied, making a face. "You guys are so morbid."

The two boys grinned and bumped their fists together.

Are they friends now? Mia wondered. It wasn't something she'd expected to happen, but she had to admit it was kind of cute.

She waited until Alex finished getting all the contestants miked up before saying, "Hi, everyone. I'll explain the rules for today's random event once we start filming. But for now, please grab a shovel. Guys, please stay where you are, and girls, please take your shovel and follow me. The snow is deep in some places, so watch your step!"

Mia led Celine, Tiana, and Shirin to the halfway point between the lodge and their cars. The snow was fresh and soft, and much deeper than she'd ever experienced in Texas. She was glad she'd decided to wear her knee-high boots.

Once they started filming, Mia said, "Contestants, welcome to Day Three of *The Cuffing Game*. For today's random event, y'all will be participating in a snow shoveling race. The guys of each cuffle will shovel to the girls, who will then shovel the rest of the way to the road. The order that you reach the road will determine the order that you pick for the next cuffings."

"And you're sure you're not just using us for manual labor?" Noah asked.

If it were anyone else, Mia would have danced around it. But since it was Noah, Mia said, point-blank, "We are, but it's for your own benefit, too. We need a path cleared up so we can safely leave the lodge for the second part of the day, a fun surprise that we'll reveal later."

"It better be fun," grumbled Celine. "All the sweat is going to mess with my makeup."

Mia was about to tell everyone to get ready when Noah cut in: "Wait. One of us—no offense, Miller—is a star athlete. How is this fair?"

"I can give myself a handicap if you want," Jack volunteered.

Tiana cupped her mouth with her hands. "Boo! Just let him be himself!"

Shirin laughed, giving her a playful shove. "You just want to take advantage of the fact that he's more athletic than all of us."

Tiana grinned. "And I see nothing wrong with that."

Jack scratched his chin. "Maybe I can just use one hand?"

"Never mind," Noah replied. "Forget I said anything, because that's plain insulting."

Matías nervously looked from Jack to Noah. "May the best man win? Or I guess person, including the girls."

"Sure." Noah sighed. "Let's just get this over with."

When her crew signaled that they were ready to go, Mia went to stand by the guys.

"Thanks, y'all," she said. "We really do appreciate your help. All right. On your mark . . . get set . . . go!"

The boys sprung to action, snow flying every which way in their wake, as the girls cheered them on. Like everyone expected him to be, Jack was amazingly fast. He easily took the lead, arms blurring as he swung the shovel up and down.

"Wow, those muscles," Alex commented, before groaning. "Note to self, delete that in post."

Mia laughed. "You're literally giving yourself more work!"

Alex gave her a sheepish grin, putting a finger up to their lips.

"Whoa, Matías!" Tiana cried out.

Mia jerked back to attention just in time to see Matías

pulling ahead of Jack, who'd started off strong but was now faltering. And Noah . . .

Mia bit her lip so she wouldn't burst out laughing. Noah wasn't even close to the other two boys, wobbling and staggering from side to side as he attempted to shovel the snow.

He clearly has never done any sort of actual hard work in his life, Mia thought. *Typical rich boy.*

Matías high-fived Shirin and passed over the shovel. She whooped and took off, clearing snow down toward the road.

"Why are you guys trying so hard?" Celine complained, folding her arms across her chest. "You don't even like each other that way!"

She looked like she was about to cry. And Mia couldn't blame her. She never expected Noah to be an athlete, but because of all his muscles, she thought he'd at least be decent. It was downright embarrassing how bad he was at shoveling snow.

"Yeah!" Jack high-fived Tiana, who also took off.

Noah hadn't even gotten to Celine when Shirin reached the road and threw down the shovel.

"Yes!" she yelled. "We did it, Matías!"

Matías ran to Shirin and grabbed her hands. They jumped up and down as they spun in a circle. From behind his camera, Damien smiled, and so did Mia.

You can definitely tell they're best friends, she thought.

Tiana reached the finish line shortly after, and Celine threw her shovel down with a growl of frustration.

Mia stepped forward so the cameras could get a good view of her as she said, "Congratulations, Matías and Shirin! You two are the winners of today's random event. You have earned yourselves the first pick of who you want to cuff with for the next round. Everyone, please come back inside the lodge, where we'll do the cuffings."

As they all headed back, Mia heard Noah say, "Sorry, this was my first time shoveling snow. I lived on the twentieth floor of our apartment building in Seoul for most of my life, so it's not something I ever had to do."

Celine sighed. "It's okay, I have cousins like that in Shanghai, so I get it."

At least that's resolved okay, Mia thought.

In the living room, Mia directed all the contestants to stand in a single-file line facing the cameras.

"It is now time to pick your cuffles for today," she said. "Shirin and Matías will go first, then Tiana and Jack, and then finally, Celine and Noah. Choose wisely, because you will be spending the rest of today skiing or snowboarding with this person."

"Skiing!" Shirin exclaimed, pumping her arms in the air.

"Yup," Mia said. "That's our fun surprise! We had some money left over from our budget, so we thought we'd treat you guys, to thank you for sacrificing a part of your winter break for us."

"Hell yes!" yelled Tiana. "Thanks, TCG crew!"

Excited murmurs came from every contestant except Matías, who'd been completely frozen since Mia said it was time to pick the new cuffles.

"Um . . ." Mia said. "Are you okay, Matías?"

"Oh, hi—I mean, yes, I'm okay," Matías replied. "It's funny because while I was shoveling, I tried so hard because I wanted to be the first person to pick. But now, I don't know if I want to actually go through with what I planned to do."

He looked at Shirin, who shook her head.

"Don't worry about me," she said. "Go for it. Choose who you really want to go on a date with. Just go first, though, because I'm still debating what to do, too."

They shared a laugh, and as Matías glanced at Jack, Mia's pulse quickened. She did her best to keep a poker face. It'd be such a bold move, to ask the one and only Jack Miller out on television *right now*, in a moment that was going to be watched by thousands of people. It was so daunting to think about. Mia wouldn't blame Matías if he didn't go through with it.

Seconds passed. Then minutes. Someone coughed, although Mia couldn't tell who.

Curiously, Matías met eyes with Noah, who nodded and gave him a thumbs-up.

"Okay," Matías finally said. "I'm ready."

"All right," replied Mia. "Matías, please go link arms with the person you want to cuff with for today."

With Damien following behind him with his camera, Matías slowly headed down the line of the other contestants.

Mia's own palms grew sweaty as Matías put one foot in front of the other, walking past Shirin, Celine, Noah, and Tiana to come to a full stop in front of . . . Jack.

Yes! Mia thought. Her heart felt like it was about to burst out of her chest, like *she* was the one about to confess. Which was never going to happen. Because she would rather die than confess to Noah that she liked him.

"H-hey," Matías said to Jack in an uncharacteristically quiet voice.

Jack's eyes widened. "Hi?" He said the word like it was a question.

Matías took a deep breath. "If you're not interested, feel free to reject me, honestly. No pressure. But I'm just going to say it. Because as famous as you are, I have no idea if I'll ever have a chance to be face-to-face like this with you again. Jack, I like you, and I've had a crush on you ever since I went to my very first college football game. I know you're out of my league and you probably aren't even into guys . . . but I tried my best on today's challenge just so I could have first dibs on you for this round."

Everyone went silent, waiting in hushed anticipation for Jack's response. Mia was sure she could hear a pin drop.

Jack scratched his head. He looked at Damien's camera and then at Matías.

Mia's stomach sank. A sudden flashback of how Jack had rejected Bethany played in her head.

Oh no, she thought. *Poor Matías . . .*

But then, slowly, Jack smiled as he linked arms with Matías. "Should we snowboard or ski?"

Matías's jaw dropped. So did Mia's and pretty much everyone else's. From behind his camera, Damien let out a shriek that was several octaves higher than his usual voice, before quickly saying in his normal tones, "Sorry, Alex."

Everyone laughed.

Alex let out a fake sigh of exasperation. "It's fine," they said. "As with all things, we can fix it in post."

Mia grinned. "Fixing things in post" was something she'd heard often in film school, especially whenever something unexpected happened and needed to be edited out. Which, she was rapidly learning, it almost always did.

Jack grinned at Matías's still stunned face.

"What?" he asked with a shrug. "I never said I was straight. People just assume I am because I play football and have a deep voice."

Mia carefully composed her face back to a neutral, "professional host" expression before saying, "Jack, listen. We appreciate you being so open about everything, but I want to make sure. Are you okay with this going public? If you're not comfortable with the whole world knowing, we can edit this out."

Jack shrugged. "I'm not exactly out, but I'm not closeted, either. Like I said, everyone just assumes you're straight if you play college football. And I never mentioned I'm bi to keep things simple. I guess I was always waiting for the right time and place to say something, if it ever came up at all. But I think I finally found someone who's worth taking that leap for. Especially since he just took a huge one for me."

He turned back to Matías, who looked like he was about to faint.

Jack lightly bumped his fist on Matías's shoulder. "We need to work out together sometime, man. Because your speed was insane. Anyway, what'll it be?"

Matías stood up straighter. "Wait, what?"

Jack gave him a patient smile. "Ski or snowboard?"

Matías let out a nervous laugh. "Oh, I'm more of a snowboarder, definitely. But more than anything else I'm a sledder. Don't let this morning fool you. I'm not *that* athletic, especially not compared to someone like you. I just have plenty of shoveling experience since I have relatives in upstate New York."

"You seem plenty athletic to me." Jack gave him a once-over, and Matías let out an excited laugh.

"Wow, okay," he said. "It's gonna take me a while to get used to that. How are you literally so hot?"

Jack blushed.

Mia smiled, feeling deliriously happy for the two boys.

But then she accidentally made eye contact with Noah. She froze. Noah had a large, goofy grin on his face, too. For one alternative-universe-esque moment, they smiled at each other, and Mia's heart beat impossibly faster.

That was the problem with crushes—some never completely went away.

CHAPTER SEVENTEEN

Noah

Mia was smiling at Noah, and he didn't know why. He could only assume they were both happy about Matías and Jack. He himself was *ecstatic* for his roommate. But why was Mia staring at *him* for so long? And *smiling*?

He narrowed his eyes in confusion, and Mia immediately scowled and looked away. Well, that was strange.

"Okay!" Mia exclaimed, addressing everyone. "That's the first cuffle for Day Three. Congrats, Matías and Jack!"

The other contestants burst into cheers.

"Now, let's cuff the rest of you," Mia continued after the applause died down. "Shirin, since Matías went with Jack, you can go next."

Shirin looked out at the rest of the contestants, glancing at first Tiana, then Noah, and then Celine, only to look at Tiana again.

"No offense," she said. "But if I had to choose, I'd choose Tiana any day. Because besides Matías, she's my bestie. And I'm sure Celine wouldn't want me to steal her man."

"Definitely not," Celine said. "Thank you so much, Shirin!"

"And, of course, I'm going to say yes to my girl, Shirin!" Tiana exclaimed.

Everyone laughed as the two friends linked their arms together.

"All right," Mia said. "That leaves Celine and Noah. Are you two going to cuff with each other?"

"Yup," Noah said. He drew his lips into a tight smile as he linked arms with Celine.

Celine also looked a bit tense, but she smiled back at him.

"Fantastic!" Mia exclaimed. "Well, thank you, everyone. I wish you the best with your new cuffles. We'll break for lunch and then head to the slopes at two. Please take some time to relax a bit before we go. We want y'all to be alert and energized so no one gets hurt this afternoon."

She raised her eyebrows at Noah, as if saying, *Especially you.*

When they finally stopped recording, Noah let out a sigh of relief and stared down at his newly blistered hands. Celine had looked so disappointed in him when he came in dead last. Now none of that mattered.

The truth was, he probably would have done a lot better if he hadn't already been so sleep-deprived. But mentioning what happened between him and Mia last night on camera seemed like a recipe for disaster. Especially when he himself was still trying to figure out what it all meant. For now, it was easier to just pretend that nothing had happened.

Noah's stomach growled. He was starving, but more than that, he was exhausted. After grabbing an Uncrustable from the kitchen, he went back to the room, only to find Matías hiding under the covers of his bed.

"Wow, Jack was right," Noah remarked. "You're fast. I didn't even see you go back upstairs."

"I bolted as soon as we stopped recording," Matías replied, his voice muffled by the sheets.

Noah sat on the edge of his own bed. "Why?" he asked before opening the plastic wrapper and taking a big bite out of his sandwich.

Matías let out a big, loud sigh but didn't say anything.

"You okay?" Noah asked when he'd finished chewing.

Matías pulled his covers down so Noah could see his face. "I don't know. What if asking Jack out was a mistake? What if the date goes horribly, and I embarrass myself in front of the thousands of people who tune in to the show?"

Noah frowned. After he'd eaten another bite of the sandwich, he asked, "Why would you? Jack said he was interested in you. Just have fun. What's the worst that can happen?"

"Oh, I don't know," Matías said with a nervous laugh.

"I could embarrass myself so badly that I start crying loud enough to cause an avalanche?"

Noah made a face. "Is that . . . something that has actually happened to you before? Wait, is that even scientifically possible?"

Matías groaned. "Probably not but who knows? I'm a loud crier, Noah. A *really loud* crier. And what if Jack only said yes because he didn't want to embarrass me in front of the cameras?"

Noah winced. Well, that sounded familiar.

"Nah," he said. "Jack doesn't seem like the type. He already rejected Bethany and sent her packing, remember?"

And he definitely seems like a more honest person than me, he added to himself.

When Matías didn't respond, Noah went on, "The guy literally came out on TV to say he was interested in you, too. You should give him more credit."

Matías's eyes widened.

"Wait," he said. "No, you're absolutely right. I've been out since before I can remember, so coming out doesn't seem like that big of a deal to me, but it's huge for Jack. Thanks for reminding me."

"No problem." Noah finished his snack, rolled the wrapper into a ball, and tossed it. The ball of trash flew into the garbage can with a satisfying whoosh.

"Nice," Matías said. "Kobe would be proud."

"Thanks. I'm gonna take a nap."

"Yeah, you look pretty tired." Matías reached down to get out his book from underneath the bed. "You go ahead. I'm too nervous to sleep right now."

Noah didn't need to be told twice. The second he lay back in bed, Noah fell into a blissful sleep.

CHAPTER EIGHTEEN

Mia

The crew gathered in the production room for lunch, but Mia was too excited to eat. Leaving her breakfast burrito untouched, she crushed her can of iced coffee and tossed it into the recycle bin.

Kallie gave her a disgusted look as she ate her own burrito. "Mia, it's barely past noon and you've already had two of those today."

Mia put her hands up in a gesture of innocence. "Hey, I'm just trying to stay awake."

Damien jabbed a forkful of salad in Mia's direction. "Try *sleeping* next time." He waved his fork, causing a piece of lettuce to fly off. "And eating *food*. Like normal people."

"You won't feel it now, but wait until you're older," Kallie said. "All that exhaustion is going to hit you like a ton of bricks."

"Oh, believe me, it's already hitting me," Mia replied. "Which is why I'm on my second can of coffee. I thought sleep deprivation was just part of film school, though?"

Alex groaned from where they were eating a half-unwrapped Uncrustable to "prevent any sticky disasters" while working on their computer.

"You definitely can't sleep if you specialize in post," they said. "Everyone's always sending you the footage last minute and expecting you to *magically* clean it all up overnight."

Mia shot them a guilty look. "Sorry, Alex." She turned back to the rest of the crew and said, "Let's finish discussing logistics quickly so we can help Alex before we head to the slopes. So it seems like every crusher is now cuffed with their crush. Which is good!"

"Is it really good that everyone's successfully cuffed with their crush already, though?" Kallie asked. "Maybe we need to spice things up a bit since it's only Day Three."

Mia bit her lip. She wasn't sure if she wanted to "spice things up," but she figured it was worth hearing what her friends had to say.

"We *could* bring in some new people to challenge the established cuffles," Damien said. "Kind of like how they have bombshells in *Love Island*. We'll have to be careful, though. Since we have limited space in the lodge."

Mia followed Damien as he walked over to his laptop. "Was there anyone who wanted to be in the show that lives close to Big Bear?" she asked.

After rapid-fire strikes of his keyboard, he replied, "Yup. There's one. His name is Kyle Yoshida."

"Will one guy be enough, though?" Kallie asked. "Maybe it's worth searching for more girls, too?"

"We can ask a few other people, since we don't know if Kyle or anyone else can even make it," Damien reminded her. "It's less than a week before Christmas. There's a good chance everyone who originally applied is now out of town or busy doing holiday things. I'll contact Kyle right now and reach out to some others, too. No guarantees, though."

"Thanks, Damien," said Mia.

Kallie thoughtfully crossed her arms. "You know, worst-case scenario, we can bring people back, right? I was thinking of Caleb's crush, Carlos? He seemed interesting. He just didn't have enough time on the show to form any connections. And he has a greater chance of still being in town, unless he booked a last-minute trip."

"Good idea," Damien said. "I'll contact him as well."

Mia settled back into her seat and finally bit into her breakfast burrito. The egg and bacon inside were now disgustingly lukewarm, so she dropped it back onto her plate and pondered upon what her friends had said instead. They definitely had some interesting ideas. Not ones she would ever have come up with herself, but not so completely out of pocket that she didn't want to go through with them.

"All right, then," Alex said as they finished eating their Uncrustable. "Adding more people sounds great, but let's keep it at a maximum of two or three. I don't want to run around like a headless chicken again."

"We can definitely do that," Damien replied. "As always, thanks, Alex. Let us know if you need anything."

To Mia's surprise, he looked up from his computer to flash the editor a smile. They returned it with a sheepish grin, which gave Mia pause. Damien and Alex didn't normally ignore each other, but they also didn't *not* ignore each other. So this little interaction was . . . unusual.

Mia cocked her head to the side, wondering if she should say something, but decided to remain quiet for now.

"While Alex is doing that," Mia said, switching gears, "Kallie, let's go look at some of the responses to the latest episode and gauge the viewers' reactions so far."

Kallie nodded. "Yup. Come take a look." She scooted to the side so Mia could pull up another chair to her laptop.

With how chaotic the second episode had been when they were filming it yesterday, Mia had no idea what to expect. To her surprise, one of the most common discussion topics in the comments was Matías and Noah's new friendship.

That moment with Matías and Noah in their room! 😍 Noah's so sweet!

I LOVE that they have each other's backs!

"I think that's one of the clips that Alex added in from the camera in their room," Kallie explained. "Apparently the two of them had a bro moment. We can watch it real quick if you want."

Mia nodded, and Kallie scrolled through the episode.

She stopped at a moment when the screen was completely black. Mia would have thought there was an error with the video if it weren't for the subtitles Alex had added in at the bottom of the screen.

NOAH: . . . if anyone gives you a hard time for liking guys or anything like that, you let me know.

"Go, Noah!" Kallie said. "Who knew he's such an ally?"

They went back a bit more and watched the scene from the beginning. Much to her chagrin, Mia couldn't resist smiling by the end. She had to admit it: Noah could really be charming sometimes. Just not to her.

"Let's go through the rest of the comments," she said.

New responses had popped up by the time they scrolled back down. Romantically, the most popular couple seemed to still be Noah and Celine. In fact, almost every other comment was now talking about them and their fireside date.

They're so cute together AHHH

It's like watching a K-drama!

That kiss!!

Mia frowned. Thankfully, before she could dwell on her own personal feelings about the date, Damien announced,

"Okay, Carlos said he can come back up tomorrow. I'm still waiting for other people to reply."

"That's great," Mia replied. "Thanks, Damien!"

She went over to sit by Alex, who was editing an extremely chaotic and hilarious clip of Noah accidentally flinging snow all around himself.

She laughed, and Alex grinned. "I'm never trusting Noah with a shovel," they said.

"Nope," Mia agreed.

This was going to be a *very* fun episode.

CHAPTER NINETEEN

Noah

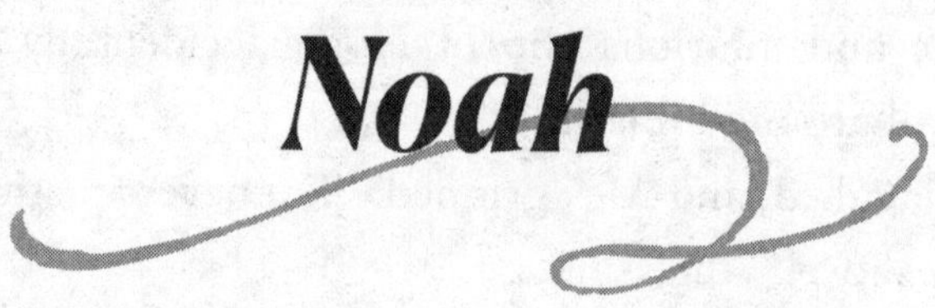

"Everyone, please bundle up and come out to the front whenever you're ready. We'll be carpooling to the slopes shortly."

Noah opened his eyes at the sound of Mia's voice and shuddered. He was never going to get used to waking up like this.

"Rise and shine!" Matías called out far too cheerfully. "It's two p.m.! You know what that means . . ."

For whatever reason, he trailed off. Curious, Noah sat up to see none other than Jack Miller leaning against the doorway of their room.

"Hey," said Jack. "Sorry, hope I'm not interrupting something."

Matías bolted up from his bed and, at that exact moment, all three boys realized Matías was in nothing but his boxers.

"Sorry!" Matías dove back into the bed and pulled the covers over himself.

"I thought you weren't going to nap," Noah hissed at his roommate.

"I didn't," Matías hissed back. "My clothes were still wet from the snow, so I took them off before I crawled into bed earlier."

Noah pressed his lips together, trying his best not to laugh. From across the room, Jack covered his mouth with his hand, presumably to also avoid laughing out loud.

"Matías," Jack said. "I was going to ask you if you wanted to head downstairs together . . . but I guess I'll just see you by the cars?"

From underneath the covers, Matías gave him a thumbs-up.

The crew split the contestants by cuffle, so that Shirin and Tiana were riding with Kallie, Jack and Matías were with Alex, and Noah and Celine were with Mia in Damien's SUV.

"Sorry for third wheeling," Mia said as she got in the passenger seat. "I didn't feel comfortable driving up here, so Damien gave me a ride here from school. There aren't any mountains where I live."

No mountains? Noah gawked, wondering how Mia could live somewhere so flat. Then again, maybe he was just too used to seeing mountains everywhere, since there were so many in Korea and in California.

Celine was uncharacteristically quiet during the drive to the slopes, and without his phone or smartwatch, Noah didn't have anything to do besides alternate between staring out the window, glancing over at Celine, and looking straight ahead at the back of Mia's seat.

He couldn't see Mia's face, but he could see the tension in her shoulders. *Mia is always so tense*, Noah observed. He could almost picture the hard-set line of her frown or even the way she sometimes bit her lip when she was deep in thought.

He leaned back in his seat, resting his head on the upholstery.

You're about to go on a date with Celine, he reminded himself. *Not Mia.*

When he turned to look at Celine again, she gave him a tight, awkward smile.

"Hey," Celine said.

"Hi," replied Noah.

"Um . . . so, we should probably decide if we want to ski or snowboard."

"I ski," Noah answered. "It's what I have the most experience with, anyway."

"I'm a skier, too," she said. "That's perfect!"

Noah waited for Celine to say something else, but she didn't. His heart sank.

Is she still mad that I came in last for the race? he thought. It didn't seem like that big of a deal to Noah, but maybe it was for her. After all, he'd been so put off by Celine talking with her mouth full. So why not her with his complete failure with a shovel?

When they arrived at the slopes, Mia and Damien unpacked three small cameras from the back of Damien's car.

"Since the school's cameras are way too expensive to use on the slopes, we'll be using these cheaper cameras to record this segment," Mia told everyone. "Damien, Kallie, and I will be recording each of the three cuffles, while Alex will be editing some clips from earlier today in the cafeteria. Please don't mind us and have fun!"

"I'll be sitting with my back against the wall so people can't see my screen," Alex added, holding up their laptop and charger. "But feel free to come to my table if you need someone to watch your stuff or if you just want to chill at any time during the day."

They split from the rest of the group to go to the cafeteria, while everyone else headed over to the rental cabin. Noah caught a glimpse of Matías happily chatting away with a grinning Jack and smiled, silently wishing them luck.

The slopes were quaint compared to the ones Noah was used to. But they were nice enough, with small log cabins at the bottom that housed the cafeteria, the equipment rental shop, and souvenir stores. After Celine and Noah had gotten their equipment, they met up with Kallie, who silently waved at them from behind her camera.

Celine remained silent as they put on their skis, and Noah shifted his attention to Damien, who was filming Matías and Jack as they started snowboarding. Impressively enough, Damien skied backward *while* recording the cuffle, somehow maintaining a relatively steady grip on the camera. How Mia found such talented individuals to be on her crew, Noah had no idea.

Speaking of Mia . . . A flash of panic shot through him when he looked around and realized she was nowhere in sight. All the other contestants and crew members were either on skis or on snowboards out in the snow. Where was Mia?

But then Mia stepped out of the rental shack in *pink snowshoes.* With a happy grin, she trotted up to Tiana and Shirin and brought the camera up to her eyes as they headed to the slopes with their skis.

"Cute!" Tiana exclaimed. "Wait, sorry, you're recording us, aren't you?"

Mia's smile widened, but she didn't say anything. The girls giggled, and Noah's mouth quirked into an amused grin.

"Um, Noah," Celine said. "Are you ready to ski?"

Noah turned back to see that Celine and Kallie were watching him. And so was Kallie's camera.

"Oh, my bad," he said. "Yeah, let's go down the hill together."

"Sure." Celine gave him a smile that was just as fake as the ones he himself practiced.

Noah winced. *So that's what it's like to be on the receiving end of one of those.*

With Kallie trailing behind them, Noah and Celine headed to the lift. A group of kids and their parents stood in line, and Noah waited for a bouncy five-year-old with a unicorn helmet and her father to properly latch themselves in before grabbing ahold of the lift rope himself.

Once again, Celine was quiet for the entire ride up.

Frustration built up inside of Noah, not because he was mad at Celine, but because of their current situation. Celine's shoulders were tense, and her eyes downcast. Noah had no idea why Celine was so guarded now. He wished they could just talk it out, both the good and the bad, like he did with—

Noah stopped himself from following that train of thought. How did he always end up thinking about Mia?

"Do you go skiing often?" he finally asked Celine when they had gotten off the lift. That seemed like a safe enough question to ask.

"No," she said. "This is only my second time."

"All right, so no black diamond slopes. Got it."

"Definitely! It's going to take all my concentration to just avoid hitting trees."

Maybe that's why Celine is being so quiet, Noah thought. *She's nervous about skiing.*

A part of him knew he was being willfully naïve, but at the same time, now that he was observing her more closely, he noticed Celine *was* unsteady on her skis. Her legs were even shaking a little.

"Remember to keep your skis parallel like French fries. And make a pizza with your feet if you want to stop."

Celine laughed. "I know that much."

"In all seriousness, anytime you want to stop and do something else, just let me know. I'm a fan of snowshoes, too. And sledding."

"Sounds good." Celine smiled at him, genuinely this time. Noah let out a sigh of relief. There she was.

By the time they finished skiing, Celine had laughed several times, even while falling on her butt. Noah was glad some of the tension between them was gone, but he was emotionally spent. His shoulders ached, not just from all the physical exertion but also the stress of having to carry the conversation. He wasn't like Matías, who talked like his life depended on it. Conversations took effort for Noah, especially when they weren't reciprocated.

They were on their way back to the rental cabin when Noah spotted something that made him do a double take. At the edge of the forest, Damien stood with his camera pointed into the woods. Noah followed his line of sight.

Underneath the cover of the snow-covered trees, Jack had his arms gently around Matías. The two boys sweetly smiled at each other, their foreheads touching for a couple beats. Then slowly, gently, Jack tilted Matías's chin up with his hand, and they kissed. It was like watching a gay Hallmark movie.

Noah smiled. At least one date was going well.

CHAPTER TWENTY

Mia

Mia had missed holding a camera.

The biggest irony of her film school experience so far was how little access she had to a camera that wasn't on her phone. Only students who'd already taken certain classes were allowed to even touch the school's equipment, which meant that as a freshman, Mia could only use the small, basic camera she had brought from home.

Her parents bought her this camera before they'd even allowed her to have her own phone. Since as far back as she could remember, she was the designated "family historian," dutifully taking pictures and recording videos of every birthday party and family Christmas production. Mia figured this was probably how she first developed an interest in filmmaking, although her parents would never admit it themselves.

Now, as Shirin and Tiana skied down the hill, Mia relished all the different emotions and details she could capture with her own two hands. The girls' conversation was casual enough, but nothing was casual about Shirin's lingering glances at Tiana whenever she thought no one was looking. Or the way Shirin bit her lip when their hands accidentally touched.

"Isn't it weird how our families have never gone skiing together even though we've known each other for, like, ten years?" asked Tiana.

"Oh my gosh, yeah. I feel like we end up unintentionally just missing each other," Shirin replied. "My family goes to Tahoe when you guys don't go and vice versa."

"I also feel like you guys go way more than we do. I'm barely holding my balance here!"

Tiana wobbled, and Shirin laughed.

Mia loved how Shirin's normally serious face lit up whenever Tiana was around. Both girls were so happy when they were with each other. It was really cute.

"Well, I'm glad we're finally skiing together," Shirin said, gently holding the other girl's arm so she could regain her balance. "I've always wanted to."

Tiana was still looking down at her skis when she replied, "Same here!"

Shirin bit her lip, and Mia found herself doing the same from behind the camera. She was so nervous for Shirin. Having to see Noah every day to record the show was hard enough. She couldn't imagine what it was like to secretly have a crush on someone who was also your best friend for *ten years*.

By the time Shirin and Tiana finished skiing, the other contestants were already in line to return their equipment.

Mia spotted Celine and Noah, who, along with Kallie, were almost completely silent. She winced. Well, that date seemed like a bust. Before she could dwell on them for long, though, she spotted Matías and Jack farther along in the line, holding hands. They both had wild, happy grins on their faces, and so did Damien as he filmed them.

"Hey!" Tiana exclaimed when she also spotted the boys. Matías came running to excitedly whisper in Shirin's and Tiana's ears. The girls cheered.

After everyone had turned in their equipment and exited the rental cabin, Matías said, "Attention, please! Jack and I have an announcement to make."

Mia's heart pounded. Something big was about to happen. She could feel it.

Matías nervously laughed when all eyes—and cameras—turned to him. He looked up at Jack, who nodded and squeezed his hand.

"We just wanted to let everyone know that we've decided to drop out of the show," Matías went on. "Since Jack already gets a lot of spotlight back on campus, we're going to try dating on the low first while there's still some time left before Christmas."

A few people gasped. Damien looked like he was about to cheer and sob at the same time. Kallie slow blinked in disbelief, while Alex clutched the sides of their head in a gesture of panic. Mia didn't blame them. Somehow the show was not one but *two* people down today. It was a good thing they'd already thought of bringing in extra people.

Shirin and Tiana loudly clapped and whooped. And soon so was everyone else, cheering on the new couple.

"Best of luck!" Noah yelled.

"Yeah, so proud of you!" Shirin said. "Baby's all grown up!"

Matías hugged Shirin and then blew kisses at everyone else while Jack waved.

As the boys went around to say their goodbyes, Kallie followed Jack with her camera while Damien followed Matías. Just in case Alex needed another angle to work with, Mia filmed Matías as he gave Noah a big bro-hug.

Afterward, Matías and Shirin spent a good five minutes whispering back and forth. Mia couldn't make out what they were saying, but from their expressions, Matías seemed to be encouraging Shirin. To do what, Mia had no idea.

When Matías came to give Mia a hug, she stopped recording.

"Thanks for creating this show," he said. "Truly, I wouldn't even have had the *slightest* chance with Jack without you."

"Nah, with your amazing personality? I'm sure you would have figured it out some way or another."

He flashed her a mischievous grin. "Maybe. But you made it a lot easier."

When Jack and Matías finished making their rounds, Damien motioned toward the parking lot.

"I'll take Matías and Jack back to the lodge, so I can record them leaving with one of the nicer cameras," Damien said. "Mia, do you mind riding in Kallie's car on the way back?"

"Not at all," Mia replied.

With a big smile, she watched as Matías and Jack literally walked off into the sunset together.

Our first Cuffing Game *success story*, Mia thought. It certainly didn't happen the way she'd expected it to happen, but she was happy for them, nevertheless.

Back at the lodge, Mia had just gotten out of the shower when she heard a knock. After living with her for the past four months, she knew it was Celine before she even opened the door.

The other girl was in her black silk pajamas, the very same ones she wore back in their dorm room. Seeing her wear the pajamas now, hundreds of miles away in Big Bear, was disorienting to say the least.

"Hey," said Mia. "What's up?"

"Hi, sorry, can we talk?" Celine asked. "Roommate to roommate?"

Mia glanced down the hall. Faint laughter came from the production room on the other side of the house, where her friends were currently finishing up the edits for today. She'd meant to join them as soon as she was done showering but . . . Celine's face was drawn tight with worry, in a way Mia had never seen it before.

"Sure." She stepped aside so Celine could enter the room. "But I have to warn you, I can't say much. In case it affects the results of the game."

Celine nodded. "It's okay. I just need someone to hear me out more than anything else. Shirin's a good cabinmate but she doesn't know Noah like you do."

"Got it," Mia replied. She sat on her bed and patted the space next to her. "What's the problem?"

With a heavy sigh, Celine sank onto Mia's bed. Then, in a rush of air, she blurted out, "Noah is *really* different from how I thought he'd be in real life."

"Different? How so?"

Celine frowned. "I mean, don't get me wrong. He's *so* hot. And he's a good kisser too . . . but he's more . . . reserved? On social media he's such a daredevil and seems so fun and outgoing. But I'm not getting any of that in person. Like, yeah, he'll say stuff. But other than our second date, it's been mostly just small talk. Is he like that with you too?"

Mia squirmed. It took all her self-control to get over the thought of Noah being a good kisser and focus on the Noah she knew from class instead. The Noah who annoyingly always had something clever to say about everything, especially during class discussions.

"Maybe he still has to warm up to you?" Mia asked. "He doesn't shut up when we're in class."

Celine's face fell. "Do you think he's being like this because of me?"

"No, not at all!" Mia exclaimed, waving her hands frantically in the air. The last thing she wanted was for Celine to blame herself for *Noah's* failings. "Maybe he's just feeling shy? A lot of people aren't themselves when they're being constantly filmed like this, even social media stars like Noah. Whatever the reason, you shouldn't blame yourself for how he's acting."

Celine sighed. "Yeah, you're right."

Mia had just relaxed her shoulders when suddenly, Celine burst out laughing. "Oh! By the way, can we talk about how horrible he was at shoveling snow today? It gave me the biggest ick. How can he still call himself a man after that?"

A burst of indignation and discomfort rose up in Mia, surprising even herself. Although she too had made fun of Noah, both in her thoughts and with Alex, it felt odd hearing Celine, the girl he was cuffed with, the girl that was *supposed* to like him, say mean things about him.

I'm just protective of him because he's a contestant on my show, Mia reasoned with herself. *It's how I'd feel about someone being mean to any of the other contestants.*

When Mia didn't say anything out loud, Celine covered her mouth. "Oops, was I being too mean? Wait, there aren't any cameras in your room, are there? I assumed not but . . ."

She looked around, and Mia gave her a polite smile. "There aren't any, don't worry. And sorry, I don't think I should contribute any more to this conversation."

Celine's face turned rigid, noticing Mia's shift in tone. With a tight smile, she said, "Right. Well, it's late, so I should probably go to bed anyway. Thanks for hearing me out and sorry if I made you uncomfortable. Good night!"

"Good night," Mia replied, unable to hide the relief from her voice. "Hope you have a better day tomorrow!"

She'd meant it as a friendly send-off, but Celine groaned. "Now you're making me wonder what sort of random event you have in store for us next," she complained.

Mia gave her another polite smile before returning to the production room.

THE IN-BETWEEN

CHAPTER TWENTY-ONE

Noah

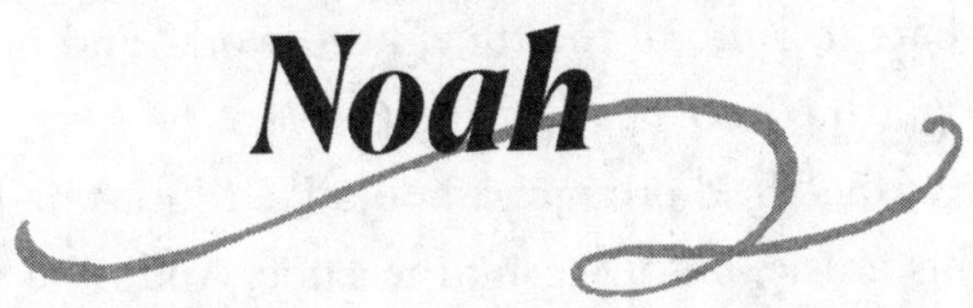

Despite going to bed much earlier than he had in the last few days, Noah couldn't sleep. Without Matías, the room was now completely still and quiet. *Too* quiet. He missed his roommate's booming voice and easy laughter. Hell, he even missed Matías's airplane snores.

It'd been so easy to forget that they were in the middle of nowhere, surrounded by snow and trees, with Matías around. But now, Noah was alone in this room with nothing but his thoughts to keep him company.

Usually when he couldn't sleep, Noah would look at his phone and scroll aimlessly until his vision blurred. He knew this wasn't something that was medically advised, but it weirdly helped him. Most of the time.

What would Mia do if I tried to take my phone back? Noah smirked just thinking about Mia's extreme look of outrage. Her reactions were always so dramatic, overtaking her face and sometimes even her whole body. They were hilarious. *She* was hilarious.

If it'd just been him and Mia, he would have definitely attempted a grand heist of some sort. But since it wasn't, he stayed in bed. The last thing he wanted to do was derail the show. He had real respect for the crew, Mia included, and he'd hate to ruin all the time, hard work, and money they were putting into *The Cuffing Game*.

He wished he'd brought a book like Matías had. Sure, he had his music, but it wasn't the same. And if he was being honest, Noah couldn't remember the last time he'd read a physical book. He usually just read Korean web novels or webtoons on his phone.

I bet Mia reads physical books, he thought. And stopped himself. Why was Mia constantly popping up in his head today?

Rolling over onto his side, Noah forced himself to think about his date with Celine, something he'd avoided thinking about ever since they got back from the slopes. Compared to how bad the beginning had been, the end had been decent. Even though they didn't talk much, they'd still shared a brief kiss—initiated by Celine—during the car ride back. Which was nice. Sort of.

Everything else about their date, though, gave him pause. Celine had barely made an effort to talk to him. And for what? Because he couldn't shovel snow?

Maybe she just hadn't been feeling great yesterday. Or maybe Noah had done something wrong. Or maybe it really was the skis, all in all. He hated guessing. Why did he have to do so much *guessing*?

Wanting to clear his head, Noah got up and went downstairs.

The house was silent, like it had been the other night when he'd talked with Mia. But this time, Noah's attention didn't stray anywhere else. As if in a trance, he made a beeline for the firepit, coming to his senses only after he'd stepped outside into the frigid night and realized he'd forgotten his coat.

A sigh escaped from Noah's lips. He sat down at the pit and lit the fire.

What was he *doing*? He and Mia had sat at the firepit *one* time. Not twice. Not thrice. But *once*. Mia had even told him that her walking out in the woods was a one-time thing.

And yet, he'd somehow ended up here, by himself, staring at the lodge and wishing a girl in a pink puffer jacket would somehow magically appear in the doorway.

He wanted to talk to Mia and hear her thoughts on Matías and Jack, on Celine, on everything.

Noah doubted Mia would ever call him a friend. But he also wasn't sure if they were still enemies like they had been back at school. What he did know was that he had genuinely enjoyed his time with her the previous night. And from the way she'd smiled and laughed while they talked, he thought Mia had too.

But maybe it'd all just been in his head.

DAY FOUR

THE CUFFING GAME

Behind-the-Scenes Contestant Interview

SHIRIN AHMAD

ALEX: Shirin, thanks for joining us today. Please look at the camera and state your name, year, major, and crush.

SHIRIN: Hi, my name is Shirin Ahmad. I'm a sophomore and I'm an engineering major. And if it's okay, I'd rather not reveal my crush's name yet, just in case I can't bring myself to confess during this show.

ALEX: That's fine. Is that why you first cuffed with Matías?

SHIRIN: Yeah. Because he was also too scared to confess to his crush. But now he did! And I'm so, so happy for him.

ALEX: Is your crush still in the game?

SHIRIN: Yes. I'm looking for the perfect opportunity to confess, but . . .

ALEX: But?

SHIRIN: It's scary. Sorry, I'm trying to be vague. Hopefully people will know why soon enough.

ALEX: That's completely fine. Whatever you're comfortable with.

SHIRIN: Thanks.

CHAPTER TWENTY-TWO

Mia

Mia woke up to countless comments on episode three screaming in all caps about Matías and Jack. People also laughed at Noah and his shovel, while others griped about how the show was a bit slow and less exciting than others.

It's because it's not supposed to be a traditional dating show! Mia thought as she lay in bed. If she'd had the time and energy, she'd have written up a response to those people explaining exactly that. But she didn't. Plus, she didn't want to be *that* person.

She navigated to the playlist of previous episodes. They were averaging around fifty thousand views per episode now. A quick search through social media revealed that people were starting to talk—and make videos—about *The Cuffing Game* on Instagram and other platforms.

"It looks like everyone loves the show so far," Kallie said when Mia showed her the posts. "For the most part, anyway. Congrats, Mia! We're making strides."

Grinning, they shared a high five.

Before she put her phone away for the day, Mia checked her notifications.

Jeannette had sent her a text reminding her to drink water, like she did every once in a while, and Lola had sent her a few dozen TikToks that she would probably never get to. Meanwhile, Cara had filled her in on her latest boyfriend drama, while their mom had sent them all more wholesome photos in the family group chat, like the ones with everyone dressed in matching Dolly Parton Christmas sweaters in front of the tree.

Mia felt a weird sting in her chest as she zoomed into everyone's smiling faces. This was her first December away from home and, already, she was missing so much. She wondered if her family had also gotten a sweater for her. If Jeannette had ordered the sweaters, probably. If their mom had, probably not. Besides sending photos in the group chat, their mom had barely messaged her since Mia first packed her bags and left for LA.

Mia had just sent Cara the best encouraging response she could manage when Kallie loudly cleared her throat.

"Yeah?" Mia asked, looking up from her phone.

"I just got a text from Alex," Kallie replied. "They didn't know if you were awake yet, which is why they texted me. You're wanted in the production room before you do the announcements for the day. I'll go with you, too."

Dread crept over Mia as she followed Kallie out of their room.

~

Mia had barely closed the door of the production room behind her when Damien asked, "Mia, are you sneaking around with Noah? Please. It's our last full day in Big Bear. Just tell me the truth so I can do damage control."

Mia reeled back. "No? Why would you think that?"

Damien looked at Alex, who hit a few keys on their laptop and adjusted their glasses.

"So . . . you know we have cameras all over the house, right?" they said. "We saw you sneak out of the lodge with Noah in the middle of the night."

"But I never left the house with—"

"You two didn't leave together, but you came back around the same time," Alex clarified. "Several hours later. Sorry, it's not like I'm trying to keep track of what you do, but I do skim through the mini-camera feeds every day before I edit, for any shots or moments we missed with the main cameras. After Day One, I made a note of you and Noah just in case it was anything significant, but then . . ."

"You sneaked out again. Last night," Damien finished for them. "Or at least Noah did. We didn't see you this time, but you know where all the cameras are, so . . . Mia, please. As the producer, according to SPC rules, I need to report to them if you *are* sneaking out with one of the talent, especially if you two are making out or—"

"No!" Mia exclaimed, spluttering at the very idea of "making out" with Noah. Trying her best to ignore the heat rising in her cheeks, she went on, "It wasn't anything like that. And I didn't even go out last night! I went to bed right after we submitted the episode. Kallie can vouch for me."

Kallie let out a nervous laugh. "I'm a deep sleeper, but I believe you, Mia. We all do, *right*?"

She shot a pointed look at both Alex and Damien. Alex hesitantly smiled and nodded, but Damien let out a long sigh.

"So Noah went out by himself last night, then?" he asked. "Don't get me wrong. I do want to believe you. But I'm just doing my job. Since we are using school resources for this project, there's a lot of paperwork that needs to be done if you're—"

"Please don't say that part again," Mia pleaded.

Damien raised an eyebrow. "Which part? The 'making out'? Mia, what's wrong with you? Do you *like* Noah Jang?"

Everyone was staring at her now.

It was a scene straight out of Mia's nightmares, the exact shot and even mise-en-scène of her friends that she hoped would never become reality.

Damien rubbed his face with his hands. "She does. Just look at her. Honestly, I've suspected it for a while, since she's a completely different person around him. I told myself, okay, she either really hates this guy or . . ." He sighed. "I'll spare you the word, Mia. Because it's clear from your reactions that you haven't come to terms with your own feelings yet."

"*Completely different person*"*?* Mia frowned. She was

about to ask Damien what he meant when Kallie said, "Wait, if Noah's your crush, then . . . why is he here? As one of the *contestants*?"

"He's also Celine's crush," Mia said. "Or he was. I don't know if she likes him anymore. She basically told me yesterday that she doesn't."

Alex groaned. "It's going to be another rough day of editing today, isn't it?"

"A rough everything, from the looks of it," said Damien. "At least we have more people joining us today."

The two of them shared a knowing look. There it was again. The faint *something* between Damien and Alex. This was neither the time nor place to bring that up, though, so Mia said instead, "Regardless of my own feelings, it's not like that between me and Noah. That one time we went outside together, we sat around the firepit and talked for a bit because we both couldn't sleep. That was all. But it wasn't planned or anything like that. I promise. And he definitely doesn't like me that way. Noah and I aren't even friends. I'll do my best to stay clear of him from now on."

Damien pursed his lips for a moment, keeping his gaze steadily on Mia's. Then finally, he shrugged.

"All right, I believe you," he said. "Let's get started with the day."

CHAPTER TWENTY-THREE

Noah

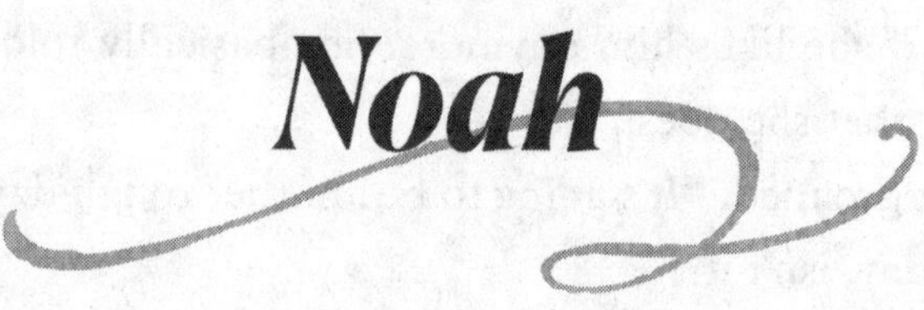

"Everyone, please bundle up in your coats and come out to the front yard," announced Mia.

That was it. That was the entire message. Compared to how verbose and friendly her previous announcements had been, this one was jarringly short.

Wondering if there was something wrong, Noah got ready as quickly as he could.

Downstairs, Alex met him and the other contestants to mike them up before they all went outside. In the front yard, Damien and Kallie were already recording, while Mia stood behind them, quietly observing everyone.

Three newcomers stood in front of the lodge. Noah froze.

"Yay, new people!" Tiana exclaimed.

Celine also cheered, but Noah stayed silent as he scanned the new faces.

The first person was Carlos, who Noah recognized from Day One, while the second was a brunette white girl he'd never seen before. The last newcomer was, unfortunately, not a stranger to Noah.

Kyle Yoshida stared back at him with a wide, toothy grin. A shudder ran through Noah's body at the sight of Thad's Little. Or, ex-Little, as Noah now knew him as.

Things between Noah and Kyle had started out normal enough. Since Kyle was Thad's Little—and thus Noah's "Grand-Little"—the three of them had hung out a few times throughout the semester. But then Noah noticed little things. Like how Kyle started styling his hair like Noah's. Or how he quoted specific lines Noah had said in his videos. It'd initially seemed like harmless imitation, so Noah never said anything. But then the lies started. Like when Kyle falsely told Thad that Noah had said certain things.

When Thad informed Noah last week that Kyle had gotten himself kicked out of Alpha Tau for lying and stealing, Noah hadn't been surprised. He'd hoped he'd never have to see his Grand-Little again.

But, unfortunately, here Kyle was. Right in front of him. On Mia's show, out of all places.

Kyle enthusiastically waved at Noah like they were close friends. A wave of disgust hit Noah, but he forced a smile onto his face for the cameras.

"Noah!" Kyle exclaimed. "I'm so happy you're still here!"

Kyle's expulsion from Alpha Tau was fraternity business, and it'd happened during finals week, so there was a good chance the *Cuffing Game* crew had no idea what kind of guy he was.

Noah had to warn Mia. He glanced over at her, hoping to catch her attention. But when their eyes met, Mia immediately stared down at her feet. He frowned, trying to puzzle out why she was *ignoring* him.

"Hi, everyone," Mia said. Apparently Noah didn't count as "everyone" because she looked around and made eye contact with everyone *but* him. "Y'all already know Carlos. Please welcome him back, along with our other newcomers, Kyle Yoshida and Violet Russo!"

Everyone politely cheered and clapped, and the newcomers went around to individually introduce themselves—or *re*-introduce themselves, in the case of Carlos—to the original cast.

Unfortunately, Kyle made a beeline for Noah. "Noah! What's up, brother?"

The younger boy held up a hand. Although Kyle wasn't a "brother" to him anymore, Noah gave him a high five to avoid causing a scene.

He had to find a way to warn Mia. If only she'd look *up* at him . . .

"Hey, nice to see you," Noah lied, masking his own disgust. "What brings you to the show?"

He'd asked the question to probe Kyle's intentions, but was wholly unprepared when Kyle replied with, "Well, you know. I wanted to meet some hot ladies. I have my eye on Celine, especially. I've been following her for years."

The word "following" in a social media context was

innocuous enough, but the way Kyle said it made Noah cringe. Kyle looked over his shoulder, and Noah followed his gaze to see that the other boy was checking to see if any of the cameras were recording them. They weren't. Kallie's camera was filming Shirin and Tiana, while Damien's was with Carlos and Celine.

Noah didn't notice Kyle leaning into him until it was too late. Noah jerked back, but not before Kyle grabbed onto his arm.

Panic shot down Noah's spine as Kyle whispered into his left ear. His tone was friendly, chill even, but there was nothing amicable about the words coming out of his mouth. Or the tight grip on Noah's arm. "I know she's cuffed with you now," Kyle said, "but come on, man, you can't have everything, you know? You have the frat . . . you're famous . . . let me have a win for once."

Noah's head spun, and he broke out into a cold sweat. He glanced over at Celine, who was still talking to Carlos by the edge of the road. Yet another girl Noah had to warn about Kyle. The list was growing by the minute.

Thankfully, Carlos spotted Noah looking in their direction and nodded at him. It took all of Noah's strength to casually hold out a fist in greeting and call out, "Welcome back!"

"Thanks, man!" Carlos replied.

Damien's camera turned in their direction, and Kyle finally let go. Noah's heart was pounding in his chest, but he briefly closed his eyes and forced himself to smile as Carlos and Damien headed their way.

Carlos bumped fists with Noah, and Kyle went to talk to Celine. And Noah was too rattled to stop him.

"Hoping to last for more than one round this time," Carlos joked.

Noah laughed, but it came out strangled. "Yeah, best of luck."

Carlos blinked as he fully took in Noah's current state. "Hey, are you all right—"

"Okay, everyone," Mia said from where she now stood in the middle of the yard. "Today's random event is these new people right here: the Gamechangers."

Noah gave Carlos a quick, grateful nod. "I am," he whispered. "Thanks." And he *was* going to be okay, now that Kyle was no longer death-gripping his arm. With every new breath, he felt more himself.

"Gamechangers," continued Mia, "you're here because you have a crush on one of these original contestants. Well, everyone except Carlos. Carlos, you're here—"

"Because I was already in the area," Carlos said. "I know. It's cool."

Everyone laughed except Noah, who managed an amused grin.

"We're glad to have you back, though!" Mia said. "Seriously. Thanks for making the drive up here again. You were the first person to respond when we asked for help."

And the only person to notice I'm not okay, Noah thought. He clapped, and everyone else joined in. Carlos bowed with a flourish, an amused grin on his face.

"Today, the Gamechangers will go first in choosing who to cuff with, which means they will each 'steal' someone else's already-cuffed partner," Mia announced. "Since we have an odd number of people, one person will be left uncuffed. This person will be in danger of being eliminated tonight, unless they can somehow take their original partner back by the end of the day."

Celine gasped. "Ooh, drama!"

Carlos and Violet looked nervous, but Kyle appeared way too excited at the prospect of stealing someone's partner. From where he now stood by Celine, Kyle shot Noah the world's most obnoxious grin. Noah clenched his hands into fists.

"Today, in your new cuffles, you will all go on cute winter wonderland–themed dates in the woods," Mia continued. "We have snowshoes by the door if you want them. But there are also paved trails available if you want to just wear boots. You can make snowmen, take walks, whatever you want to do. Please be sure to stay within the view of the crew and not wander off on your own, for safety reasons."

She paused to gesture at Kallie and Damien, who nodded back at her.

"At the end of the day, each person who has cuffed with a

Gamechanger will have a choice. Switch back to the person you were with before or stay in your new cuffle. Whoever fails to cuff with someone by the end of the day will be eliminated, and the final three cuffles will move on to the finale."

Noah braced himself. There was no doubt Kyle was going to steal Celine from him. Which was fine in and of itself. But not when Kyle was . . . well, Kyle. Hopefully Noah could warn everyone about Kyle before getting eliminated himself. Or somehow get Celine back so Kyle would be automatically eliminated.

"Okay," Mia said, recapturing his attention. She was still avoiding him, looking at everyone *else* as she continued, "Is there a Gamechanger who would like to pick first?"

Kyle's arm shot in the air. Because of course it did.

"Me!" he yelled. "I pick Celine, my crush!"

Celine's jaw dropped, and a low murmur arose from the rest of the contestants. A pressure built up inside Noah as he felt several pairs of eyes on him. Some people even gave him looks of pity.

Noah kept his face blank. If he spoke out about Kyle now, everyone would just think he was being jealous. The only thing he could do now was watch.

"I'm your crush?" Celine asked. A small, hesitant smile appeared on her lips.

"Yes, ma'am." Kyle held out his hand in a flourish.

Celine squealed and ran to him, linking arms with him without even a second glance at Noah.

Noah suppressed a groan.

Yeah, he thought. *I'm not getting her back*.

After yesterday, he had a feeling something like this would happen. Celine just didn't seem that interested in him anymore. Plan A it was. He had to warn Celine as soon as possible, since Mia wasn't even looking at him today. For whatever reason.

Violet raised her hand. "I'd like to go next. If that's okay?"

Mia nodded, and Violet pointed right at Noah.

"I choose Noah," she said. "Hi!"

Noah blinked. Violet shyly waved at him, and a million thoughts flew around in his head like a swarm of bees. But he still managed a friendly smile back. The last thing he wanted was for Violet to be collateral damage. "Hi."

He linked arms with the new girl. Violet was shorter than both Mia and Celine, so the height difference was a bit of an adjustment. But with her long brown curls and button nose, she was cute. All the girls were. And now, Noah had to somehow go on a date with one girl while trying to keep the other two safe from a guy who was essentially a ticking time bomb.

Noah's stress levels were through the roof. *Pretty girls* would *be my downfall*, he thought. *And an overzealous wannabe*.

Carlos stepped up to choose next. He wrapped his arms around his head in a gesture of distress as he looked at Shirin and Tiana, like he was having a nervous breakdown.

"Okay," he said. "Full disclosure, I was someone's crush, so I didn't come into this show with a crush of my own. So I have to choose between you two on the spot, saving one while possibly eliminating the other. This is the worst day of my life."

"That guy is weird," Violet whispered to Noah. "But in a good way. He's funny."

Noah nodded in agreement. "You should have seen him when he got eliminated on Day One," he whispered back, grateful for this small moment of humor. It was a nice break, and hope fluttered in Noah's chest. If only he could just freely hang out with Violet without having to worry about Kyle. Or Celine and Mia.

Carlos let out a noise of frustration. "Okay, I hate to be doing this, but it's better than eeny, meeny, miney, mo. Pick a number between one and twenty."

"Ten," Shirin said almost immediately.

From beside her, Tiana grinned. "You *would* pick ten."

"It's the halfway point," Shirin replied with a shrug. "What do you pick?"

Tiana looked at Carlos and said, "I'll go with eight. My favorite number."

Carlos glanced from Tiana to Shirin, and then back again. "It was seven."

Tiana and Carlos linked arms, and Shirin said, "Goodbye, world, I guess."

She sounded casual enough, but there was an edge to her

voice that made Noah cock his head. To add to the intrigue, from behind the cameras, Mia bit her lip, like she did whenever she was worried. What was going on?

Out of all the girls in the game, Shirin was the most mysterious to him. For some reason, she seemed to not like him almost right off the bat. Which was fine, but Noah couldn't figure out her role in the show at all. The girl had mostly only cuffed with or talked to her friends. Noah wasn't sure if she was even here to date.

"Okay!" Mia said loudly, making Noah jump. "There we have it. Our three new cuffles for the day. Shirin, feel free to tag along with the crew for now. Everyone else, have fun but keep safe, since there might be wild animals in the woods. And remember, whatever you do today will affect the viewers' opinions of you. During our live streamed finale at four p.m. Pacfic Time on the twenty-third, the winning cuffle of *The Cuffing Game* will be determined through audience voting."

"No pressure," Violet said.

"I don't know which I'm more terrified of, the wild animals or the live stream," Noah deadpanned.

Violet giggled, a bright bell-like sound that made him smile.

Alex came by to hand out walkie-talkies to the other crew members. "I'll be staying behind at the lodge to edit, so at least one person will have cell service at all times," they announced. "So if there's an emergency, please find one of the other crew members and we'll call for help."

Everyone nodded. Noah was glad that, as always, the crew seemed to know what they were doing.

Mia, who was *still* refusing to acknowledge Noah's existence, expertly led them through the woods. As he stared at the back of her pink puffer jacket, Noah was reminded of the late-night conversation they had earlier this week.

Maybe she'd been location scouting that night but didn't want to tell me, Noah thought.

Her dedication continued to amaze him.

The sunlight streaming down through the branches warmed Noah's face. Feeling hot, he unbuttoned his coat and caught sight of Mia glancing in his direction. When he met her gaze, she quickly looked away.

They soon came to a clearing with some trails leading deeper into the woods. An untouched layer of snow covered the ground, and Noah overheard Carlos say to Tiana, "This is perfect snowman-building snow, right here!"

"Yes, build that snowman!" Mia exclaimed. "Have a snowball fight. You can do whatever you guys want. I'll be here, behind the cameras, if anyone needs me."

With that, she walked to the back of the clearing, giving all the contestants some space.

Carlos and Tiana started rolling snow into a ball, and before Noah could see where Celine and Kyle went, Violet pointed at one of the paved trails and said, "Hey, do you want to go for a walk over there?"

"Sure." Noah followed Violet, searching for Celine and

Kyle as they went. The other cuffle was nowhere in sight.

"You know, as a kid, I thought snow was reindeer poop," Violet suddenly said.

"Wait, what?" Noah snapped to attention to see that Kallie was currently recording both him and Violet. From behind the camera, Kallie gave him a look that said *What are you doing?*

Noah winced. Right. The date. With a smile, he looked back at Violet. "And why did you think that?"

Violet smiled back, but there was the faintest bit of hurt in her eyes. She'd noticed he'd been distracted. Guilt crawled up inside of him, and Noah turned his body to give her his undivided attention.

"Don't get me wrong," she continued. "This was when I was young. Like, not even five. My older brother convinced me that snow was whatever fell on the ground whenever Santa and his reindeer were flying overhead. In my defense, it always snows around Christmas where I'm from, so it made sense to my four-year-old brain."

"That's adorable," Noah replied.

Part of him wished he could stay here like this, listening to Violet's stories about her childhood and just having a peaceful day with her. But the knowledge that Kyle was out there, somewhere in the woods with Celine, pressed down on his shoulders like a heavy weight.

I have to find them, quick, Noah thought, *so I can give Violet my full attention after I've dealt with Kyle.*

"I felt so stupid when I found out my brother was lying to

me this entire time," Violet went on. "But now, I think it's cute too. Because of that, whenever I see snow . . ."

There. Past Violet's head, at the far edge of the clearing, Noah spotted Celine and Kyle walking down the trail that led deeper into the woods. And after Mia explicitly told them to stay close too. Not even five minutes in, and Kyle was already breaking the rules.

"Sorry," Noah said. "I'll be right back. I just need to take care of something first."

Before Violet could even reply, he took off running after Celine and Kyle.

CHAPTER TWENTY-FOUR

Mia

What had started as a peaceful day out in the snow quickly became . . . not that.

Just a few minutes into his date with Tiana, Carlos abandoned the big ball of snow they'd been rolling to throw himself, back first, onto the ground, spraying white powder in all directions. Tiana shrieked, and Damien cursed under his breath as the snow hit his camera.

"LA native here," Carlos said. Mia wasn't sure who he was talking to. Tiana? The camera? "This is the most snow I've ever seen in my life!"

Damien wiped the lens clean carefully, then resumed recording as Carlos swooped his arms and legs up and down in the snow.

With a laugh, Tiana joined in, and so did Shirin and Violet. The four contestants let out loud whoops as they made snow angels. The big smiles on their faces made Mia smile, too.

As happy as she was to see them have fun, Mia also felt

lightheaded. It felt like the Earth's axis had shifted under her feet, like it often did for her when things didn't go according to plan. This whole snow day was supposed to be a *romantic* day for the cuffles. Not whatever this was. Shirin wasn't even supposed to be joining in with the rest of the contestants!

But at the same time, she had to admit the present moment was cute. Wholesome, even. A nice change of pace from the structured days they'd had in the past week. Maybe they all just needed a small break.

Damien came to stand next to Mia, his camera still pointed at the contestants as they stopped making snow angels to resume the snowman Carlos and Tiana had started.

"Children," Damien said under his breath. But the slight smile on his lips told Mia he thought this moment was adorable, too.

This was the nature of reality TV, she was beginning to realize. You set the rules and gave people instructions, but in the end, they did what they wanted anyway. And sometimes, they did things that were much better than you originally planned.

Mia had barely attempted to think positively when she caught sight of something that almost made her heart leap out of her chest.

"Damien!" she hissed. "Zoom in on Tiana and Shirin."

While Carlos and Violet were off to one side, continuing to roll a big ball for the snowman's torso, Shirin and

Tiana were rolling a smaller one for the head. As the girls worked, their hands brushed together, too many times to be accidental. They laughed, staring into each other's eyes with the sort of heat that threatened to melt their snowman before he could even stand.

Mia's ship was finally sailing. Just not how she thought it would. She smiled and rested her chin in her hands.

Her head still woozy with secondhand euphoria, Mia was looking around to see how everyone else was doing when she realized someone was missing. Or rather, multiple someones.

"Wait," she whispered to Damien. "Where's Noah? Or Celine and Kyle?"

She glanced around at all four corners of the clearing. But all she could see were trees, snow, and more trees.

From behind the camera, Damien shot her a concerned look.

"Is your walkie-talkie muted?" Mia hissed.

He nodded.

Mia grabbed her walkie-talkie, rushing away so the contestants' lav mics wouldn't pick up on her voice.

"Does anyone have eyes on Noah? Over," she asked. "And Celine. And Kyle. Over."

Alex's response came first. "Shit, did we lose *all* of them? Over."

Mia looked around, her stomach lurching when she realized she couldn't find Kallie either.

"Wait, where are you, Kallie? Over."

There was a long pause. Mia's body began to tremble from head to toe. Somehow, her worst nightmare had come true, and she hadn't realized it until it was too late.

She was about to tell Alex to call for help when her walkie-talkie crackled back to life.

"Hi," Kallie said. "I'm with all of them right now, over. About a ten-minute walk north of the clearing."

Mia breathed a big sigh of relief. They were fine. She freaked out for nothing.

But then Kallie continued, "I think Noah and Kyle are about to fight. Mia, come quick!"

CHAPTER TWENTY-FIVE

Noah

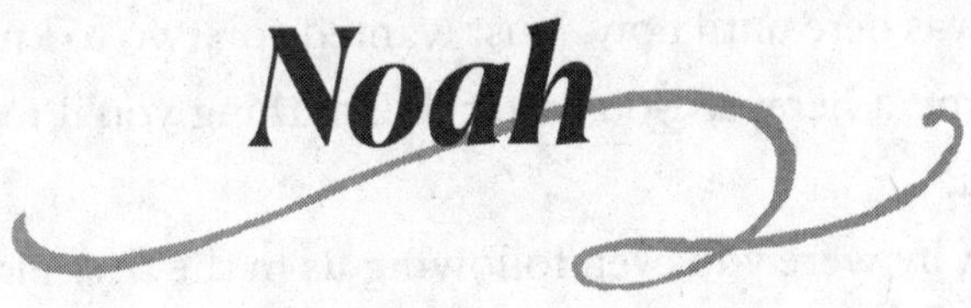

Noah came across Celine and Kyle making out with each other in the woods. Which wasn't wholly unexpected. But it certainly made things awkward.

"Hey, what's your problem?" Kyle asked when Noah approached them. "Are you jealous or something?"

All the friendly "bro-eyness" was gone from Kyle's voice, replaced by the sharpness of a serrated knife. Well, that hadn't taken long.

"No," Noah simply said. Because it was true, he realized. He wasn't jealous of them at all.

Before anyone could say anything else, Noah stepped aside to reveal Kallie standing behind him with her camera. Noah himself hadn't known Kallie was following him until he heard her whispering into her walkie-talkie, calling Mia for backup. He didn't want Mia to have to deal with . . . whatever this was. He resolved to take care of this mess before she arrived.

Kyle cursed under his breath. And Celine, who'd been

glancing between the two boys in horror, said, "Noah, how could you? We just wanted some privacy."

"For the record, I didn't tell Kallie to follow me," Noah replied, keeping his voice low and even. "I didn't even notice she was here until now. I just wanted you two to know there's a camera here, so you won't do anything you'll regret being aired."

"Why were you even following us in the first place?" Kyle snapped. "Aren't you supposed to be in your own cupful or whatever?"

"It's cuffle," Noah said, matter of fact. "Respect the terminology. And you guys both know you're not supposed to be out in the woods like this. You heard what Mia said."

Celine dropped her gaze to the ground, but Kyle retorted, "Okay, Mom. Jesus. We're not in the frat house anymore, Noah. And even if we were, I'm no longer part of Alpha Tau, so you can't tell me what to do."

Noah ignored Kyle, opting to talk to Celine instead. That was why he was here, after all. Not to have a pissing contest with someone who was three years younger.

"Celine, I know this isn't something you'd want to hear from me. But I just wanted to warn you about Kyle. He got kicked out of Alpha Tau for being an all-around asshole."

Celine's jaw dropped. Kyle rolled his eyes and said, "Oh, come on—"

"Given the kind of guy he is, I don't think Kyle has the best intentions," Noah went on, cutting him off. "I'm pretty sure he's only trying to date you because he wants to be me."

"You take that back!" Kyle yelled, with just enough outrage that told Noah he'd struck a nerve.

But before either boy could say anything else, Celine exclaimed, "Noah!" Anger burned in her eyes as she hissed, "First you waste my time, and now you *stalk* me and the guy who's actually into me, just to burst in and say weird things about him?"

Noah took a step back. This was *not* how he expected this conversation to go at all.

"What do you mean, waste your time?" he asked. "And *stalk*? I wanted to make sure you were okay."

A slight movement caught Noah's attention. Kyle was shaking his head, which annoyed the hell out of Noah. But at least he was staying quiet. Noah was surprised Kyle was even doing that.

"But why?" Celine asked Noah. "You don't even care about me. I liked you, Noah. A lot. I DMed you so many times. You ghosted me, but I figured you got busy, like you said you did. Then on the show, you just led me on!"

Noah sighed, not because of Celine, but because he was frustrated with his past self. He needed to get better at communicating with other people, both online and face-to-face. "First of all, I'm sorry. Truly, I never realized how me being busy could hurt someone like that." He softened all the edges in his voice before continuing, "But on the show,

I wasn't leading you on. I was genuinely trying to get to know you. I just don't think . . ."

He hesitated, wondering if he should say this next part.

Celine crossed her arms. "What?" she asked. "Say it."

Noah briefly closed his eyes. People were going to make him into a reality TV show villain because of this, but *someone* had to be honest. "Look, our first two dates were great. But I'm not sure if we're compatible. Or if you even *like* me. You were literally out here kissing another guy."

Tears erupted from Celine's eyes, but Noah wasn't sure if it was because his words had hurt her feelings or because he'd forced her to confront the truth on camera. Maybe a bit of both.

"I tried, too, you know!" she exclaimed. "You just weren't the guy I thought you were."

It took all of Noah's self-control to not visibly react to *that* revelation. "Right, and there's nothing wrong with that . . ." He trailed off. Nothing in Celine's face told him she was willing to listen, to meet him halfway so they could come to a peaceful resolution. It'd been a mistake for him to follow her here.

He took another step back.

"Wait, where are you going?" Celine grabbed his hand.

Noah flinched away. He'd already been tense from Kyle grabbing him earlier, but now, he'd reached his limit.

Noah glanced around the forest and caught sight of

Kallie's camera. He gritted his teeth. He hated that it was there, capturing him at his worst. Everyone was going to see him like this. The students at Marlon, the viewers on YouTube, and the who-knows-how-many of his followers that watched this show.

Suddenly Noah couldn't breathe. His body started shaking from head to toe.

"Hey," Celine said, sounding genuinely concerned. "Are you okay?"

"Should we call for help?" Even Kyle looked worried. Which was just great.

Noah opened his mouth, but nothing came out. He had to go. Now. Before he completely shut down and made even more of a fool of himself.

He forced out a breath and tried again. "Sorry," he said. "But I can't do this right now."

And then he ran away. Away from Celine and Kyle. Away from the camera. And away from Mia's show.

Beyond the trail, the woods were thick and unforgiving, sending Noah tripping and falling multiple times into the snow. But he didn't stop. *Couldn't* stop. His heart was pounding too loudly in his ears. His head, hammering along with it, a confusing and jumbled rush of thoughts and memories.

He'd moved an entire ocean away from home to flee from a life where he'd spend endless nights watching movies and TV shows to even just momentarily escape from reality.

In his head, Noah knew that this was different, that his current situation on *The Cuffing Game* was not at all like the circumstances he faced back home. But his body took a lot more convincing.

I never should have come here. Noah had thought Mia's show would be a fun challenge, but maybe it was one he hadn't been ready for.

His legs gave out beneath him, and he got a face full of snow. A quiet "oof" escaped from his mouth. He turned over and lay there for a moment, chest heaving.

Snowflakes began falling around him in the twilight of the forest. It was beautiful. Peaceful, even.

Noah sat up when he felt like he could breathe again.

When he'd been running, he'd felt hot and cold all over, but now, as the icy wind cut through him, he was freezing. He stood up and began retracing his steps.

Noah had always thought he had a good sense of direction, but apparently that didn't apply to the woods. Every tree, stump, and rock looked the same, worsened by the now steady snowfall that was slowly covering everything in sight.

He could have sworn he'd run for only ten, fifteen minutes tops, but he was still lost after he'd walked for much longer than that. Shadows stretched and lengthened as the sun sank. Soon, Noah was trembling again. He was still wearing his coat, but the cold pierced into the exposed skin of his face, his lungs, everywhere.

Is this how I die? Noah thought.

For the sake of his pride, he hoped he was at least miles and miles away from the lodge. It'd be so embarrassing if his frozen, lifeless body ended up being discovered just five minutes away from everyone else.

His legs were about to give out again when he saw it: a small cabin in the woods not unlike the one he'd seen in a horror movie.

I'll take my chances out in the cold, Noah thought.

He'd only taken ten more steps when a coyote's howl pierced the thin air.

Noah turned around and dashed for the cabin.

At least most of the deaths in *The Cabin in the Woods* were quick.

THE IN-BETWEEN

CHAPTER TWENTY-SIX

Mia

Noah was missing, and it was Mia's fault. Granted, it wasn't like she'd told Noah to go off running into the woods. That was definitely a logical failing on his part. But they'd been out there because of *her* show. And she'd failed to keep everyone safe.

They'd ended up calling for help and halting production for the rest of the day. It wasn't ideal, but it wasn't like the show could go on with Noah missing and Celine sobbing inconsolably, even after Mia had tried her best to comfort her.

They were all back at the lodge now, and as the sun dipped below the horizon, Mia watched the recording of what happened from Kallie's camera. She had some *thoughts*. But they had to find Noah and make sure he was safe first.

She was waiting to hear back from the search and rescue team when she got a call from an unknown number. Mia feared the worst. What if this was someone calling to say they'd found Noah's dead body? Her hands shook so much she almost dropped the phone. "Hello?"

"I hate to disappoint you, but I'm still alive."

It was obviously him. Relief swept over Mia like a huge tidal wave. But she kept an edge to her voice as she said, "I'm hanging up. I hope you freeze to death."

Noah laughed, but the sound was weaker than usual.

Mia bit her lip. "Where are you?"

"I don't know if you know, but apparently an old lady owns the lodge we're renting right now. It used to be her family home before she got older and built a smaller cabin for herself about ten minutes away. I got here and passed out for a bit. Sorry, I would have called sooner but I just woke up."

No wonder no one could find Noah out in the woods. "You're in Ms. Merritt's cabin?"

Noah paused. "You know who she is?"

"Not personally, but I read about her when Damien and I were booking this lodge. Look, we called the police and there's a search and rescue team looking for you right now. I'll let them—"

"Odd request, I know," Noah cut in, his voice uncharacteristically sharp, "but can you come get me yourself? Only if you feel comfortable driving now, of course."

"What? Why?"

She glanced out the window. It was dark outside, but it'd stopped snowing a couple hours ago, so it was probably safe. She'd just need to borrow someone's car . . . *if* she wanted to go get Noah. He didn't seem like he was in any real danger. Or at least, not anymore.

"I was able to talk to Ms. Merritt through her smart doorbell, and she remotely unlocked the cabin door," Noah explained. "But there's no food because she's in the Bahamas for the holidays. That's where I should have gone, too, honestly. No offense."

Mia rolled her eyes. Sometimes she *wished* Noah were quieter with her like he was with Celine. "I'll come get you. But only under one condition."

"And that is?"

"Say please."

She'd expected him to protest or give her some pushback over her "inane" request. But he only said, "Please, Mia? It's been a long day, and I don't know how many more people I can take."

It occurred to Mia that Noah didn't include her in "people."

She'd do this for any of her contestants, Mia reasoned. Not just Noah.

"All right," she said. "I'm on my way."

The only times Mia had ever driven in wintry conditions were the once-a-year days when it snowed in her hometown in Texas. Ms. Merritt's cabin was only ten minutes away. Twenty, since Mia drove Kallie's SUV at a snail's pace. But it felt like an eternity.

By the time Mia arrived at the cabin, her hands ached

from how hard she'd gripped the steering wheel. She parked the car in the driveway and stared, taken aback by what she saw.

Compared to how luxurious and huge the lodge was, the cabin was the exact opposite—small and simple, and almost eerie in the dark of the night. It looked haunted.

Mia wondered if she'd somehow navigated to the wrong house. But then the door opened, revealing the warm glow of a fireplace and a *shirtless* Noah.

Mia started the engine back up and rolled down her window to shout, "I'm leaving! This is obviously a trap."

A flash of confusion crossed Noah's face. Then amusement as he looked down at himself.

"Sorry!" he called out. "My clothes got wet from the snow. I'm drying my shirt right now."

He was smiling at her, but there was tension in his face. Everything about Noah looked haggard. His skin had gone pale and almost ashen. He was also . . . shaking.

Mia had one bar of cell service, so she sent a quick text to tell the crew she'd found Noah and that they were okay. Then she got out of the car, making sure to grab the bag she'd packed from the kitchen.

"You brought food!" exclaimed Noah, his entire face lighting up.

"You said you were hungry," Mia replied. "And however much you might think otherwise, I'm not a *complete* sadist."

Noah took the bag from Mia and walked her back to the cabin.

"No, definitely not," Noah said. "Maybe an evil mastermind, though. If what you did with *The Cuffing Game* is any indication. You know, when I first gave you that idea, I didn't expect you to . . ."

He trailed off. Mia glared at him. "Expect me to what?"

Noah shrugged as he pushed open the door. "I don't know. Be really good at it. I thought you hated reality TV."

"I do, but a show is a show. And I've planned out many others before. Plus, I grew up watching random clips, thanks to my sisters. And I did my research."

Mia paused when they entered the cabin. Despite how awful and scary the small house had looked on the outside, inside, it was actually very nice. Antique, priceless-looking furniture with plush upholstery decorated the living room, while the quaint kitchen had beautiful white fixtures and porcelain faucets. A lush white rug covered the hardwood floor, and around the lit fireplace were . . . turquoise lounge chairs.

"Apparently Ms. Merritt's favorite color is turquoise," Noah said as he placed the bag of food on the kitchen counter. "Thus, the lounge chairs."

Mia gave him a questioning look. "Did you get her entire life story over the doorbell?"

Noah shook his head and motioned at an antique turquoise telephone by the couch.

"She told me her number so I could call her after she let me into the house. We chatted briefly after that. I think she wanted to make sure I didn't need immediate medical attention before we hung up."

"Ms. Merritt is getting *all* the good reviews," Mia remarked. "And I'm going to ask Damien to suggest her to anyone else at Marlon who needs a lodge for shoots. So she gets more bookings."

"That's a great idea," Noah replied.

As he started rummaging through the bag, a random thought occurred to Mia.

"Wait," she said. "You memorized my number? Is that how you called me using the landline?"

Noah didn't look up from the bag. "Yup. You know, just in case. Pro tip: always memorize the numbers of production heads before every shoot in case something goes wrong. Just one of the many things you'll learn later in film school."

"Right."

Suddenly Noah beamed. Before Mia even knew what was happening, he'd opened three separate Uncrustables and stacked them together into one big sandwich.

"I packed actual food, too!" Mia protested.

Peanut butter and jelly oozed together as Noah chomped down on his monstrosity of a sandwich. Mia looked away with disgust and saw Noah's coat and shirt hanging by the fire.

"If you're okay now, we should get back to the lodge as soon as your clothes are dry," she said. "There's still a lot we have to do for today's episode."

Noah nodded, thankfully opening his mouth again only when he'd swallowed his last bite. "Definitely. And don't worry about production delays. Since it's my fault, I'll cover for any extra costs."

He got out a water bottle from the bag and started guzzling it.

"Slow down!" Mia exclaimed. "You're going to choke."

Noah lowered the now half-empty bottle. Already, he looked more like himself, color back in his cheeks and light back in his eyes. Solemnly, he said, "I thought I was never going to be able to drink bottled water or eat an Uncrustable ever again."

A laugh escaped from Mia's lips. "Really? You like Uncrustables that much?"

Noah nodded. "One of mankind's best inventions. In my opinion, anyway." He ambled over to the fireplace and checked his clothes. "Hey, they're dry already. We can probably start heading out . . ."

He trailed off, cocking his head to the side as he listened.

"Mia," he said, his face suddenly serious. "The wind's picked up. I can hear it through the chimney."

Panic speeding up her heartbeat, Mia opened the door and got a face full of snow. Howling wind buffeted her, shrieking in her ears. She cried out as she fought to close the door.

Something solid and warm pressed against her as, suddenly, the door slammed shut.

She looked up to see Noah standing over her. His bare chest was just inches away from her face.

They were trapped. *She* was trapped in this small cabin with a half-naked Noah.

CHAPTER TWENTY-SEVEN

Noah

Noah was sure he was going to die today. First the cold, and now *this*. Mia's face burned tomato red. Her eyes flamed twice as murderous as she glared up at him.

Noah moved away and grabbed his shirt from where it hung by the fireplace.

"Sorry," he said. "I was just trying to get the door."

Mia didn't say anything until he'd put on his shirt. Then, in a low, vaguely concerning voice, she said, "We should probably stay here for the night. I can't drive in this kind of weather."

"It's okay. Neither can I. It's probably going to get worse, too."

Mia put her head in her hands and groaned. "Damien is going to kill me. And I don't even want to think about what the SPC is going to do when they find out about this."

Noah held his hands up in the air. "It's okay. As far as I'm concerned, you did nothing wrong. In fact, you saved my life."

"What if word gets out that you and I are spending the night together? In the cabin that belongs to the *owner* of the lodge we're renting for five days?"

Mia was panicking. That much was clear. Noah glanced around the cabin for something that could distract her. But all he saw was old lady furniture, and he didn't know anything about that.

"No one has to know," Noah replied, looking at Mia again. "This is just between you and me. If someone asks, we can say we found a vacancy at an inn or something. In separate bedrooms. And Ms. Merritt doesn't have cameras inside the cabin. I checked."

At the mention of bedrooms, Mia's face scrunched up with even more panic. "How many bedrooms does this cabin have? The roads won't be safe until they clear them tomorrow morning."

"One. But I can sleep in the living room."

"You're too big to comfortably sleep on the lounge chair!"

Noah placed his hands on Mia's shoulders, looking right into her eyes. "Mia, breathe. It's okay. You're okay. I'm okay. That's all that matters for now. We can deal with the rest when we're back in the lodge. And you can take the chair, since you're smaller. But only if you don't mind sleeping in the living room. I'm good with whatever."

He'd hoped to comfort her, but Mia's eyes widened.

"Wait," she said. "Are you . . . *touching* me? Willingly?"

Noah blinked, looking down at his own hands. They were indeed calmly resting on top of Mia's shoulders.

"Oh," he said, stepping away. "Yeah, I was. Wait. How do you know I don't like physical contact?"

"Well, the footage from earlier today, for one. That was painful to look at."

Noah winced. "Oh, you watched it."

"Yeah," Mia said with an apologetic frown. "But that's not the only time. You didn't shake my hand when we met at Ground Smoothie. And when you did touch me to help me up, you looked unhappy. At first, I thought it was because you couldn't stand *me,* but you looked so uncomfortable the first few times *Celine* touched you, too. You seem to only be comfortable with physical contact when people give you bro-hugs or fist bumps. Or when you and Celine kissed. Maybe you just hate being taken by surprise? Which, I can kind of relate with, since I don't like surprises either."

Noah shook his head in awe. "You're really observant."

She shrugged. "All I've been doing since I got here is watching people from behind the camera. I've been watching every contestant, not just you."

"Right."

Mia didn't say anything else, didn't probe and prod him to ask *why* he hated being touched. And Noah was glad. Because if he was being honest, he had no idea why. At first, he'd thought it was because it'd been too long since he had any substantial amount of contact with another human being. But after today, he was beginning to realize it was more than that.

In the comfortable silence that formed between him and Mia, Noah finally put together the words he needed. Softly, he said, "You're right. I don't like being touched, but only when someone takes me by surprise. Like, I'm perfectly fine at a concert or other crowded areas because I *expect* it, you know? If I had to guess, it's probably because my life back home wasn't always . . . peaceful. I hate it when people raise their voices, too."

Mia's face softened. "Oh, I'm sorry, Noah." After a moment of thought, she clapped her hands in a decisive manner. "We don't need to include the part with you and Celine in the forest if you don't feel comfortable with us airing it."

Noah let out a dry laugh. "How will you guys explain the production delays then? Just include a title card saying I randomly disappeared?"

"I don't know. But we can figure it out later. That's not what's important."

Noah stared down at Mia, fully taking in the sincerity in her kind eyes. His heart beat a bit faster as he looked away. "You can keep it in. I specifically came on this show to challenge myself. And to show a part of myself no one's seen before. If people unfollow me because I had a panic attack, then so be it."

When Mia didn't say anything in response, Noah turned

back to see that she was staring up at him again, quietly biting her lip. In this present moment, she looked so adorable that Noah didn't know what to do.

"What?" he asked softly.

"Sorry if I'm totally out of line for suggesting this," she said, "but have you considered therapy?"

Noah let out a sharp laugh. There was the Mia he knew. As blunt as ever. A grin slipped onto his lips.

"It's been suggested to me, yes. But I never thought things were bad enough for me to need it. Today made me realize I might, though."

Mia made a face, as if she was wondering why he was *smiling* while talking about therapy. He got his face back under control as she replied, "Therapy isn't something you can only go to when things are terrible. It can help you in other times, too. Seeing someone helped my younger sister, Cara, when she was having a hard time adjusting to high school."

Noah nodded as he sat back down on one of the turquoise lounge chairs.

At the beginning of every year, Noah liked to pick up one new activity, whether it was longboarding or learning to use a particular editing software. Perhaps next year's new venture should be therapy. The idea both excited and intimidated him at the same time. It seemed pretty timely, especially with all the changes he'd soon face with graduation.

Mia, who'd gone over to sit at the dining-room table, suddenly asked, "Wait. What about when you helped me up at Ground Smoothie? Or when you refused to shake my hand?"

Noah frowned. "What about it?"

"You looked *really* uncomfortable then. And it wasn't like you weren't expecting to make physical contact with me."

Just thinking about what it was like to hold Mia's hand for the first time, the unexpectedly pleasant warmth of her skin against his, made Noah's face burn. Desperately, he hoped Mia wouldn't notice. "Oh. That's not why . . ." He hesitated, and then quietly said, "I don't dislike touching you, Mia. Not at all."

"What . . ." She paused, as if putting two and two together. And then Noah wasn't the only one who was blushing.

Before he could dwell on the rosy pink of Mia's cheeks for long, though, she quickly turned her back toward him. She started typing on her phone, so Noah sat back in his chair, relaxing his muscles against the upholstery.

He must have dozed off, because when he next opened his eyes, Mia was sitting across from him on the other lounge chair. Her expression was unlike how he'd ever seen it before, her dark-brown eyes and cherry-red lips soft instead of being tense and rigid.

Her face immediately hardened when she noticed he was awake.

"You can go into the bedroom and sleep, if you want,"

she said flatly, getting up from her seat. "You've had a long day."

Noah stiffened. "No, it's okay. You can sit back down. And thanks, but I'll go to bed when I want to. Unless you want to sleep now."

"Nah." She settled back into her chair, and they stayed there for a long moment, face-to-face in the warm glow of the fire like that night at the firepit. Noah's heart raced at the familiarity.

"By the way, did you want to talk about what happened with you and Celine?" Mia asked. "Like, what caused the confrontation in the first place. You don't have to if you don't want to, but . . . I got Celine's side earlier today. So I can also listen if you want to tell me your side, too, to make things fair. Feel free to vent."

"Vent?" Some of Noah's old walls came back up at the foreignness of the word. In theory, Noah knew what the word "vent" meant. He'd encountered it on American TV shows and had heard girls say the word around campus. But this was the first time anyone had offered to listen to *him* "vent" before. Back home and at the fraternity house, *he* was the one who usually listened.

Noah stared into the fire. "There's not much to talk about," he finally said. "Celine and I aren't compatible. And I'm a jackass."

He braced himself, expecting Mia to agree with him. But she just leaned forward. "And why is that?"

Noah let out a slow breath. The familiar pressure was starting to build up inside him again, making it hard for him to shape his thoughts into concrete words. But he managed to say, "Before the show, I accidentally led Celine on by replying to her messages and comments. To me, I was just doing my job. Responding to people boosts engagement. But she thought I was being genuine."

Mia groaned. "You *do* do that a lot. Flirt with people, I mean. Which is why I never read the comments of your videos."

Noah raised his eyebrows at Mia. She wasn't looking at him, instead staring into the fire like he was a few seconds ago. Her cheeks were red, but he couldn't tell if that was because of the heat or something else.

"Wait. How many of my videos have you watched?" he asked. "Do you follow me? I thought you just watched my stuff to do research on me."

"Let's go back to the original topic," she said, blatantly avoiding his questions. "You apologized to Celine, though, right? Or at least, it seemed like you did."

"Yes."

"Good. And how about on the show? Were you leading her on here in Big Bear like she said you were? And *why* did you think it was a good idea to run after her and Kyle?"

"I'm not proud of what happened today," Noah said with a sigh. "But I swear, I was only trying to help. And no, I was not leading her on. I *was* actually interested in her. Or at least I was trying to be. If I'm being honest, my first impression of her wasn't that great. She talked with her mouth full, and—"

Mia groaned again. "No! That's literally her worst habit. I forgot to tell her not to do that before she went on the show . . ." She trailed off as she realized what she was saying.

"Wait," Noah cut in. "Is Celine your *friend*?"

"Roommate. She's the reason you were brought on to the show."

"Right. She said I was her crush on the first day." He nodded thoughtfully, putting all the puzzle pieces together. "So you and Celine are roommates. She likes me. And that's why you looped me on to the show as her crush. Okay, everything makes sense now."

Mia bit her lip and avoided his gaze. Noah cocked his head to the side. There was something else there. Whatever it was, Mia clearly didn't want him to know. In fact, she looked downright uncomfortable about it.

Noah figured it was best for him to move past it, whatever it was. She respected *his* boundaries, and now it was his turn. "Anyway, bad first impression," he said. "But I liked her again after the second date, when I got to know her better. I wouldn't have kissed her, otherwise. But then . . . today, I don't know. It really sounded like we just don't like each other. I mean, she was kissing another guy! Sure, I was on a date with Violet, but we were just talking. And it's not like I had a choice."

Noah paused, shocked by how easily the words had tumbled out of his mouth. Here he was, spilling his guts all over the place. And his body wasn't freaking out like it had with Celine. His heart was still beating fast, sure. But he wasn't sweating. And he didn't feel like he needed to run.

It's because Mia is actually listening to me, he realized. *Instead of screaming in my face.*

And it was true. Like she had the night at the firepit, Mia was taking in everything he was saying with a thoughtful look on her face. She didn't try to change the subject, nor did she dismiss him and tell him he was lying or being too much. She just let him be.

This Mia was so different from the Grumpy Mia he knew from class that Noah's head hurt. But he guessed both sides of her *could* be true. After all, when things previously got prickly between them, it was usually about their opposing opinions about movies or filmmaking. Not actually important things like *feelings*.

When Noah didn't say anything else for an extended amount of time, Mia blinked once, and then twice. She opened her mouth and closed it again, like she did whenever she was gathering words for a response in class.

The familiarity helped him relax. Just a bit.

"I see what you mean," Mia said at last, her tone neutral and careful. "Well, we got the conversation on camera. And don't worry. We're not like those other TV shows that manufacture people's responses or edit scenes to make people look bad. The viewers will see you as you are. And they'll interpret everything the way they want."

Noah shrugged. "And that's fine with me." He paused, remembering what had crossed his mind earlier in the forest. "Hey. Do you think it was a mistake for me to come on here?"

Mia furrowed her eyebrows. "What do you mean?"

Even with his usual ease with Mia, this part was harder to share. He ran a hand through his hair. "I came onto your show because I wanted to meet someone, yeah. But I also came here because it's hard for me to talk to people."

When Mia gave him a look that said *What the hell are you talking about?* he amended, "Yes, being social is part of my job. But I'm bad at having *real* conversations about things like feelings." A shudder ran through him at just the thought of his conversation with Celine. "I've never been in a relationship before. And after today . . . I'm realizing maybe a person like me shouldn't have come on a *dating* show in the first place."

Mia stared at him for a moment. And then, she began to laugh.

Noah went cold. He shrank into himself as he looked down at his feet. He'd taken down all his walls, only for Mia to laugh at him.

"Sorry," she said. "But Noah, have you listened to

yourself for the last hour or so? I kind of wish I had a camera with me."

"Why?" Noah said with a sharp grin. "So everyone can make fun of me?"

"No!" Mia replied. "So you could watch it back. You say you're bad about talking about yourself, but you're not. You're very articulate *and* relatable."

Noah shook his head. "I'm really not. At least, not normally. I'm only like this with . . ."

You. The last word died on his lips as he met eyes with Mia over the warm glow of the fireplace. Her face reddened, and this time it was unmistakable that she was blushing because of *him.*

They stared into each other's eyes for a long beat. And then another.

Mia broke away, clearing her throat.

"I mean, you were pretty good at it during your second date with Celine," she said. "I think you just need more opportunities to practice being more authentic. And what better time to work on that than a reality TV show being watched by thousands of people around the world?"

She gave him a small grin that told Noah she was joking.

I don't need a whole reality TV show, he thought. *The only person I want to talk to is right in front of me.*

But what he actually said out loud was "Don't remind me."

DAY FIVE

THE CUFFING GAME

Behind-the-Scenes Contestant Interview

VIOLET RUSSO

ALEX: Hey, Violet! Thanks so much for joining me, and for joining the show on such short notice. Please look at the camera and state your name, year, major, and crush.

VIOLET: Hi, it's no problem. I'm Violet Russo. I'm a junior and a dramatic arts major. And my crush is Noah. Or at least, I thought it was Noah. Now I'm not sure.

ALEX: Oh? And why is that?

VIOLET: He kind of just . . . ran off during our date. It was so bizarre. And apparently he made one of the other girls, Celine, cry? Before disappearing into the woods? Sounds like a huge red flag to me.

ALEX: Yeah, it's been a wild twenty-four hours. He's fine, now, though. Mia found him.

VIOLET: Well, that's good. But in any case, that's a bit too much for me. Plus, I met someone else on the show who's a lot more . . . stable.

ALEX: Oh, that's great!

VIOLET: Yeah. *[smiles]* He's really sweet. Funny, too.

ALEX: Cuff with him, please!

VIOLET: I *do* want to cuff with him. But I don't know. Things are really complicated right now. And I don't know if he feels the same way.

ALEX: Well, there's only one way to find out, right?

VIOLET: I guess. But I don't want to create extra drama, you know?

ALEX: Listen, this is a reality TV show. Made by *college* students. And this is the last day before the finale! As the editor, I give you permission to go wild. Just, if you can, try to wear the same outfit and keep the same hairstyle all day. To make things easier for me.

VIOLET: Okay . . . if you say so.

CHAPTER TWENTY-EIGHT

Mia

Mia drove them back to the lodge as soon as the roads were safe. Compared to how scary the drive had been the previous night, in the early morning light, it was nice. Pretty, even. Golden sunlight streamed down through the trees as they drove on the newly plowed roads. Mia even felt comfortable enough to speed a little, which earned her a "slow down, partner" from Noah.

She glared at him at the next stoplight. "You know people in Texas don't actually talk like that, right? Or at least not the people I know."

He gave her a mischievous grin. "My only exposure to Texas has been old westerns. And you."

Mia groaned. "Most of the old westerns weren't even shot in Texas!"

For the rest of the car ride, Mia gave Noah a condensed summary of a fifteen-page essay she'd written this past semester about the "Hollywood-ification" of Texas. It pretty much all boiled down to "everything you see is a lie" and "that's actually California or Arizona."

When she finished, he rested his chin on his hands and said, "Fascinating," like he really was pondering the fact that John Wayne was an Iowan who had never lived in Texas. It was a cute gesture, one that almost brought a smile to Mia's lips.

The lodge was completely silent when they arrived, and so were the surrounding woods covered by the heavy snow. If everyone's cars hadn't still been parked in front of the house, Mia would have thought they had all left.

She carefully parked Kallie's SUV behind Damien's. As Noah grabbed the now half-empty bag from the back seat, Mia's eyes lingered on his hands, thinking about how he'd placed them on her shoulders the previous night.

Noah's gentle but firm fingers had surprised Mia and, of course, she couldn't forget about what had happened by the door . . .

She shook her head as heat started rushing into her cheeks. She had to focus on the shooting day ahead.

In the early hours of the morning, Damien had texted her a revised production schedule for the rest of the show. Luckily, they'd had the foresight to schedule today as a travel day. When Kallie and Damien first suggested it, Mia had been hesitant to include the buffer, worried that it'd slow down the pace of the show. But now she was grateful for her friends' wisdom. She always was.

Besides the catch-up work they had to film, edit, and upload yesterday's episode onto the SPC YouTube channel, all they had to do was drive down to their beach house rental.

As they got out of the car, Mia sneaked a glance at Noah. From what she'd heard from both Celine and Noah, it didn't look like that cuffle was going to survive past today. Celine would undoubtedly pair up with Kyle, but where would that leave Noah? For the first time, Mia worried he would be voted off the show. An uncomfortable feeling settled in her stomach.

They'd reached the front door when Mia heard it: the faint burbling of water.

Noah frowned, hearing it too.

"Is there a hot tub nearby?" he asked.

"There's one in the backyard, but it's been covered up all week," Mia replied. "Unless . . ."

They glanced at each other with wide eyes before heading to the back of the lodge.

In the now very much uncovered hot tub, Carlos and Violet were making out, their bodies faintly illuminated by the tub's lights. Thankfully, they were wearing swimsuits. But they might as well not have.

A small squeak escaped from Mia's lips. The effect was immediate.

"What the—" Carlos whirled around, so quickly that he almost slipped. Violet screamed. Noah burst out laughing.

"Sorry! Sorry!" Mia exclaimed, waving her hands back and forth. "I promise we both just got here. We didn't see anything, I swear. Well, besides the kissing, but that can stay a secret if—"

"What in the world is going on?"

Damien came running out into the yard, followed closely by Alex and Kallie. Damien was in sweats, like he'd just been working out, while Alex and Kallie were still in their pajamas. Kallie was carrying a camera, obviously recording.

Noah laughed even harder, bending over with his hands on his knees. Mia could have sworn she saw a tear leak from the corner of his eye.

Carlos and Violet stood up in the hot tub, dripping wet.

"Noah, I can explain," Violet started.

Noah straightened, finally growing serious. "No need. I'm completely fine with this. In fact, I'm happy for you guys. I'm the one who abandoned you first."

Violet gave him a grateful smile. "Okay, thanks."

Carlos looked directly at the camera.

"It feels so good!" he exclaimed with a big smile. "Finally being wanted by someone."

"We *need* to talk to Carlos about not breaking the fourth wall," Damien whispered to Mia.

She smiled as Violet said, "You can say that again. I can't remember the last time someone liked me back!"

Mia resisted the urge to say "aw" out loud. She was genuinely happy for them.

"But also," Carlos said, "I'm *freezing*!" He sat back into the swirling hot water. "Maybe we should go back inside and shower."

Kallie stopped recording and approached the two contestants as they got out of the tub.

"I started filming before I left the lodge, just in case," she said. "But I wanted to double-check. Are you guys okay with this hot tub scene appearing in the episode?"

Carlos and Violet looked at each other and shrugged.

"Yeah," Violet said. "It's not like we did anything besides kiss. And by the time you came out, we weren't even doing that. I'm surprised you guys didn't come out earlier, since . . ."

Violet turned to look at Alex, who shrugged.

"I encouraged her to go after the person she liked," they said, glancing back and forth at everyone. "Was I not supposed to do that?"

"Oh yeah," said Kallie. "I was filming that. I thought it was super cute."

Damien groaned. "Technically, we're not supposed to interfere . . . but I honestly don't care what happens at this point." He raised his eyebrows at Noah and Mia before clearing his throat. "Contestants, please go back to your rooms and wait for the morning announcements. Crew . . . please come with me to the production room for a brief meeting before we officially get started with the day."

"Good luck," Noah whispered to Mia. Before she had a chance to respond, he walked back inside the lodge.

The production room was even more of a mess than usual, with candy wrappers and snack bags strewn across the floor.

"Sorry," said Alex as they went around picking up some of the trash. "Damien and I were stress eating."

Damien sat at his desk. Interlacing his fingers with each other, he cleared his throat and stared right into Mia's eyes.

"Mia," he simply said.

Mia looked at all her friends, one by one. "First of all, I'm so sorry about last night," she said. "I had no idea the snow was going to start up again. I didn't mean to abandon y'all like that, I swear."

Kallie shrugged. "I'm just glad you and Noah are safe."

Damien and Alex nodded.

"And before anyone asks," Mia added before anyone else could respond. "Nothing happened last night. Really. I slept in the living room. Noah slept in the bedroom. And we just talked."

Damien sat back in his seat. Mia's thoughts raced as he met eyes with Alex, an unspoken message passing between them.

"Something did happen last night," Alex blurted out. "Well, here at the lodge, I mean. Damien and I are officially dating!"

Kallie and Mia gasped.

Kallie looked shocked, but Mia almost burst from joy. Finally! Her instincts had been right after all. Something *had* been going on between Damien and Alex.

"Wait, what happened last night while I was gone?" Mia asked. "Besides the stress eating."

"Well . . ." Alex glanced at Damien. "Do you want to tell them, babe? Or should I?"

"*Babe*!" Mia and Kallie shrieked.

Damien covered his ears. "I'll do it," he said. He sighed and rubbed his face with his hands before continuing, "Basically, I was having a nervous breakdown. About being behind schedule, about what I should tell the SPC if one of you went missing for good, what I should do if one—*or both*—of you ended up *dead* . . ."

Mia winced. "Sorry," she said. "I tried to text whenever I could."

"And I appreciated that. Truly," replied Damien. "And, like Kallie said, the most important thing is that you and Noah made it back safely. But yes, I was stressing and Alex . . ."

He looked to Alex, who nodded and took over.

"I was freaking out, too," they said. "Because for the first time since we got to Big Bear, I couldn't finish editing the episode! Since we still need to film the final cuffings. And I had nothing left to edit after dinner."

Mia scrunched up her face. "Wait, you were freaking out because you *didn't* have anything to do?" she asked. "Isn't not having work a good thing?"

"I'm a workaholic, okay? Most editors are. But no, not in this instance. I knew it would mess with the postproduction schedule, and then I worried about how I should organize the episode when there are two separate days of filming instead of one . . ."

Kallie narrowed her eyes, like she was trying to solve

a challenging math problem. "Okay, so," she cut in, "to summarize . . . you two were both freaking out . . . and then you kissed? Wow, so much happened after I went to bed last night!"

Damien buried his face in his hands for a couple beats before saying, "I hate that it can be so easily condensed like that. But yes. I think I've liked Alex for a while now, but I never realized it until we roomed together and were together almost every day."

Mia gasped, remembering how Damien had been so grumpy whenever Alex swooned over Noah's posts. Now it all made sense.

Alex grinned widely. "Yup, and I've always been kind of intimidated by him, but only because he's so perfect."

Damien's eyes widened before he covered his face with his hands again.

Kallie snickered and Mia burst out laughing.

"I'm so happy for y'all!" Mia exclaimed. She threw her arms out by her sides, and they all came together in a big group hug.

"Sorry for the reason behind it," she continued, "but I hope you feel better about everything now. And that the catch-up work isn't too bad."

Alex gave her a pained look. "I doubt it. But thanks, Mia. Luckily the SPC was pretty chill about us uploading this episode later than usual. No one's in the office right now, but Carl—he's one of the staff members I was able to reach over email—just told me to submit whenever I can today before we leave Big Bear. He's already put up an announcement on social media that there were some production delays with this episode."

"Oh, I know Carl," Damien remarked. "He used to be one of my TAs. Nice guy, albeit a very hard grader."

Mia nodded. "Well, I didn't bring much," she said. "So it won't take long for me to pack my bag. If anyone needs an extra pair of hands today before we leave, I'm all yours."

Damien gave her an appreciative nod, while Alex said, "Thanks, Mia."

"Now that we've all caught up, we should get started for today," Kallie said. "The quicker we film the cuffings, the faster we can finish and upload the episode, right?"

"Agreed," Damien replied. "Let's do the announcements. Ready, Mia?"

"Yup." Mia bit her lip.

She had no idea what was going to happen at today's cuffing, but all she could do now for Noah and the other contestants was wish them luck.

CHAPTER TWENTY-NINE

Noah

Noah was lying in bed, his suitcase packed and ready to go, when Mia's voice came from the overhead speakers.

"Attention, all contestants," she said. "Please gather around in the living room for the final cuffing."

As it always did, the previously quiet house came to life with the hustle and bustle of everyone making their way downstairs.

Noah closed his eyes for a brief moment, listening to the footsteps and creaks of the floorboards. This, he realized, was the last time he was going to hear that sudden rush of noise. It was their final morning in Big Bear. He was determined to enjoy it—and make whatever amends he could before he left.

Downstairs, he joined the line of contestants standing in front of the cameras in the living room. Kyle's jaw dropped, and many of the other contestants also shot glances at him, like they were surprised he was still alive. The only person that didn't acknowledge his presence was

Celine. Which was understandable, given what'd happened yesterday.

He stole a glance in the girl's direction, just to check on her. Her eyes were still puffy, but other than that, she looked as beautiful as ever. She'd even added extra glitter under her eyes, so she was sparkling.

He knew Celine, like him, was great at hiding under a mask. But as far as he could tell, besides the puffy eyes, she genuinely looked okay. Maybe Kyle was good for her after all.

"Good morning, everyone," Mia said. "We apologize for the delay due to some . . . unforeseen circumstances. This morning, we will do our final cuffings, after which three cuffles will move on to our finale tomorrow. If you were one of the people chosen to cuff with a Gamechanger yesterday, please step forward."

The three contestants stepped forward. Noah and Celine stood ramrod straight, completely ignoring each other. In his peripheral vision, he saw Tiana nervously shift her weight.

"We will now cuff people in the order that the Gamechangers picked their match," Mia announced. "So that means Celine will pick first, then Noah, and then finally Tiana. Please remember that all cuffings must be mutual to be valid, meaning both people will have to want to be in it. Whoever is not in a cuffle at the end of this round will be eliminated."

It occurred to Noah that now that Violet was with Carlos, Noah had no idea who he was going to choose. He frowned before putting back up his mask of neutrality.

"Celine," Mia said. "Please pick who you'd like to cuff with for the finale of *The Cuffing Game.*"

Celine didn't look at Noah for even a second before saying, "Kyle. Because unlike some people, he's actually a gentleman."

"Oh yeah!" Kyle cheered, pumping his fist in the air.

It took all of Noah's self-control to not visibly react as the others gasped.

Kyle? A *gentleman*? Without his phone, he had no idea whether Thad was keeping up with the show at his ski resort in Aspen, but Noah hoped he was. Just for this one hilarious moment.

He wanted to laugh and cry at the same time as Celine walked past him with a flick of her hair. But the only outward reaction he allowed himself was running a hand through his own hair, a little gesture to relieve some built-up tension. After what had happened yesterday, it felt good to be in control of himself in front of the cameras again.

Celine and Kyle linked arms, and Mia turned to Noah.

"Okay then," Mia said. "Noah, as Celine's previous partner, you're up next."

Noah coughed and looked around at the remaining contestants, glancing one by one at Violet, Tiana, and Shirin. Violet, after what he'd seen this morning, was a definite no. For both her sake and his. And Shirin, probably no as well, since she'd shown zero interest in him all week. Maybe Tiana?

But then he saw it. The tiniest exchange of glances between Tiana and Shirin. Shirin, to her credit, was managing to keep an indifferent expression, but Tiana's eyes widened in panic.

And then, it finally clicked.

Noah shrugged. "Respectfully, I'm dropping out."

Damien's camera immediately focused on him as Kallie's swept across the other contestants' shocked faces.

Noah smiled. He was going to miss being on this show. It'd been challenging, but also weirdly fun.

"Yup, you heard me right." Noah pointed right at Damien's camera this time, breaking the fourth wall. "I'm out."

Damien cursed under his breath, swinging his camera away from him.

Okay, people are probably going to make fun of me for that.

Noah walked away from the camera and came to a stop in front of a wide-eyed Mia. Bits and pieces of the conversation he had with her last night lingered in his head.

"Hey," he said to her, quietly so Alex's boom mic couldn't pick up on the sound. "Can we chat privately before you leave Big Bear? I want to talk to you about something."

Mia gave him the faintest of nods. Noah got out of her way so she could go back in front of the cameras.

"Um, okay then. Well, that was interesting." She let out a nervous laugh that was echoed throughout the room. "Tiana? How about you?"

Tiana looked positively giddy as she said, "I'd love to cuff with Shirin, again!"

She and Shirin linked arms and cheered.

"Okay then!" Mia said. "So, this isn't what we originally planned, but since we have two people left . . . Carlos? Violet? Would you like to cuff together and be the final cuffle?"

From where he now leaned in the doorway, Noah grinned at how well Mia was playing the part of the clueless MC. If he were hosting, he probably couldn't have resisted throwing them a wink. Or otherwise alluded to the hot tub incident this morning.

Carlos and Violet looked at each other with huge grins on their faces. "Yes!" they exclaimed.

"Well, there you have it, folks," Mia said, smiling brightly as she turned back to the cameras. "Your final three cuffles of *The Cuffing Game*! Tune in tomorrow at four p.m. Pacific time to vote for your favorite pair during the live streamed finale. Congratulations, finalists!"

Everyone cheered. Smiling, Noah fully ducked out into the hall, knowing he'd made the right choice.

THE IN-BETWEEN

CHAPTER THIRTY

Mia

Since the drive to the beach house was not safe without cell service, especially in current winter conditions, Mia returned the finalists' phones. As she did, she made them all promise to not check social media or the SPC's YouTube channel. Most of them were probably going to do it anyway. But she hoped they would at least think twice about it.

After helping Alex out as much as she could before they shooed her out of the production room, Mia went downstairs. Noah, who'd also gotten his phone back, had texted her to meet him in the backyard. So while Mia expected to find him outside, what she *didn't* expect was to find him in the hot tub, which was still bubbling and steaming from when they'd left it on this morning.

He was shirtless again, so Mia had a clear view of his wide shoulders sticking out of the water.

This guy can't keep his shirt on. She swallowed but crossed her arms and did her best to look indifferent as she deadpanned, "Wow, did you quit my show so you could use the hot tub? You know you could've just asked to use it anytime, right?"

Noah smiled. "Nah," he said. "I wanted to enjoy it for a bit before I left. Do you want to join me?"

For a brief moment, his grin faltered, like he couldn't believe he'd actually asked the question out loud.

Every inch of Mia froze except her racing heart. She definitely couldn't get in the hot tub with Noah if he were still on the show. But what were the rules now that he wasn't? Mia thought about texting Damien, but she couldn't figure out how to word the message without being super awkward.

Hey, can I get into the hot tub with Noah? was definitely not a text she ever wanted to send. To anyone.

Damien and Kallie had gone ahead to set up the beach house and double-check shooting locations, so the only other person she knew for sure was still at the lodge was Alex. She wasn't sure if all the *contestants* had left yet, but for now, no one was in sight.

Even so, Mia hesitated. Some part of her knew that if she took Noah up on his offer, there'd be no going back. Having a fireside chat was one thing. Getting into a hot tub with her crush was a whole other level of intimacy.

"You don't have to join me if you don't want to," Noah said when Mia didn't respond. "And I can come out from the tub, too. If that's what you prefer."

Her body moved before she'd fully made the decision, taking off her shoes and rolling up her pant legs before her logical side caught up. As she dipped her feet into the water, Noah's warm brown eyes steadily met hers. Suddenly all she could hear was the beating of her own heart.

From where she sat on the edge of the hot tub, she had the perfect view of his high cheekbones. He was beautiful, and it was both amazing and infuriating how hot he was.

Mia's face burned.

Noah's lips parted ever so slightly. And that was all it took for Mia to imagine what it'd be like to sink down into the water and kiss him. It could have been her imagination, but Noah seemed to shift closer, ever so slightly.

Immediately, Mia pulled back, gripping the hot tub's edge with both her hands to avoid toppling over. Noah raised his eyebrows in surprise.

"So, why did you drop out of the show?" she blurted out before Noah could remark on what had just happened.

Noah also leaned back, placing his arms around the edge of the tub. This unfortunately gave Mia a clearer view of his broad chest.

"Well, I knew Tiana would much rather cuff with Shirin," he said. "And I wanted Violet and Carlos to have the chance to be an official cuffle together."

Mia frowned. "You didn't care that you'd be sacrificing your chance to win the game?"

"Nah," he said, running a hand through his hair. "I

never really cared if I won or lost. I came here to find love." The second the words landed, Noah winced. "Wow, that sounded cheesy. It's a good thing I'm not being recorded right now."

Mia snorted, and he gave her a lopsided grin that took her breath away. Yup, his real smile was much cuter than his fake one.

She held her elbow up to hide her face and coughed.

Noah's grin widened, and he slowly looked up at her as he said, "If I'm being honest, I don't feel that strongly about any of the *Cuffing Game* girls. They're not who I have a crush on."

Mia let her arm drop and widened her eyes ever so slightly, barely managing to catch herself from having a bigger reaction. For all she knew, Noah could have been about to say he secretly had a crush on Kyle.

Carefully, she replied, "I thought you didn't have a crush."

Noah stared down at the swirling water below before meeting her gaze again, deliberately this time. "I didn't. But I'm starting to realize that I do like someone now. And I think it'd have made everyone's lives easier if I figured it out sooner."

What is happening? Goose bumps prickled her arms in a tingling wave. Mia had a feeling she knew where this conversation was going. But she asked anyway, "What do you mean? Who's your crush?"

At some point during their conversation, it'd started

to snow, and now it was just her and him in the hot tub together, surrounded by the wintry quiet as the white flakes fell around them.

She should have never gotten into the hot tub with Noah. They'd crossed into a whole new territory, past a point of no return. She'd thought being stuck in the cabin with him last night was bad, but this was ten times worse.

Noah's lips parted ever so slightly as he leaned forward. Before she could stop herself, Mia dropped down to the water and leaned in as well. Her clothes got wet, but she was beyond the point of caring, not stopping until her and Noah's faces were just a few inches apart. He gently placed a hand on her cheek, and the sudden warmth of his skin made her let go of a breath she hadn't realized she was holding.

I don't dislike touching you, Noah had said. Mia swallowed.

With a shaky breath, Noah said something, so quietly that it was more of a whispered prayer than an actual statement.

"Wait, what?" she asked softly.

"You," he repeated, more loudly this time. "I have a crush on you, and I wanted to tell you before I left. I thought I hated you at first. You took yourself so seriously in class and I loved making fun of you for it. But then I got to know you better, and I realized you're actually really cool. And after seeing you work on the show and witnessing firsthand how much you care about everyone and everything . . . I tried my best to ignore my feelings for you, but I can't deny them anymore. It might sound impossible, but I really admire you, Mia. And I like you."

She pulled back. This was a dream. A nightmare even. How could the star of her own reality TV show fall in love with *her*? How could her *secret* crush like her back? "You can't *like* me," Mia said. "It's been less than a week!"

Noah blinked in confusion. "Okay," he replied, drawing out the word. "That's a little hypocritical for someone who created a six-day-long dating show to say, don't you think?"

"First of all, that part wasn't my idea," Mia said. "The SPC set that short time period since it's more affordable. Second, this is different. Most of the contestants on our show knew their crushes for a long time before they came on here, either up close or from afar."

Noah crossed his arms to his chest. "But what about the people who didn't know each other before? Like Violet and Carlos? Compared to them, you and I have known each other for much longer."

He made perfect sense. And Mia knew it. But at the same time, she couldn't get past the sheer, ridiculous notion that he liked her back. Or that, within a few days, he'd done a complete one-eighty from pestering her in class.

She had no idea what her face was doing, but whatever it was made Noah's expression soften.

"Mia," he said gently, slowly reaching a hand toward her. "Why is it so hard for you to believe that I like you? You're amazing."

Pressure built up inside Mia's chest. Her hands shook. Some part of her wanted to shout *Guess what, Noah,* actually, *I've had a crush on you for as long as I can remember. That's the entire reason why I created* The Cuffing Game *in the first place!* But she didn't. He'd changed his mind so quickly about her, like he'd changed his mind about Celine . . . too many things had happened for her to ignore.

Mia opened her mouth, and then closed it again, fully parsing out what she could and couldn't say. Finally, she decided on, "Noah, what about Celine?"

He frowned. In a low, confused voice, he asked, "What about her? I can't like you just because your friend had a crush on me?"

"Well, you kissed her."

He sighed. "Yeah, but that's before I knew better. Celine didn't even like me for me. She was only interested in me because I'm famous. She knows it, too. Which was why she dumped me the moment she found out what I'm really like, which is hilarious, since her new guy wants to be me."

Mia made a face of disgust. She'd heard him say that to Celine in yesterday's footage, too, but she had no idea what he meant. "Why are you so adamant that Kyle wants to be you? Because you've got more followers? You're so full of it."

Noah ran his hand through his hair in frustration. "He used to be in Alpha Tau, and I had some weird interactions with him in the past. There's a reason why he got kicked out of our fraternity. But I don't want to get into all that right now. I want to focus on *us*."

"Noah," Mia said, "there can't *be* an us. Not before we figure the other stuff out. Celine—"

"Can we please stop talking about Celine?" Noah cut in. "I know she's your friend, but she literally threw herself at me the moment we got here, confessing I was her crush and not even giving me a *chance* to talk to anyone else. During *speed dating*! But the moment she got to know me, the real me, she lost interest. No, she wants a real 'gentleman.'"

His tone was pure ice now, his voice mocking and cruel in an all-too-familiar way.

Anger rushed into Mia, replacing whatever hot tub–inspired feelings she'd been previously experiencing. Could she really like someone who saw people this way? Who looked down on people like Noah did with Kyle, Celine, and even herself back in school?

"You do realize you sound like a complete jerk, right?" she asked.

Noah gritted his teeth. "I've been nothing but honest with you," he said, practically growling. "And you've listened to me and nodded along like you understood this whole time, until now. Why are you bringing up all this other stuff instead of just believing me when I say I *like* you?"

Mia couldn't take it anymore. "Why *should* I believe you? You're a rude, pretentious frat boy turned influencer who negged me all semester before wildly doing a one-eighty. And you always act like you're better than everyone else, while the only reason you're attending film school here in the first place, even when you have zero respect for real cinema and barely pay attention in class, is your daddy's money!"

Noah flinched back like she'd slapped him.

Mia's mouth dropped open in shock. She couldn't believe she had said that hideous jumble of thoughts out loud. Her gut twisted with guilt.

"Noah, I'm sorry. I went too far," she said, reaching for his hand. "I just panicked—"

Noah jerked back so roughly that water splashed up. His face twisted with anger and hurt. "Is that what you really think of me? After everything I did for you and your show? After I literally eliminated *myself* so other people could get a chance at their happy ending?"

Mia remained quiet. The snow was coming down in full force now, an overwhelming blizzard that made it hard to see the world around her, slowly erasing Noah bit by bit. Before, when she was all flared up, she hadn't felt the cold. But now the wind seemed to cut through her.

Noah took a long, shuddering breath. And then, as Mia watched, his expression flattened out, becoming the emotionless mask she'd seen many times in his videos. It was terrifying how he could switch it on and off.

"I'm going back to LA," he said, turning away from her. "Sorry, this whole conversation . . . it was a mistake. After last night, I thought maybe, just maybe, you might like me too. But I clearly read you wrong."

He shivered as he got out of the tub. Without looking back at her, he said, "God, it's cold. Don't stay out here like that for too long, Mia. You'll get hypothermia."

After all that, he's still looking out for me.

She grabbed his hand, finally fast enough to make contact. "Wait, are you okay to drive like this?"

Noah froze. Still expressionless, he stared down at their joined hands until she let go.

"I am, thanks," he said flatly.

He walked away, and Mia watched in silence as he was swallowed up by the snow.

CHAPTER THIRTY-ONE

Noah hated everything. He hated the snow. The wind. And perhaps most significantly at this very moment, himself.

"*I am, thanks*," he repeated his own words to Mia in a mocking way as he leaned his forehead on the steering wheel of his stalled Jeep.

The colorful row of rubber ducks on his dashboard smiled at him in a vaguely sinister way. Or maybe Noah was just tired.

His Jeep had all-season tires *and* snow chains, so Noah thought he'd be fine. But then a deer had crossed in front of him, and he'd swerved, driving off the road and into the snow.

All things considered, Noah knew he'd been very lucky. His car could have easily veered into a tree or off a cliff. And fortunately, he hadn't been going fast enough to cause significant damage.

But he was stuck. He was miserable. And he just wanted to go home.

Thankfully, he'd charged his phone up before he left the lodge, so he'd been able to call for help. A tow truck was on the way, but with no real ETA because of "a heightened number of accidents in the area." Noah had heard about how dangerous the roads in the Big Bear area were during snowstorms. And he'd still decided to drive. All because he'd wanted to run away from a girl.

What a loser, he thought.

Noah stretched his hands out in front of him as he thought about how Mia had grabbed him. And how *he'd* touched her cheek, before everything blew up in his face.

Even when he'd been mad at her, her touch had *still* felt nice. It was a new experience for him, not just liking but *wanting* to be touched by someone else.

Even when that someone hated him.

Noah was hopeless.

From everything that had happened this past week, and after everything he and Mia had talked about over the last couple of days, he was now sure he needed therapy. Jae-hyun had first suggested it to him a couple years ago, claiming it'd "worked wonders" and helped him move on from their "hellhole of a childhood." But Noah had replied he was too busy. And he really had been, back then. But now that he was about to graduate in a few months, things were a lot more chill. And he definitely had plenty of time now, alone in his snowbound car.

He picked up his phone from where he'd tossed it on the passenger seat and started looking for therapists near

Marlon. He had only one bar of cell service, and it seemed unable to decide if it wanted to stick around, so he didn't make much progress before he got a call from Thad.

"Bro. Bro!" Thad's voice was distorted from the bad cell service, but Noah could still make out what he was saying. "Wow, you're finally picking up! I've been trying to call you all week! Are you still in the game?"

Noah frowned. "What game?"

"*The Cuffing Game*! The show you're on!"

Ah. So, Thad *had* been watching.

"I'm not in it anymore," he said. "I'm actually on my way back home."

"Oh, bummer. I'm sure you gave it your all, though. Everyone in Alpha Tau has been talking about it these past few days."

Noah raised his eyebrows. He'd never thought Thad—or anyone in his fraternity, really—would be the type to watch reality TV shows. But he stood corrected.

"Wow, you guys must really be into it," Noah said.

"It's so good! I'm pretty sure everyone who goes to Marlon watches it now, especially after the show made college sports headlines when Jack came out. Even my parents are watching it with me. All I've been doing this Aspen trip is ski and watch *The Cuffing Game*."

That meant everyone and their mom—literally—was going to watch Noah's little freak-out, if they hadn't seen it already. He groaned, leaning back into his seat.

"Hey," Thad continued. "So—"

The line went dead. In the sudden quiet, Noah's heart still pounded in his ears. The whole conversation had been stressful, but he also didn't want to leave his friend hanging. He sighed and called him again when the tiny bar was back.

"Sorry, lost service. I'm back now, though."

"Wait, lost service? I was *wondering* why your voice sounded so weird. Where are you?"

"Long story," Noah said.

"Um, okay. Are you all right, though?"

Noah stared out his windshield, at where his car was half-submerged in snow. "Yeah," he lied.

"Anyway, who is this Mia chick? Does she like you or something? She keeps staring at you in *every* episode. Like, I know she's the host but—damn, she glared at you right now! Sorry, I started watching the new episode they just uploaded."

Noah froze. "What do you mean?"

"Huh? Well, apparently something happened last night so they had to delay—"

"No, about Mia. What did you mean, she *stares* at me?"

He *had* noticed Mia looking at him a few times here and there throughout the last few days. But had it really been that much? His heart still stung from her rejection today. He wasn't sure he could take any false hope.

"Oh man," Thad replied. "Listen. This is something you have to see for yourself. Is your cell service good enough to watch the show?"

"Probably not."

"Okay, well, just trust me and watch the show whenever you get the chance."

Thad sounded so confident, enough that it piqued Noah's curiosity. "All right," he said. "I'll talk to you later."

"See ya," Thad replied. "Have fun!"

Noah hung up. After bookmarking the webpage of therapists, he searched for *The Cuffing Game*. Blood rushed to his face as the screen slowly loaded with all the different results.

Thad was right. The show had become really popular. Not only did the show already have entire articles *and* its own subreddit, but a couple of episodes themselves had several hundred thousand views.

It was going to take forever to load up the episodes with his fickle service.

But luckily, Noah had plenty of time.

DAY FIVE (CONTINUED)

THE CUFFING GAME

Behind-the-Scenes Contestant Interview

KYLE YOSHIDA

[Internal note: unaired; recorded shortly before we left Big Bear]

ALEX: Hey, Kyle. Thanks for dropping by on your way out. Please look at the camera and state your name, year, major, and crush.

KYLE: *[looks directly at camera]* Hey, what's up? My name is Kyle. I'm a freshman and I'm majoring in business. My crush is Celine, the little hottie.

ALEX: Um, okay! And you just cuffed with her in the previous episode. Congratulations! How is that going?

KYLE: Pretty good. I'll be honest. At first, I was only interested because she's *hot*. But we're a lot more compatible than I thought we'd be. We're going to drop out of the show. You know, like Matías and Jack? I watched the first few episodes before I came here so I know that's allowed. I want to take her to Vegas for the holidays.

ALEX: Oh! That's rather . . . fast. I mean, I'm not judging, but uh . . . that's amazing! Did you already tell everyone else?

KYLE: Yeah. We told Mia and got her approval.

ALEX: And what exactly are you guys going to do in Vegas? If you don't mind me asking.

KYLE: I'm doing what Noah couldn't do.

ALEX: Uh, okay, well, I hope you guys have an amazing time in Vegas. I'm so jealous!

KYLE: Yeah, I'd be too, if I were you. You film people work way too hard.

ALEX: Right. Okay, bye, Kyle. Have a safe trip.

CHAPTER THIRTY-TWO

Mia

Two hours into their drive out of Big Bear, Mia was deep in her thoughts about her conversation with Noah when Alex said, "Hey, so, you know how everyone else left before us?"

Something about their tone made her sit up from where she'd been moping in the passenger seat.

"Yeah?" she asked. "What about it?"

"Some people *did* have things to do. But it was also because of another reason," they said, shooting her a nervous glance. "A surprise. And normally, I wouldn't say anything. But Damien said we should give you a heads-up, because, well, you're you."

Mia bit her lip. After growing up in a household with four sisters, where a "surprise" could mean anything from a disastrous makeover to a completely inedible but well-intentioned homemade birthday cake, Mia had grown to hate surprises. In fact, most surprises—and other unexpected occurrences—gave her a lot of anxiety.

"But it's a fun surprise!" Alex continued. "I promise. Just a little something the rest of the crew and I prepared for you. You know, to congratulate you on being almost done with the show."

They sounded so excited that Mia pulled her lips up into a smile.

"Aw thanks!" she said, doing her best to force her voice to be bright and cheery. "I'm looking forward to seeing what it is."

By then, they'd arrived at the beach house, a white, modernly designed cubic building with two stories and floor-to-ceiling windows. It was somehow even bigger and more grandiose than it looked in the photos, a stark contrast from the nice yet understated exterior of the lodge they'd stayed in at Big Bear.

Alex parked their car in the driveway and got out the boom mic from the back of the car. As she stepped outside, Mia let out a quiet breath of relief. It wasn't warm, not by LA standards, at least. But after spending the last several days in Big Bear, even fifty degrees seemed nice and pleasant.

She'd just shut the car door behind her when Damien and Kallie came out of the house. Damien was empty-handed, but Kallie had her camera pointed right at her. Before Mia knew what was happening, Alex moved to stand behind Kallie's camera with the boom mic.

"Since today is our fun travel day episode," Damien said, joining Mia in front of the camera, "I thought it'd be nice if we filmed some moments with the crew, too. You know, since it's the last recorded episode before the live streamed finale tomorrow."

Mia nodded. Filming cute behind-the-scenes footage of the cast and crew was something they'd discussed before, although they never figured out when to do it. She guessed that time was now. "That's totally fine," she said. "But why are we recording now?"

Damien exchanged glances with Alex, who nodded.

"I gave her the heads-up about the surprise," they said.

Mia smiled. Out loud, it sounded so ridiculous that she needed a *heads-up* before a surprise. But after months of working on *The Cuffing Game* together, her crew accepted her as that type of person. It felt nice to be known.

"Excellent," Damien said. "And Mia, just trust us on this, okay?"

She nodded and bit her lip.

"Mia," Damien said again, but in his formal "producer" voice. "You've been the driving force behind the show. And I speak for the contestants as well as the rest of the crew when I say that we appreciate all that you've done for everyone."

He got out a blindfold from his pocket. Mia froze but let her friend cover her eyes with the piece of fabric.

"Y'all are literally the only people in the world I trust enough to do this with," Mia remarked. "You know that, right?"

"I know," Damien replied in a singsong voice. "Thank you for trusting us."

He securely tied the blindfold around her head and led her up the steps to the house. Mia heard the door open and close behind them, and after they'd gone a few feet inside, Damien said, "Okay, loosening the blindfold."

The fabric fell away, and it took a few seconds for Mia's eyes to adjust to the lights. And when they did, she blinked rapidly to avoid bursting into tears.

"Surprise!" Kallie exclaimed. "We're having a beach house party!"

"Not everyone could make it of course," Damien amended. "Since it's three days before Christmas. But this is still a decent turnout. We know you hate surprises, but hopefully you'll like this one."

Streamers and balloons decorated the dining room of the house. All the finalists except Celine and Kyle were there, along with Jack and Matías. They all stood around the kitchen island, where a large white cake sat on the counter.

Back home, Mia was always the one throwing parties for her sisters, since, although she was the oldest, Jeannette had good ideas but wasn't very good at executing them. This was the first time Mia had never had a party thrown for *her.* Her heart swelled with gratitude as more tears fell from her eyes.

"Wow" was all she could say out loud. "Thanks, y'all."

She looked around for Celine and Kyle but remembered what Damien had said. *I guess they have some things to take care of before we start recording again*, she thought.

Closely followed by Kallie and Alex, Mia approached the

kitchen island and peered closer at the decoration on the cake.

Thanks, Mia! it said in gold and black frosting. *From The Cuffing Game Family.*

Gold and black were Marlon's school colors. After a whole semester of feeling lost and out of place, seeing her name in those colors made her chest squeeze.

It was like she finally belonged.

Damien filled small champagne flutes with sparkling apple cider and Mia passed them around. When everyone had their drinks, Kallie exclaimed, "We love you, Mia!"

The others joined in, cheering as they raised their glasses. Tears fell from Mia's eyes. She smiled so widely that her cheeks ached.

When she first came to Marlon, "friends" were the last thing on Mia's mind. She was laser focused on her own dreams and ambitions, and that was it. But somehow, her crush on a particularly annoying frat boy, and the show she'd created to avoid her feelings for him, had led her to a whole group of people that had become her second family, thousands of miles away from her biological one.

As people mingled, Matías and Jack approached her.

"Mia!" Matías exclaimed. He squeezed her so tightly that her feet lifted off from the ground.

"Hey!" she said when she could breathe again. "How are things?"

"*Amazing*," Matías replied with a big smile.

"We're still really grateful," Jack added.

Mia beamed, even more than before. "Any fun plans for the holidays?"

"Jack is flying home to Atlanta tomorrow, while I'm going back to New York. Sadly it was too late to make Christmas plans together."

"You could always hop on a plane and surprise Jack's parents," she joked. "They probably already know you from the show."

Matías's eyes went wide. "I know you're kidding, but you're absolutely right. They *do* already know me, thanks to the show. Apparently they want to meet me soon . . . just not at Christmas. Which I understand. Plus, I can't abandon my family last minute! Christmas is a big deal in my household."

Mia laughed. "I totally get it, because same!"

She mingled some more, checking in to make sure everyone was okay. She was enjoying herself, but some part of her couldn't help but wish Noah were there. And that they hadn't had their horrible fight.

When the sun had almost set, Mia wandered over to where Damien was chatting with Alex and Kallie, who'd put down their equipment to enjoy the party.

"So when are Celine and Kyle coming to the beach house?" she asked her crew. "It's getting kind of late."

Alex's mouth dropped open. Their eyes widened with panic as they looked from Mia to Damien and then to Mia again.

Mia's heart thudded in her chest. "What?" she asked. "What is it?"

Damien put a hand on Alex's shoulder, as if to reassure them. "I'd already left by then, but Alex told me that since Kyle was the last crusher to be interviewed, they pulled him into the production room before he and Celine left."

"Kyle and Celine were the last contestants to leave the lodge," Alex explained. "You were in your room, I think."

Mia groaned. After the hot tub fiasco with Noah, she'd gone back upstairs to take a hot shower and change into new clothes. She'd had to unpack and repack her bag. It'd been super annoying, and she'd had no one to blame but herself.

"I haven't edited it yet, since it's supposed to air before the finale tomorrow," Alex continued. "But Kyle told me he and Celine are dropping out of the show. And he said *you* approved it and told them they could go to Vegas."

"I definitely didn't say that." An uneasy feeling settled in Mia's stomach. "And Celine already has plans to visit her family in China over the break. She said so during her interview on Day One."

Granted, Mia had only met Celine four months ago, but her roommate didn't seem like the kind of person to change plans so drastically.

"Sorry, Mia!" Alex moaned. "I should have asked you about it directly. You seemed to have a lot on your mind already, so I only told Damien."

"And I thought it was strange," Damien replied. "But I

figured you had a conversation about it with Celine in private since she's your roommate."

"What can they even do in Vegas?" Shirin asked. She and the other contestants had drifted over at some point into the conversation. "They're not even twenty-one yet, right? They can't gamble, drink, or even get a hotel room by themselves in most places."

"But they can elope," whispered Matías.

Everyone gasped, turning to look at him.

"But it's only been a couple of days!" Tiana said. "They're not *actually* going to get married . . . right?"

Alex scrunched up their face. "Yeah, I don't know," they said quietly. "I hope not. Kyle said a lot of weird stuff, like how they're more compatible than he thought they'd be and how he wants to do what Noah couldn't, whatever that means."

Deciding enough was enough, Mia called Celine. The line went straight to voicemail.

Celine was probably fine, but the *not* knowing was what killed Mia. She called her roommate again. Voicemail.

Everyone was watching Mia, waiting for her to decide what to do. For the first time since they'd started this show, even Damien seemed at a loss.

Tears of frustration sprung into her eyes as she stared down at her phone. She wanted to scream, but of course, she couldn't. Not now, anyway.

"Crew," she finally said. "Emergency production meeting, now."

THE IN-BETWEEN

CHAPTER THIRTY-THREE

Noah

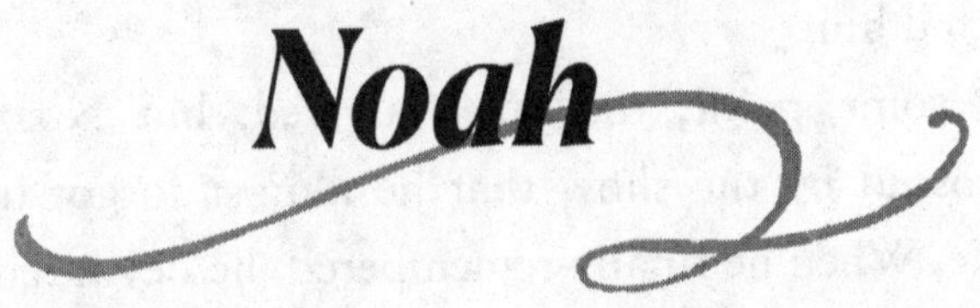

As luck would have it, the tow truck got to Noah in an hour. He'd had to rent another car for the week while his Jeep was in the shop, but he was able to return to the fraternity house by sunset.

In the end, because of bad cell service, he hadn't been able to get through more than the first five minutes of episode one while waiting in his car. Now, he relished the power and speed of high-speed internet. The fraternity house was empty, like it always was during the holidays, so Noah ordered pizza and queued up all four available episodes of *The Cuffing Game* onto the smart TV before throwing himself onto the living room couch.

Living out in the woods had been fun, up to a certain point. But it sure felt good to be back in civilization. He took a slow, deep breath and pressed play.

From the very first second, Noah was enthralled. Alex had done an amazing job, piecing together all the different moments from the past several days into extremely binge-worthy episodes. This was Noah's first time seeing himself—*as* himself—in long-form content. It was painful how *douchey* he came off as in some scenes, even when he hadn't meant to be a jerk. God, no wonder Mia had rejected him.

At some point, the pizza arrived, but Noah was so engrossed by the show that he almost forgot to bring it inside. When he finally remembered, he devoured the food as he kept watching and laughed so much he almost choked on pepperoni when he saw himself *try* to shovel.

When Matías cuffed with Jack, Noah got up on his feet, clapping and yelling, "Let's go!" like he hadn't witnessed the moment in person. And during the most recently released episode, he paused his fight with Celine to book a session with the earliest available therapist.

Jesus, he thought. *I'm such a mess when I don't edit myself.*

What was amazing about the cameras was how they picked up on little details that he'd missed, even when he'd actually been there at Big Bear himself. Like how Shirin and Tiana *definitely* liked each other as more than friends. And how, like Thad had said, Mia kept *staring* at him, especially in moments when Noah was looking away from her.

And apparently, he and Thad weren't the only ones who noticed.

Can we talk about how the host is always either looking at Noah or looking at everyone *but* him? I'm obsessed.

HELLO, does Mia like Noah?? Are they secretly dating or what??

Just me on my nonexistent pipe dream Mia and Noah cuffle ship!

The comments weren't all over the place. In fact, only a handful of people even mentioned Mia compared to the countless viewers who talked about Noah, Celine, or the other contestants. But Noah felt hopeful just seeing they were there.

Fully spent after his emotional roller coaster of a day, Noah had finally gotten into bed when he noticed he'd received a DM request from a @chismetias.

After sounding out the name in his head a couple of times, Noah opened the message.

CHISMETIAS: HEY IT'S MATÍAS. FROM THE CUFFING GAME.

Noah grinned. Somehow, Matías texted exactly how he talked. Since the message had been from a couple hours ago, Noah replied immediately.

NOAHDJANG: hey, how are you? thanks for remembering to reach out.

CHISMETIAS: GOOD. AND YEAH, OF COURSE!!! WE SHOULD HANG OUT AFTER BREAK. I DON'T KNOW IF

YOU HEARD BUT THERE'S A LITTLE SITUATION WITH THE SHOW. I WAS AT THE BEACH HOUSE EARLIER TODAY.

Noah had so many questions. Why was Matías at the beach house? And what was the situation? He responded with the best way he could summarize his thoughts.

NOAHDJANG: ?

CHISMETIAS: CELINE IS MISSING. AND SO IS KYLE. WE THINK THEY'RE IN VEGAS BUT WE'RE NOT SURE. EVERYONE IS REALLY WORRIED. MIA CRIED. THOUGHT I SHOULD LET YOU KNOW. I WATCHED THE SHOW AND YOU SEEM TO LIKE HER. AND MAYBE ALSO CELINE???

Noah made a face at his phone. So many things were said in that one message that he didn't know where to start. But most importantly . . .

Mia cried.

After thanking Matías and promising to hang out with him after break, Noah called Thad.

Thad answered on the first ring, like he always did. "Hello?"

"Hey," he said. "Can you tell me Kyle's phone number? And maybe also his address? Don't tell anyone, but Celine is missing, and we think she's in Vegas with Kyle. You have his information on file somewhere, right? Since you were his Big."

"Oh man," Thad said. "He did mention he has some relatives in Vegas, although his parents are in LA. But I don't think I'm allowed to share anything else beyond—"

"I graduate in a few months, so I don't care," Noah replied, matter-of-factly. "I'll take full responsibility if we get into trouble."

Thad chuckled nervously. "All right then! We're really doing this, huh? But if anyone asks . . ."

"We never had this conversation."

CHAPTER THIRTY-FOUR

Mia

At 2 a.m., on the morning of the finale of *The Cuffing Game*, Mia sank into her bed. This wasn't how she'd expected to start the last day of her show, but here she was.

In the end, Mia and the other crew members had decided to do a vote. She'd abstained, and everyone else had unanimously chosen to keep filming.

"We only have the finale left," Kallie had said. "And they're both adults. For all we know, Celine could be making out with Kyle at an EDM show right now. I just don't think it's fair for everyone else to stop production now."

They'd also asked the contestants, who pretty much said the same thing.

Mia knew everyone was right. Celine *was* most likely fine. But she still couldn't shake off the guilt and worry that pressed down against her chest.

First Noah, and now Celine. Somehow, Mia had gone into the show with her crush and roommate and walked out with neither. And not just on camera, but off, too.

Maybe the mistake was having my roommate and crush involved in the first place. Mia winced. But it wasn't like she had a choice this time around. As a freshman, she'd had virtually no power. She promised herself to only cast complete strangers for her next show. If she was ever allowed to have another one. Right now, with two missing cast members, her chances were getting slimmer by the minute.

In her bed, Mia mentally went over what had happened yesterday. There were so many little interactions to sift through, to turn over and over again like a rock in the palm of her hand. She went through everything that had transpired both on and off screen, wondering if she could have somehow prevented things from happening the way they did.

She'd just drifted to sleep when her phone rang.

It was Celine.

Mia bolted out of bed.

Not wanting to wake up Kallie, she grabbed her phone and ran out of the room. Some part of her brain was still stuck in Big Bear, so when she opened up the back door to a stunning view of the moon shining over the dark-blue waters of the Pacific Ocean, Mia did a double take. This was something she could never see back home.

Breathing in the cool, salty air, Mia answered her phone. "Hi."

"Hey," Celine said. Mia could barely hear the other girl's voice above the rush of people. Music blared nearby and, at first, Mia wondered if Kallie had been right and Celine really was at an EDM show. But then she heard sporadic car horns. So, Celine was outside. But where?

"I got your messages," Celine continued. "All ten of them."

After she had heard about Kyle's plans for Las Vegas, Mia had spiraled and left Celine a broad spectrum of messages in the last twelve hours, ranging from the quick and casual "Just checking in!" to the heavy-handed "Hey, please call me back so I know you aren't dead."

In retrospect, they were all so embarrassing.

"Are you okay?" Mia asked. "You're in a safe place, right? And you and Kyle didn't elope?"

Celine laughed. "Wait, what? Of course not! He did ask me to be his girlfriend, but I told him it was way too soon. And I'm okay!"

A loud car honk burst through from the other line. Mia jerked her phone away from her ear and brought it back in time to hear a guy—Kyle?—laugh. Celine giggled and cheerily said, "Sorry! That was Kyle jaywalking. We just got out of a show and are headed back to the car right now. Should get a lot less chaotic in a few minutes. Hold on."

More loud voices and traffic noises ensued. Mia held her phone at a distance until she heard the car door slam shut. The background noises subsided, and Celine yelled, "Be quiet, please! I'm having an important conversation with Mia on the phone!"

"Hello?" Mia asked. "What's going on?"

"Hi, yes," Celine said, her voice a lot more audible than before. "I'm in the car now. Sorry, it's been a wild twelve hours. My phone died while we were at Big Bear, and after I dropped off my car back at school, Kyle drove us to a show in Vegas! I thought everything would suck since we're not twenty-one yet, but we've been finding a lot of fun eighteen-plus things to do, especially since it's only a couple days until Christmas."

Celine sounded happier than she had all week. Somehow.

"That's . . . good!" Mia did the math. The drive back from Big Bear to school was at least two hours, and then the drive to Las Vegas was another four. And that was *without* factoring in SoCal traffic, which added even more time. To a "plan everything" type A individual like Mia, that kind of long-distance, last-minute trip sounded like a nightmare. She always knew she and her roommate were different types of people, but she never realized just how different they were from each other until now.

"Sorry I left you and everyone else in the dark," Celine continued. "If I'm being completely honest, I didn't think you'd care that much. Considering we're not exactly friends. But then I listened to all those voice messages . . . and I was surprised."

Mia blinked. "You were?"

"Yeah. I mean, come on, you barely talked to me in the entire semester we lived together," Celine said with a sharp laugh. "You were always off doing cool film school things with your cool film school friends. You only really started chatting with me after I agreed to be on your show and got Noah involved."

Mia looked down at the white sand beneath her feet, processing Celine's words. It was true that she had always thought of Celine as more of a "roommate" than a "friend." But she was surprised to hear Celine's side of things.

In Mia's eyes, *Celine* had been the one that was almost never in their room, always going out to the coolest parties or hanging out with influencer friends who would never give the time of day to dorky freshmen like herself. Until now, Mia had no idea that it went both ways. That while she was feeling left out by Celine, Celine was feeling left out by her, too.

"I do care about you," Mia said. "Roommate, friend, whatever. And I care that you're happy and doing well."

She told Celine about how *she'd* been feeling the past several months, and the other girl let out a long sigh.

"Being someone's roommate isn't easy, huh," she replied. "But yeah, it's okay. Now we know. And I'm fine! I've just been trying to relax and have fun. This week has been hard. I thought I knew who I liked, and I thought I knew what kind of person he was. I was *so* wrong on both counts. And to top it all off, I discovered that the roommate who invited me to be on her show actually has a crush on the very same guy as me!"

Mia dropped her phone in the sand. After picking it up again, she asked, "Wait, what? How did you . . ."

Celine laughed. "Okay, so, at first, when you told me you knew Noah, you were *so* intense. I was, like, wow, she must really hate him. And while I was on your show, I got a sense that *something* was up, but I was too busy with my own drama with Noah to figure out what. But after watching the show on our way to Vegas, I realized that intensity is part of your dynamic with him. You hate each other, but you like each other just as much. Maybe more. Either way, you two are obsessed and there are entire *fan edits* out there shipping you guys! I watched a few of those, too."

"Oh no," Mia groaned. She'd accidentally stumbled upon a couple on social media earlier today herself. It was all so embarrassing. "Celine, I'm so sorry. While it's true that I had a crush on Noah, I never thought it'd be reciprocated. I would have never brought you and him onto the show otherwise."

"Yeah, well . . . no real hard feelings. Because we both got what we wanted in the end. Don't get me wrong, what happened on the show was *really* awkward, and I'm glad we're getting a few weeks off from living together during the break. But I'm also low-key grateful because the show helped me realize that Noah isn't the kind of guy I like *at all*. Kyle is."

"Kyle?"

Celine giggled at Mia's disbelief.

"Okay, I think you got a really bad impression of him from Noah," Celine replied. "But he's not that bad,

I promise! He's just a rebel, which I like! Kyle is what I thought Noah would be like in real life. Based on his social media, I mean."

Mia made a face at the thought of Noah being like Kyle. She remembered what Noah said about Kyle wanting to be like him and cleared her throat. "Well, even though you said it was okay, I'm still sorry for the mistakes I made. Really. I promise to be a better roommate—and *friend*—next year."

"Same here," Celine replied. "I'm glad we're having this conversation, honestly! We've talked more now than we did all semester."

Mia winced. "Yeah, we should definitely fix that in the new year."

"Agreed!"

Mia was thinking back to her conversations with Celine when she remembered an important detail. "Wait," she said. "So are you not going to see your family in China this year? The main reason I thought you were kidnapped or something was because you said you already had plans for break."

A few seconds later, Celine replied, "Oh, yeah, okay. I can see how that made you worry. But nah, that flight isn't until tomorrow. And I asked my parents if I could skip this time around. I love my family and all, but we go every year! I'd rather hang out with Kyle."

"And they just let you skip?" Mia's mouth fell open in

disbelief. Dropping out from a family trip *and* going to Las Vegas with a boy were both things *her* parents would never let her do. Her life and Celine's were so different from top to bottom.

"Yeah," Celine replied. "I mean, they don't know I'm in Vegas right now. But I'm going back home at around noon to drop my parents off at the airport, so everything should be fine. That reminds me. Could you *please* do me a favor and edit out any mention of Kyle and me going to Vegas? And about me going missing? Please, roommate to roommate? I don't want to get disowned."

Mia grinned. "Sure. Not just roommate to roommate, but friend to friend. It's the least I can do after everything I put you through this week."

"Thanks, Mia," Celine replied. "You're the best."

Mia smiled. From her voice, she could tell the other girl was smiling too.

She was about to say bye when Celine said, "Oh, also. Mia? Now that we've cleared the air, can you tell Noah to *please* go back to LA? He and Kyle had a pretty intense dance-off at the concert we were at, and now I'm watching them try to one-up each other outside of the car. I feel like I'm third wheeling on my own trip."

"Wait, what? Noah is in *Vegas* right now? With you and Kyle?"

"Oh, I thought you knew! Yeah. He got here an hour ago, and he kept pestering us to tell you I'm okay. Which is why

I called you as soon as we got out of the show. Whoa, Noah just did a backflip!"

Mia's heart felt funny, jittery, and nervous in a way it'd never felt before.

"Okay," she said. "I'll call him right now. Thanks so much, Celine. For everything. Happy holidays and I'll see you next year!"

"You, too!"

They hung up. After taking a few calming breaths that would make Jeannette proud, Mia called Noah.

CHAPTER THIRTY-FIVE

Noah

"You're in *Vegas*?"

Noah couldn't tell if Mia was happy or mad. She sounded like she was a bit of both.

He pressed his phone closer to his ear and looked down from where he and Kyle were parked on the rooftop level of the parking garage.

Even from where he was standing, he could hear the excited chatter and drunken laugher of the holiday revelers on the street below. Noah held up a hand as Kyle got back into his car and drove off with Celine.

"Hello?" Mia asked. "Noah, are you there? Are you really in Las Vegas with Celine and Kyle?"

"Sorry," he replied. "Yeah, I was waiting for them to leave." Noah cleared his throat. After talking nonstop with Celine and Kyle for almost an hour, his voice was a bit hoarse as he continued, "It's a long story. Basically, I heard from Matías about what happened, and then I was able to track Kyle down. I would tell you how, but then I'd have to kill you."

Mia snorted. "Frat business again?"

"Don't know," Noah deadpanned. "Also, it's *fraternity*."

"Noah . . ."

In a big rush, he blurted out, "Matías said you cried and then, the next thing I knew, I was driving to Vegas. It just kind of happened, and I know you hate me, but—"

"Thank you," Mia said, cutting him off. "Really. You didn't have to go all the way to Vegas to talk to *my* room—friend. But you did. Also, I don't hate you."

"Is *room friend* the term first years are using these days? Weird, but okay."

"I'm being serious."

Noah heard sniffles on the other line. "Wait, are you *crying*?"

A woman shot him a dirty look as she walked back to her car. He turned away and whispered, "Mia, I did everything so you *wouldn't* cry."

"No, I know, sorry," she replied, her voice tight and pinched. "It's just . . . it's been a stressful week. And this is the nicest thing someone has ever done for me. I can't believe you spontaneously drove four hours to make sure my friend was okay."

I'd do a lot more for you, Noah thought. But he didn't say that part aloud. He was coming on too strong already.

Mia sniffed again.

From where he was standing, Noah could just make out the edges of the big Christmas tree set up downtown. He stared at the glimmers of light as Mia asked, "Wait, so what happened between you and Kyle? Celine mentioned a dance-off?"

Noah groaned. In the last five hours, he had sped hundreds of miles through the desert, yelled over enough loud EDM to make him never want to hear another beat drop again, and had no less than two dance-offs. He was exhausted, but he'd thankfully been able to make peace with both Celine and Kyle by the end of the night.

"Yeah, it was a lot, but we worked everything out, eventually," he told Mia. "Kyle is super competitive, but I think he genuinely likes Celine."

"That's good. But . . ." A small giggle came from the other line.

"But?"

"He's not the one that did a backflip, though, right?"

Noah laughed. "I never said *I'm* not competitive, too."

Someone honked, and Noah got back inside his car. The rental's interior wasn't as nice and roomy as his Jeep's, but at least it was speedy. He connected his phone to the car via Bluetooth and leaned back in the seat.

"But yeah," he continued. "I'm pretty satisfied with the outcome of the night. Celine called you, and Kyle agreed to get his own personality next semester."

"His own personality?"

Noah could picture the way Mia scrunched up her nose in confusion. "He admitted to copying me. Apparently, he was just having some kind of first year identity crisis. I almost felt sorry for the guy."

There was a long stretch of silence, and Noah wondered if Mia had fallen asleep when she said, "Thanks, Noah. Again. And sorry I didn't trust you the first time. It sounds like you've had a busy night."

"It's fine. Thanks for the apology." Noah couldn't resist asking the question for any longer. "Now do you believe that I like you?"

Another pause.

In a quiet voice, Mia said, "Yeah, I do. But before anything happens between us, there's something you should know about me, Noah. That everyone should know about me."

Well, that was concerning. Noah frowned. "What is it?"

"Just watch tomorrow's episode, the one we're airing before the finale. I'm guessing it'll come out around noon."

"Are you revealing that you're a vampire? Because that would explain why you don't sleep—"

"Noah! I'm hanging up."

"Okay, okay," he said with a laugh. "I'll watch it."

DAY SIX

THE FINAL DAY OF *THE CUFFING GAME*

THE CUFFING GAME

Behind-the-Scenes Creator Interview

MIA YOON

[Internal note: to be broadcasted instead of Kyle's interview.]

ALEX: Hey, Mia. Thanks for joining us for this exclusive behind-the-scenes interview of *The Cuffing Game*.

MIA: Hi, Alex. Thanks for doing this so early in the morning.

ALEX: It's no problem. Luckily I was able to finish editing the other parts of the episode last night so I can just add—Oops, the viewers probably don't care about all that, good thing I'm going to edit myself out. Anyway, how do you want to start?

MIA: The same way we always do.

ALEX: So you want me to ask—

MIA: Yep.

ALEX: Okay. Please look at the camera and state your name, year, major, and crush.

MIA: I'm Mia Yoon. I'm a freshman majoring in film production, and my crush is Noah Jang.

ALEX: *[silence]*

MIA: Um, Alex? Are you okay?

ALEX: Sorry. I needed a minute. So, you're really doing this, huh?

MIA: Yup.

ALEX: Okay then. What brings you in front of the camera today?

MIA: The contestants on the show have been so vulnerable and brave. So I wanted to do the same. As everyone knows by now, I'm the creator and the host of *The Cuffing Game*. But what people *don't* know is that I'm the original crusher of this show.

ALEX: And what do you mean by that?

MIA: Growing up, I made up shows to deal with things I couldn't control or didn't understand. When our family dog died when I was a kid, I came up with my own version of *Bluey*. But not Australian. When the girl I liked dumped me after homecoming and my parents were homophobic about it, I wrote a pilot episode and used it to get into Marlon's film school.

ALEX: Good for you!

MIA: Thank you. But yeah, when I developed a crush on *Noah*, who I originally *hated* . . . making a show about other people's crushes was easier than dealing with my own. It was never supposed to actually have Noah in it. We were just trying to save the show, and things snowballed from there. I regret its origins, but I don't regret *The Cuffing Game*. I love our cuffles, and I hope our audiences do, too.

ALEX: Aw, that's so sweet. Do you have any final words for our audience? Or for Noah, perhaps?

MIA: If you're watching, Noah, please know that I don't regret my feelings for you. Just maybe how I went about things. I'm sorry for pushing you away and being mean just because I wasn't ready to come to terms with how I truly felt. I hope you'll forgive me. And as for everyone else . . . welcome to the last day of *The Cuffing Game*. The live stream starts at four p.m. Pacific time.

CHAPTER THIRTY-SIX

Mia

This is the messiest show I've ever seen.

She made this entire TV show because she likes someone? Instead of just *telling* him? That's so wild!

My pipe dream cuffle ship! It's coming true!

After they uploaded the last recorded episode of *The Cuffing Game* at noon, Mia lay in her bed and scrolled through people's various reactions to her interview. She'd propped the windows open, and the cool ocean breeze filtered into the room. She could hear the seagulls, as well as the cast and crew members playing out on the beach. The vibes were amazing, but they did little to ease her nerves.

She'd expected Noah to call her. Or even send a text. *Something* to indicate that he'd seen her confession. But when the one response she'd wanted never came, her heart sank. She'd thought Noah, as dramatic as he was, would appreciate this public confession over a private one. But maybe she'd just embarrassed him—and herself.

To distract herself, Mia watched *The Cuffing Game* in its entirety, something she'd been too busy to do until now. Celine had been right. It was almost comical how many times Noah glanced off camera, presumably to look at Mia. Or how she and Noah snuck glances at each other when they were on-screen together.

She'd just finished watching the latest episode when she got a FaceTime call from Jeannette.

Mia picked up instantly, eager to talk with her sister for the first time since she'd left for Big Bear. She'd been expecting only Jeannette and was caught off guard when all four of her sisters crowded the phone screen.

A chorus of "Hi, Mia!" and "Hey!" greeted her. Tears erupted from Mia's eyes.

"Hey, y'all," she said, her voice cracking on the first word. "How are things?"

Lola's jaw dropped open, while Cara and Marie gave her weird looks. Jeannette's face went dead serious as she brought the phone close to her face. "Mia? What's wrong, hon? You okay?"

Mia shook her head, unable to lie to anyone for any longer. "No, I messed up. Big-time."

"Did something happen with the show?" Jeannette asked. "It's okay. Tomorrow's Christmas Eve. I can change your flight to tonight, if you want me to."

"It's not that," Mia said. "I messed everything up."

"What happened?" Jeannette asked. "Talk to me."

Mia had avoided telling her sister much about the show, mainly out of guilt and fear that she'd only disappoint her. But now, she told Jeannette everything, from how her crush on Noah had inspired the show to what she'd said during her interview this morning.

Jeannette reacted appropriately, gasping or cursing at the right moments. As they talked, Mia realized just how much she'd missed her sister. *All* her sisters. Back home, they'd talked almost every day about what was going on in their lives. Jeannette especially had been her guiding light, her closest confidante. And Mia had felt so lost without her.

When Mia was finally done, Jeannette took a deep breath before she said anything, as was customary in the Yoon household.

"Mia," she said, "I have a confession to make. Actually, we all do."

Her sisters were suddenly all back, crowding the screen as Jeannette repositioned her phone.

Mia swallowed. "What?" she asked, unable to keep the panic from her face. "What is it?"

"We watched the show!" Lola blurted out.

Marie and Cara giggled, and Jeannette gave her an apologetic look.

"We got curious," Jeannette explained. "I found it on

YouTube, and I'd only meant to show them the first episode but then—"

"It was amazing!" Lola exclaimed. "We couldn't stop watching."

"And Noah is super cute!" Cara exclaimed. "Wow, so hot."

Mia opened her mouth to protest when Jeannette beat her to the punch.

"Catherine Ji-ah Yoon," she said, "Noah is way too old for you."

Cara started arguing back, and Mia was smiling at the familiarity of watching her sisters bicker when she had a horrifying realization.

"Wait," she said. "How did y'all *all* watch the show? You couldn't have unless you watched it on the living-room TV. And that means . . ."

"That your dad and I watched it, too." Mia almost dropped her phone as their mom came into view.

"It's quite impressive, dear," she continued. "When I was your age, I was just trying my best to sneak into frat parties."

"Tried that," Mia quipped. "Didn't like it."

She winced the moment the words came out of her mouth. Her mom had *complimented* her work for the first time in her life, and *that's* how she'd responded to her? Old habits sure died hard.

Her mom gave her a tight smile. "Well, we all have our own likes and dislikes."

"And we *all* liked your show," Jeannette replied, grabbing her phone away and saving the day as usual. "Even Dad."

"Daddy was gasping and yelling the entire time." Lola snickered. "Like he was watching a Cowboys game."

"Anyway," Jeannette said, taking the phone and walking away from everyone else, "we're all so proud of you, and if Noah doesn't come *running* after all that, well, screw him! He's not that cute."

"Except he is," Cara hissed.

At least three different voices shushed her.

"Thanks, y'all," Mia said, wiping away the tears that had started falling from her eyes again. She could barely process what had just happened in the last ten minutes, but she was grateful for everyone's support, nonetheless. "My flight gets in tomorrow afternoon, so I'll see you soon."

"Can't wait," Jeannette said, blowing her a kiss. "Good luck with today's live stream! We'll be waiting for you at DFW in our Dolly Parton Christmas sweaters."

"Please don't," Mia groaned.

"Come on, I know you secretly love them. We bought you one, too!"

A small smile crossed her lips as she thought back to how, just a few days ago, she'd sadly looked at her family's matching sweater pics, hoping they hadn't forgotten about her. Now, all of that seemed silly. Of course they hadn't.

"Okay, I'll allow it. See y'all soon."

"Love you!" exclaimed her sisters in varying pitches and volumes.

"Love you too."

By the time they ended the call, the light of the late afternoon sun had started coming through the curtains of her room.

Mia got out of bed. It was time for the finale of *The Cuffing Game.*

She used another of Celine's videos—one that Celine had *personally* recommended to her—to achieve what she thought was her best look yet: a face full of makeup that actually accentuated her features, a sleek white evening gown, and her favorite pair of red heels. She felt good about her outfit, even more so when her friends did double takes when she walked down onto the beach.

Alex whistled, and Kallie exclaimed, "Damn, Mia!"

Even Damien gave her an approving smile. "Now, let's finish this show of ours."

Mia smiled back and nodded at her friends.

Damien and Kallie had set up two tables on the beach: one with a camera connected to the laptop they were using for the live stream, and another smaller, decorated one where the cuffles were going to have their final dates. Everything looked beautiful under the golden hour light. The brilliant white tablecloth, the glass candle holders sparkling in the sunshine, and the bright bouquet of pink and red flowers capping the middle of the table. Even the equipment on the other table looked gorgeous in the setting sun. Or at least it did to Mia.

Carlos and Violet, the first cuffle for today, came down in their evening finest. Carlos was in a white tuxedo while Violet wore a bright yellow dress that glowed golden in the sun.

When the contestants and crew were all ready, Mia took a deep breath and stepped into the frame. Going live was nerve-racking, but in a good way. The adrenaline cleared Mia's head of all distractions. *Including* a certain frat boy with a cute smile.

"Ready?" Kallie asked.

"Ready," replied Mia.

Damien started the live stream.

"Hi, everyone," Mia said, looking into the eye of the camera. "Welcome to the live finale of *The Cuffing Game*. I'm sorry to say that Celine Huang and Kyle Yoshida have decided to drop out of the show. But we wish them nothing but the very best! Stick around until the end of the live stream to vote for the winning cuffle. That lucky pair will win the cash prize of five thousand dollars."

She paused to look up from the camera. Damien nodded, and so did the rest of her crew.

"Our first cuffle took everyone by surprise, even themselves!" Mia continued with a smile. "But they're still very cute. Please welcome Carlos Manalo and Violet Russo!"

She stepped away from the camera, and Carlos and Violet began their date.

"So," Violet said. "I can't believe we made it to the finale. I can't believe *I'm* here, honestly. Like, I just got here! I feel bad since I'm so new to the show!"

Carlos shrugged. "It's okay, I was one of the original contestants *and* I was the first one to be eliminated, so we balance each other out. I, for one, can't think of a better person to be by my side today."

"Aw, same!"

Mia watched the laptop screen as the viewer count ticked steadily up. Fifty people tuned in . . . then a hundred . . . five hundred . . . a thousand. Then suddenly, ten thousand, fifteen thousand . . . seemingly in the blink of an eye.

Her palms started to sweat. She wondered if her own family was watching, too.

Comments, emojis, and unfortunately also spammers flooded the chat, too quickly for Mia to read everything. But she did see several people talking about how cute Carlos and Violet were.

In a weird way, it's like they were meant to be.

Violet's yellow dress is so cute!! Does anyone know where she got it from?

Aw Carlos <3 Violet

"Since we just met each other a couple days ago," Carlos said, recapturing Mia's attention, "I want to make things clear. I don't want you to feel pressured to get into a relationship with me because we're on the finale of this show, okay? We can treat this as a normal second date if that helps."

Violet smiled. "Sounds good. But also, I *am* really interested! Like, I appreciate you setting expectations and all that, but trust me, I wouldn't be here if I didn't want to get to know you more. I do have to ask you something, though. Before we go any further."

"Hm?"

"Do you like anime? Sorry for the random question, but the last guy I was with . . . he didn't like that I love nerdy stuff like anime and Marvel movies. And I don't really want to be with anyone who shames me for my hobbies."

Carlos clapped his hands. "Are you freakin' kidding me? I *love* anime! And comic books, too! I literally grew up going to Comic-Con."

"That's amazing!" Violet exclaimed. "I've always wanted to go, but I usually don't stay in California during the summer."

"We should totally go next year! Wait, sorry, is it too soon to make plans like this?"

Violet giggled. "Not at all. I'd love to go with you."

As the cuffle continued their conversation, Mia smiled. After seeing how much of a not-so-good time Carlos and

Violet had on the show, she was glad they had found each other. Their date raced by, and in what seemed like almost no time at all, Mia stood in front of the camera again to say, "We'll be right back with the second cuffle after a short break."

Damien paused the stream, and the crew prepared for the next cuffle date. Sunset was fast approaching, so Mia went around to light the candles on the table while Alex set up light panels to brighten the space. Kallie adjusted the camera while Damien double-checked the stream connection. The way they worked in perfect harmony made Mia smile. She was going to miss her crew. She hoped this wouldn't be the last time they could all work together.

Shirin and Tiana couldn't stop smiling at each other when they came out for their date, so much so that Mia felt euphoric just watching them. Both girls looked amazing; Tiana wore a Cinderella-esque sky-blue chiffon dress while Shirin was in a sleek, long-sleeved black evening gown.

"Okay," Mia said once the girls were settled in their seats. "Ready to go?"

"Yup," replied Shirin.

"It's now or never," said Tiana.

Mia stepped in front of the camera again, and Damien raised his hand to signal he'd resumed the stream.

"Welcome back, everyone, to the final date of *The Cuffing Game*," she said. "Our current cuffle has been best friends for *ten* years, truly showing the power of friendship. I, for one, am very much excited for this date. And I hope you are, too."

Mia retreated to the laptop to watch the audience reactions coming in.

OMG, they look so nice!

Wait, are they JUST FRIENDS or do they actually like each other that way?

AH! I hope Shirin confesses to her crush!

From across the candlelit table, Tiana shyly smiled at Shirin. "Hi."

"Hi," replied Shirin. She glanced at her friend and then at the camera before continuing, "Before we get started, I want to say something. Just so it's clear. This is not a friend date. Or at least, it's not for me."

Damien's jaw fell open, while Alex stifled a gasp with their hands. Kallie's entire body tensed, and from the way she was practically vibrating, Mia could tell she was trying her best not to physically react for the sake of the camera.

Slowly, Tiana smiled. "I know."

People immediately flooded the chat with *AHHHH*s and celebratory emojis. Mia smiled.

"Wait, what?" Shirin asked. "You knew I liked you this entire time?"

Tiana shook her head. "No . . . it's complicated. I think some part of me always liked you in that way, too. I was just deep in denial at first, and then I was too afraid to act on my real feelings. So when I got the invitation to go on this show and saw that you were also going to be on it, I had my hopes! But I wasn't sure. It got *really* obvious toward the end, though. Sorry I kept you waiting."

She reached out and took Shirin's hand. The other girl stared at their joined hands like she wasn't sure if she was dreaming or not.

"Y-you're fine," Shirin said. "It took me a long time to admit it, too."

"At least you did *something*. And I'm so grateful you did."

The girls grinned at each other; their fingers interlaced as they kept talking.

The Cuffing Game had been a mixed bag for everyone, including herself, but as Mia watched this final date, her chest swelled up with pride and joy for everything that had led to this final episode. Shirin and Tiana were so cute together, as were the other cuffles that had met through the show.

She looked at her friends, who were also smiling as they watched Shirin and Tiana's date. This had always been the goal for Mia and her crew, after all. Making a show where *other* people confessed to their crushes. Not herself. She had to remind herself of that.

In the soft glow of the candlelight, the two girls ended their date with a kiss. Everyone cheered as they walked offscreen.

Mia stepped back into frame. "Thank you, Shirin and Tiana. There you have it, everyone. The final two cuffles of *The Cuffing Game*. For the next fifteen minutes, please cast your votes using the poll link provided in the comments. We will announce the winner shortly—"

"Wait!" someone said, off in the distance. "I have something to say!"

"What kind of joke—shit, I forgot we're live!" Damien slapped a hand across his mouth, and Alex snickered.

"Sorry, babe," they said. "I can't fix things in post this time."

Mia ducked behind the camera to check the responses that were coming in on the laptop screen.

LOLLLLLLL

WHAT IS HAPPENING? Whose voice was that??

This show is a wild ride from start to finish!!!

Wait, it's our boy, Noah! Look at him run!

Alpha Tau! Alpha Tau!

Mia's heart pounded in her chest as quick footsteps approached, muffled by the sand. When she looked up, Noah was there, standing right in front of the camera. He was panting and breathing heavily, like he'd just run a race.

When their eyes met, Noah held out his hand.

"Hi, Mia," he said. "Can you please come stand here with me?"

CHAPTER THIRTY-SEVEN

Noah

Noah had no idea what he was doing. All he knew was the swirling, jumbled mess of big *feelings* he had for Mia, and the fact that he wanted the whole world to know how he felt.

Mia was right after all, he realized, groaning internally as he thought about that fateful day in the lecture hall. *I* am *the type of person to obnoxiously show off the person I like to everyone.*

Mia's face was blank with surprise as she asked, "Noah, what are you doing?"

Fear belatedly struck his heart as he realized Mia could shoot him down when he was the most vulnerable. He slightly lowered his hand but pressed on.

"Sorry I didn't respond sooner," he said. "I watched today's episode and then drove here as fast as I could from Vegas and then *ran* across the beach because I realized I was going to miss the stream, thanks to LA traffic. The whole time, I was thinking about how to best give you my answer. And now seems like the best time. Only if you're okay with it, of course."

Biting her lip, Mia took Noah's hand and let him guide her to the front of the camera.

Reassured by the warmth of her hand, Noah addressed the camera directly. "For anyone who's been sleeping under a *rock*, this is Mia. She's the creator of *The Cuffing Game*, as well as the host. And it took me a while to realize it, but *she's* the person I want to cuff with on this show."

Several gasps came from behind the camera. Noah looked up to see that Shirin, Tiana, Violet, *and* Carlos had come out onto the beach to rejoin the crew. Some of the cast and crew members seemed taken aback, but no one looked truly surprised.

He turned around to address Mia directly. Her eyes were wide, and her mouth slightly agape.

"Mia, you're amazing, and I like you. I know I've already told you this in private. But I wanted to tell you this in front of *everyone* so you have no doubt that this is what I think of you. You're super observant and ambitious and just *so* caring. Yes, you initially made this show to forget you like me"—a few people chuckled, and Noah smirked before continuing—"but there's no doubt you care deeply about everyone here. People who aren't in film school don't realize how much blood, sweat, and tears a single production like this takes. They don't realize the countless sleepless nights and *months* of preparation it takes to make everything happen. But I do. And people may think it's weird you created this show instead of just telling me how you feel. But you know what? You were totally justified in what you did. When we first met, *I* was a complete asshole to you. And I had so many walls up that made it hard for you—for anyone, really—to get to know the real me."

"So he's self-aware," Mia said. "Finally."

Her words were as blunt as always, making Noah laugh.

"Yeah," he said. "Sorry it took me so long to get to this point. Hell, I would have made a show to avoid my feelings for me, too. Actually, a movie, since I like films more. A thriller, maybe?"

Mia made a face, and Noah pressed his lips into a line so he wouldn't burst out laughing again.

"Anyway, I like you, Mia. And after watching your interview, I'm *pretty sure* you like me, too. So, without further ado . . ."

Noah put his hand on his waist, so that his arm formed a circle. An invitation.

Mia blinked, as if she could hardly believe what was happening.

"I've always wanted to do this," she whispered. Then slowly, as everyone around them burst into applause, she linked her arm around his.

Noah was about to ask Damien to cut the live stream when, so softly that he almost missed it, Mia asked, "Can I kiss you?"

Noah's heart beat faster. She was asking him for permission. In these current circumstances.

He suddenly understood what people meant when they said they "*swooned.*" Because that was exactly what he was doing over Mia right now. His entire body felt hot, and not in a bad way.

"You can always kiss me, Mia," he said, with a grin so wide and genuine that his mouth hurt a little. Then Mia stood up on her tiptoes to finally, *finally* kiss him.

CHAPTER THIRTY-EIGHT

Mia

Mia's show was completely going off the rails, a situation right out of her nightmares. But instead of feeling like she was spiraling out of control, Mia was on cloud nine.

Noah's lips were softer than she could have ever imagined, gentle yet firm in a way that made her knees weak. He wrapped his arms around her waist and pulled her close, steadying her as he kissed her harder and deeper. She was about to lose herself in the moment when—

"Wait!" Alex hissed. "We're still live!"

Mia stiffened, and Noah let go, gently so she wouldn't lose her balance. Right, the show. They had to finish the show. Catching her breath, she glanced at Alex and the rest of her crew. Damien nodded before jotting down something on a piece of paper and passing it to her.

Mia cleared her throat. "Everyone who is a finalist in *The Cuffing Game*, please step in front of the camera," she said. "Noah . . ."

Noah was also out of breath, and *not* because he'd been running this time.

"Totally fine," he said, moving away. "I'll step back. We can continue this later."

When the four finalists had gathered around her, Mia opened Damien's note.

"According to the votes and audience reactions," she said, "Shirin and Tiana, you two are the winners of *The Cuffing Game*. Congratulations! Not only do you win each other, but you also get the cash prize of five thousand dollars. We wish you nothing but the very best!"

Shirin and Tiana squealed, jumping into each other's arms.

Violet and Carlos looked momentarily disappointed, but then they smiled and hugged each other.

"This is just the beginning for us!" Carlos said with a shrug.

"Yup," Violet replied with a big grin. "Pretty amazing beginning, if you ask me!"

They shared a kiss, and Mia turned back to the camera with a big smile on her face. "There you have it, folks. Thank you so much for watching *The Cuffing Game*, the dating show for Marlon students, by Marlon students. Happy holidays and we'll see you next year."

Damien cut the live stream, once and for all. Then, in an uncharacteristically cheery voice, he yelled, "We did it! We actually pulled this show off. I'm free!"

"*We're* free!" Alex pulled him in for a hug, and so did Kallie. Mia joined in, squeezing her friends tight.

"Thank you so much, y'all," she said. "I couldn't have

done any of this without you. And I'm really proud of all of you."

"Are you kidding?" Kallie asked. "We're proud of *you*! I can't believe you're just a freshman. What are you going to do as a senior? Start your own studio?"

"As of now, that's not in my four-year plan," Mia joked. "But maybe I should pencil it in?"

She was still laughing with her friends when there was a gentle tug on her arm.

Noah stood behind her, his expression a mix of happiness and anxiety.

"Hey," he said. "Can we talk?"

"Um, I want to," Mia replied, "but we have to clean up and prep for the wrap party—"

"Damien, Alex, and I have it all taken care of," Kallie cut in. "Go! Be a freshman for once and *have fun*."

"Yes, *go*!" Alex yelled.

Damien raised his eyebrows at Mia, as if to say *What are you waiting for?*

Mia shot her friends a grateful look before taking Noah's hand.

The loud celebrations of the cast and crew faded away as Mia and Noah walked along the beach. The moon was rising, big and white in the night sky. Waves gently crashed down on the shore and around their feet, shimmering in the moonlight.

"I wanted to let you know that everything I said back

there . . . it wasn't just for the camera," Noah said. "Or even social media. I couldn't care less about other people when it comes to us. I only care about *you*, and I wanted to make sure there was no way for you to doubt that I like you this time. Sorry I interrupted the show, though. I—"

Mia laughed. "Noah, it's okay. You're completely fine."

They shared a smile before Noah looked away, his eyebrows wrinkling with concern. "Maybe it's the type A film school student in me," he said. "But I want to talk logistics, especially since I'm graduating next semester. I'll most likely stay in LA after graduation, to finish a few projects and to make my own long-form content, but I'm not one hundred percent sure. You're a first year, so obviously I don't want you to be tied down to me in case something happens . . . but . . ."

"But?"

"I don't want to lose out on a chance to be with you, either," Noah said. "Even if I end up having to return to Seoul and fly back and forth across the Pacific Ocean, I'll do everything within my power to make us work, I promise."

Before Mia could respond, Noah ran a hand through his hair. "God," he said. "We literally just kissed for the first time and I'm talking *logistics*. Not exactly sexy, now is it? Should I just shut up and take off my shirt?"

Mia snickered. Celine had been right. The real Noah was definitely *not* the unobtainable, devil-may-care boy from his social media. But he was perfect. Or at least he was perfect for Mia.

"What are you talking about?" she asked. "Logistics are *so* sexy. They're practically my love language."

Noah froze, his eyes slightly widened with surprise. Then, without warning, he pulled her in for another kiss that left her breathless.

Mia knew this relationship wasn't going to be easy. They were both workaholics, and she herself would only get busier as she started loading up on classes and internships. If she was being completely honest with herself, she had never even *considered* factoring in a relationship, much less a possibly soon-to-be long-distance one, into her four-year plan. And for a good reason, too.

But at the same time, looking back at the past few months, she saw how things had gotten so complicated *because* she'd tried to control matters when it came to love.

She stared into Noah's eyes, which were as passionate and dedicated as her own. They were both extremely busy people, neurotic in their own ways. But they also gave everything to the people and things they loved, no matter what. If they couldn't make it work, no one could.

"I want to give us my all, too," Mia finally said. "I'll create a shared calendar for us."

Noah leaned closer, peering up at her from underneath his dark eyelashes. In a low voice he said, "Okay, you were right. Logistics *are* sexy."

Mia wrapped her arms around Noah, and he pulled her tight.

They kissed, again and again, underneath the moonlit night sky. And Mia realized that some of the best things in life—like the most priceless moments on TV—are unplanned.

Acknowledgments

This book—or my entire career, really—wouldn't have been possible without the University of Southern California, my alma mater, and the students, professors, and other staff members I met during my time there. Marlon is, of course, a fictional university, and it's definitely not an exact replica of USC, but Mia's and Noah's collegiate world is based on my own memories of being a student. Sometimes, I think back to my college years in LA and wonder, *Was that all just a big dream?* Spending nights tediously editing dailies in the film school's freezing basement computer lab while bundled up in a hoodie like an angry gremlin, getting up hours before sunrise to stand behind a camera in the cold morning mist to capture the perfect shot of the rising sun (and failing!), realizing I'm classmates with celebrities and other influencers and feeling *incredibly* small, crashing frat (sorry, fraternity) parties and failing spectacularly at beer pong . . . I could go on and on.

I don't miss being a *college student* and having all those

paralyzing worries about *the future*—being in your thirties is much better, trust me!—or the frantic moments of yelling, "We'll fix this in post!" But I do miss being able to learn and create in that zany, chaotic environment with so many other passionate and talented individuals. It's a period of my life that I didn't fully appreciate until it was too late, a chapter that set the foundation for the storyteller I am today. Also, RIP Ground Zero Performance Café, which I paid homage to with Ground Smoothie. Truthfully, I still dream about their milkshakes. And their immaculate, artsy vibes.

The Cuffing Game would also not have been possible without the various creative works that inspired it, namely Jane Austen's *Pride and Prejudice*, ITV's *Love Island*, Netflix's *Single's Inferno*, and Studio N's *Our Beloved Summer*. If you, reader, like any or all these things, please, let's be friends.

Speaking of friendship, Mia's social circles are beautifully diverse and (sometimes) queer because mine are. Thank you to everyone who helped this workaholic bisexual get out of her writer's cave during the making of this book, namely: Chelsea Chang, Luke Chou, Gernae Alexander, Sally Matinfar, Margaret Zeng, Anoosha Syed, XinYi Xan, Sean Dixon, Brian Lee, Holly Leung, Hyunju Bush, Kris Wong, Juri Ahn, Brianna Horgan, Kaiti Liu, Angelica Tran, Patrice Caldwell, and Alice Zhu. Thank you always to Annie Lee, Elly Ha, Stephanie Lu, Michelle Chan, Bernice Yau, Aneeqah Naeem, and Sarah Wu for the virtual, long-distance love. A million thanks go to Francesca Flores for somehow trusting me enough to go on a trip *literally* up the snowy mountains so we could learn how to snowboard, ski, and honestly just experience *so much snow* for the first time in our lives. Key parts of this book wouldn't exist without you. I miss our little trips. Thank you also to Anita Chen for our SoCal trip that was instrumental to the writing of this book.

Thank you to Sara Schonfeld and Mabel Hsu, the brilliant editors I had the pleasure of working with during the process of writing this book. This was a wild beast of a project, my most ambitious one yet, and I couldn't have wrangled it without you. Thank you to Molly Fehr and Leni Kauffman for making this book so *beautiful*, inside and out. And of course, a big thank-you to my agent, Penny Moore, as usual, for everything.

I am eternally indebted to the musical artists whose songs fueled this book. Beyoncé's "CUFF IT" inspired the title, and Mia's personality only came together after I listened to Olivia Rodrigo's "all-american bitch" on repeat and scream-sang the chorus. Meanwhile, Noah's personality didn't fully coalesce until I danced with reckless abandon to DPR Ian's "So I Danced." BTS, Taylor Swift, Benson Boone, Joji, and Glass Animals provided additional key emotional beats for Noah, while Ariana Grande, TWICE, Miley Cyrus, Sabrina Carpenter, BLACKPINK, and CHUNG HA provided them for Mia.

Finally, thank you, H, for loving me in all my chaos and for being the perfect partner. Love you.